THE
NAZARENE'S
PRICE

ENDORSEMENTS

"You must beware that what you hold dearest doesn't become what holds you." *The Nazarene's Price.*

What if the rich young ruler's story didn't end the way we all imagined? Donna does a beautiful job telling his story in a hope-filled way true to scripture and history. She drew me in, leaving me feeling like I knew Matthias, Peter, and other New Testament characters. Best of all, I finished with a deeper understanding of Jesus's compelling love to seek and save us all. This left me with a yearning to surrender and follow Him.

"Come. See. Believe." *The Nazarene's Price*
—**Brenda Gates**, author of, *Anna's Song: Cries From the Earth,* and organizer of The Carbondale Christian Writer's Group in Southern Illinois

I plan to recommend *The Nazarene's Price* to every non-believer I know. Donna has done an exquisite job of rendering Jesus and his message using both good-natured human and spiritual brush strokes. I found it an awesome, terribly poignant version of this eternal story."
—**Mary Rebecca W. Johnson**, MT(ASCP)

THE NAZARENE'S PRICE

DONNA K. STEARNS

ELK LAKE PUBLISHING INC

PUBLISHING THE POSITIVE
Plymouth, Massachusetts

COPYRIGHT NOTICE

The Nazarene's Price

The Holy Bible, King James version, in the Public Domain
The Complete Jewish Bible by David H. Stern. Copyright © 1998. All rights reserved. Used by permission of Messianic Jewish Publishers, 6120 Day Long Lane, Clarksville, MD 21020

All other references to Christ's words and specific scriptures are the author's paraphrase for the purpose of readability, without sacrificing meaning.

Cover and Interior Design: Lana Ziegler, Derinda Babcock
Editor(s): Mary Johnson, Cristel Phelps, Deb Haggerty

PUBLISHED BY: Elk Lake Publishing, Inc., 35 Dogwood Drive, Plymouth, MA 02360, 2022

Library Cataloging Data

Names: Stearns, Donna K. (Donna K. Stearns)
The Nazarene's Price / Donna K. Stearns

348 p. 23cm × 15cm (9in × 6 in.)
ISBN-13: 978-1-64949-655-3 (paperback) | 978-1-64949-656-0 (trade paperback) |978-1-64949-597-6 (trade hardcover) | 978-1-64949-598-3 (e-book)

Key Words: Jesus of Nazareth; the Messiah; Life of Jesus; Passover; Resurrection; Eternal Life; Miracles

Library of Congress Control Number: 2022942780 Fiction

DEDICATION

The Nazarene's Price is dedicated to you, the reader. Many prayers have been offered for you to know and grow in the understanding of the pursuing love of Jesus Christ, God the Son.

ACKNOWLEDGMENTS

The Lord has provided many to encourage, teach, and pray for me in this writing journey—beginning with my Granny. She would rejoice to see the fruit of her investment.

I am thankful for the following and the unnamed who have been a part of seeing *The Nazarene's Price* become published.

The Carbondale Christian Writers, who critique and encourage one another

Chad R. Allen, writing coach and creator of Book Proposal Academy

Deb Haggerty, who welcomed me into the ELPI family of authors

My patient and talented editors, who taught me red ink is my friend on the road to making my story the best it can be. Thank you.

Thank you Derinda Babcock and Lana Ziegler for designing a beautiful cover.

The Lord, for going before me each step of the journey.

INTRODUCTION:

The Lord gives each of his children a mission to declare his story to the world. He gives us many avenues to accomplish this work. Writing is one of those ways. Jesus told many stories to illustrate truth. *The Nazarene's Price* is biblical fiction showing the truth of Jesus's pursuing love for each of us through the account of the rich young ruler. Many of the people are real individuals who lived during Jesus's time on earth. The Bible records events found in my story. Biblical fiction expands the characters' personalities according to the writer's understanding of scripture and imagination, creating a relationship between the characters and you, the reader. In reading biblical fiction it is important to remember, it is fiction built on a foundation of truth with bricks of possibilities.

The Gospel of Mark includes the insight which produced, *The Nazarene's Price*. Mark wrote, *"Then Jesus beholding him loved him ..."* My prayer and hope for you is to know and grow in the persevering, pursuing, love of the Nazarene.

PART ONE

Behold the Lamb of God which taketh away the sin of the world.

—John 1:29 (KJV)

CHAPTER 1

The fear of death he wore each night as a shroud began to melt as the sun's morning rays warmed the rocky Galilean shore. The sea sang its song on waves of empty promises. The white sea birds called to one another, soaring and diving in pursuit of a feast. A hesitant smile pushed despair into the dark places of his mind for a moment. Morning brought hope—a false hope? He wasn't sure. The gentle waves whispered words of life to his hidden fears.

Matthias shaded his eyes from the flickering fingers of sunlight playing on the water. In the distance, a fishing boat rocked its way to shore. Simon and Andrew's, no doubt, which meant James and John would be in the one coming alongside. These men were rough as camel's hair but good fishermen, making a good living. They weren't rich, but merchants welcomed their coins at the marketplace, where Matthias supplied them with sweet grapes and figs. The men, boats, and sea moved in a rhythmic dance as they neared shore.

"Zebedee!"

Only one man could bellow like that. Simon's voice matched his size. All Capernaum knew when the big fisherman came ashore.

"If those two quick-tempered sons of yours were as quick to work as they are to argue, we would all be rich!"

Simon's baritone laughter echoed across the water. The brothers shot hot glances his way, never missing a tug on the full net. Zebedee shrugged his shoulders.

Matthias turned toward home. The approaching cadence of feet and unmistakable slap of leather halted his steps. The fishermen's chattering behind him ceased as a dapple gray stallion and rider came into sight.

The centurion's bronze breastplate gleamed in the morning light. He held the reins short, causing the steed's head to bob in rhythm to the dance of his prancing high steps. They made a matched pair, heads held high, noses in the air, full of their own power.

Matthias stepped off the road as the centurion and a dozen foot soldiers bristling with spears and swords drew near. Three tethered men in ragged tunics and bare feet stumbled behind the centurion's horse.

The middle captive's arms sagged. A quick jerk dropped him to his knees and forward into the dirt, covering his face with grime. The two prisoners standing lunged for their partner, until the crack of a whip gave them pause. But the one on the right raised his tied hands to his head, persisting in his attempt until the centurion halted his stallion and turned in the saddle.

"You! Back in line. You, on your feet."

The horse's head danced against the tight reins as it snorted and stomped. Matthias's quick step rescued his feet from danger. The centurion's dark-eyed dead stare insinuated Rome's power to be his own, filling Matthias with a wave of fear he fought to control. The centurion looked him up and down impassively.

"You're a ruler of Capernaum's synagogue."

Not a question, but a challenge. Rage roiled Matthias's gut. His red mantle with its blue border made no secret of his position, but his youth had obviously caused the centurion to question him. His muscles tensed.

"Yes, lord, I am one of the rulers."

"Warn them. Only one reigns supreme. Caesar." He clasped a fist to his chest. "Any other claims are destroyed." He yanked the prisoners' tethers. "Treason ends in death. You ungrateful Jews need to accept this and enjoy our generous gift of your synagogue."

The centurion hawked and spit in the dust in disdain. "I can't imagine why a Roman centurion honored your people with such a gift."

"Yes, lord." Matthias clenched his jaw and gave the man a conciliatory nod.

The centurion nudged the dapple gray and moved southward toward Tiberius, Herod's capital. As the prisoners passed Matthias, they stared out of the eyes of the already dead, knowing their end. He watched, as did the fishermen, until the troop moved out of sight.

Matthias's tense muscles began to relax as he stroked his short, black beard.

Those ragtag, unkempt men looked the part of Barabbas's band of thieves.

He dismissed the thought. Barabbas made no claims to being the Messiah. He murdered and robbed anyone fool enough to travel alone, under the guise of inciting insurrection against Rome.

"Shalom. Matthias, isn't it?" called Simon.

Matthias turned and moved toward the fishermen.

"Yes, I am Matthias, son of Zebulun."

"You talked with the centurion. What were the crimes?"

"Treason, probably claims of being the Messiah. In Rome's interpretation, a king, and a threat to Caesar."

Simon returned to checking his nets. "Is it too much to hope their crosses will not line the roads to Jerusalem when we travel to Passover?"

Matthias puzzled over who Simon was addressing—himself or the others—until Simon spoke again.

"Andrew, John, watch yourselves speaking openly of this John the Baptizer and his supposed Messiah."

"Shalom," muttered Matthias. "I'm no more than a piece of information." He started to move away when bits of John's reply pricked his ears and slowed his steps.

"John the Baptizer ... repentance ... kingdom of God. Messiah. Come, hear him."

Matthias couldn't make out more of the fishermen's conversation. He twisted the curled sidelock dangling beside his ear tighter, as he headed for home.

Rumors of this Baptizer being a prophet are coursing through the land. Could the long-awaited Messiah be walking in Israel even now?

No prophet of the Lord had spoken in Israel for over four hundred years. All Israel, himself included, waited for their Messiah to come dispose Rome's rule and place a true king of Israel on the throne—not the pretentious Herod, who played at being an Israelite. The vision of the three men returned to his mind.

Crosses, that's where such ideas end. Better not to dwell on these things.

Yes, he waited for the Messiah, too, but at what price? The greater the distance between himself, the itinerant fishermen ready to cast bait toward any hope, and the soldiers with their catch soon to be drying in the sun, the easier he would breathe.

Matthias's legs cried for respite as he topped the steep hill where home waited. The need for air alleviated the anxiety raised by the vision of the prisoners. But John's words lingered in his mind.

He reached for the mezuzah on his doorpost, kissed it, and mouthed its contents.

"Hear, O Israel: The Lord our God is one Lord: And you shall love the Lord your God with all your heart, and with all your soul, and with all your might ..." Upon completion he kissed and returned the scroll to its place before entering his house.

A whiff of Deborah's hot cakes welcomed his rumbling stomach. He handed his robe and turban to Eliezer, revealing long black curls that matched the color of his eyes. Matthias meticulously bathed his hands, on the off chance he had come in contact with any unclean person or object, before he reclined on the couch to wait for Eliezer to wash his dusty feet.

The gentle touch of his servant worked in vain to lighten the weight in his heart.

"That will do, Eliezer. If my mind would quit prodding me like an ox goad, I could stay longer." Matthias sat up. "But I can't. Do Deborah and Leah have my breakfast ready?"

"Yes, Master. But surely you can rest a moment." With a tilt of his head, Eliezer pointed an accusatory finger at Matthias as if he was an unruly child and added, "You know Deborah will scold you with some proverb about haste in eating not being good for the body, mind, or soul." He smiled, folded the towel across his arm and offered his master assistance.

Matthias grinned at the mention of his grandmotherly servant.

"She clucks like a mother hen, and you worry like a father over a wayward son." He grasped Eliezer's outstretched hand and pulled himself to his feet. "Father was right to put you as head of the household. I'm not sure what I would do without your care and wisdom. You make my days without him bearable."

"Your father was an honorable man. He dealt fairly in business and faithfully served the people in the synagogue. And ..." Eliezer smiled at Matthias as he continued. "He raised a fine son. Now, young sir, your meal is waiting for you in the inner court." Eliezer bowed and extended his arm, gesturing the way.

Matthias related instructions to his servant as they walked past the stone well in the garden courtyard. "I'll be leaving on personal business as soon as I have eaten. I need you to take care of some items for me here."

"Yes, Master."

"I hope my quest doesn't cost me more than I'm willing to pay."

"Master?"

Matthias faced his servant with a measured stare. "Have you heard the newest rumors of the Messiah and this John the Baptizer?"

Eliezer nodded slightly. "I have heard rumors."

"Leah," Matthias called to his house maid who currently stood guard over the bread oven. At the sound of his voice, she stopped strangling her apron and approached with timid steps.

She's such a little mouse.

"Bring food for me and Eliezer."

Eliezer didn't move from his place.

Matthias saw his uncertainty and waved him forward. "It's not like this is the first time I've asked you to eat with me. Come, dear friend. We'll sit under the fig tree."

The tree stood taller than most figs, providing a canopy of shade in the far left corner of the garden. Already its budding leaves held the promise of early summer fruit. As a child, Matthias had wondered why his father kept a gnarled ugly tree in such a place of honor.

When he questioned his father, the old man had smiled. "As my father told me, I tell you. It is a testimony to Israel's history. Its beauty lies not in its appearance but its fruit. The fig tree holds the Lord's promise of peace and prosperity. It was born in our past and points to our future."

Matthias hadn't understood then. Now no longer a youngster, his contentment at his own prosperity brought momentary pleasure. Prosperity promised peace. He glanced at the light filtering through the limbs and tender leaves.

I have the prosperity. Where is the peace that was promised?

Leah interrupted Matthias's reverie as she set the tray of bread, assorted fruits, and cheese on the table. She retreated and returned with large mugs of buttermilk. "Will there be anything else, Master?"

Her demeanor set his nerves on edge. "Yes. Speak up and set those mugs down."

"Forgive me, Master."

Matthias shot her a stern glance and cupped a hand behind his ear as if to indicate he couldn't hear her.

"Forgive me, Master." She stood as tall as her small frame allowed, as if a taller stature would give volume to her trembling voice. "May I be dismissed to help Deborah, Master?" She stared past Matthias into nowhere.

He dismissed her with a wave of his hand. "Go."

Matthias took the bread and offered it to the Lord. "Blessed are you, Lord our God, King of the world, who brings forth bread and all good things from the earth." He broke it into two pieces and offered a piece to his servant. They dipped it in the dibs, a sweet syrup made from his grapes.

"Eliezer, tell me what you've heard. Servants have ears everywhere."

Eliezer laughed. "Yes, young sir, there is always much talk. I will tell you what I have heard, although I am not one to repeat old women's fables and gossip."

"Is that true?" Matthias grinned before finishing the fresh buttermilk in a single gulp.

"Master, you know I am not a talebearer." Eliezer's face clouded until he caught sight of his master's smirk.

"Continue, Eliezer. I will be good."

Eliezer could hardly keep his hands still as he recounted the latest news from the marketplace.

"Master, all Israel longs for our Messiah's appearance, hoping he is on our horizon. People voice their hopes even at the market. There I overheard Hannah speaking of the Promised One."

"Hannah?"

"A servant of Jairus, Master."

Matthias nodded, making a mental note to see Jairus, the chief ruler of the synagogue.

Eliezer continued. "Hannah and another woman I did not recognize spoke of the Messiah while looking over the fruit merchant's produce. But she may have been, let me think, maybe I do know her ..."

"Eliezer, I don't care about her name. I only want to hear what they said."

"Yes, Master. Forgive my wandering. Hannah said Jairus traveled to the Jordan River where the one called John the Baptizer preached repentance and baptized the people in preparation for the coming of God's kingdom."

"Jairus has heard of him, then. But that's not all. What else did you hear? Tell me now."

"Yes, Master, but it may not be true. Their words were not always clear."

"Finish it. I'll decide for myself."

"Hannah overheard her master and wife speaking of the event. As the Baptizer preached, one stepped from the crowd for baptism. The Baptizer refused at first ..."

"If that's why he came, why would the Baptizer refuse? Was the man an unrepentant sinner?"

"The women did not say. But they did say the Baptizer finally relented."

Eliezer intertwined his fingers into a fist with his forefingers and thumbs pointing upward—then he spoke. As his voice grew louder, his hands flew apart and punctuated each word.

"The moment the one he baptized came up from the water, a dove rested on the baptized one. Then a ... a ... a sound came from heaven."

"A dove? And a sound? Who is this man?"

Eliezer leaned closer to Matthias and spoke softly.

"Some said the sound was thunder. But Hannah said Jairus spoke of a voice."

Matthias could see in Eliezer the anticipation of an unsure reaction.

"A voice? From heaven?" Matthias covered his smile with his hand. "And did Hannah report what the voice said?"

"I heard her say only the words 'my beloved Son.' Then a merchant interrupted their conversation. But as to the man's identity, there were whispers of a lamb and a Messiah." Eliezer sat back.

Matthias leaned away from his servant and scowled at him.

"Messiah? Is this one proclaiming he is the Messiah?"

Eliezer straightened and lowered his eyes to the table. Silence filled the air like an unwanted guest, until at last, he answered.

"That is all I heard, Master."

Matthias rose, and Eliezer began clearing the table. The sunlight filtering through the fig tree turned Matthias's thoughts into a prayer.

"Lord God of our fathers, who hears our cries, reveal your truth."

He waited. He listened, but the only answer came in the quiet rustle of leaves whispering—not unlike the dangerous rumors swirling through the land.

CHAPTER 2

"I'll go to market for you. I'll get a good price for the barley and salt. Gramma will return shortly to help with the baking," Rebekah pleaded with her mother.

"Go, child, go." Sarah waved a flour-covered hand at her daughter. "Gramma is bound to be more help than you, with your head filled with the sea."

"Immah, I am not a child," retorted Rebekah, hand on her hip. "I am of marrying age now." With her dignity restored, she grabbed the few coins laid out on the table and hurried out the door with her mother calling after her.

"Of marrying age, yes, but always a child. I'll pray for the young man who'd try to tame your spirit. And don't tarry long at your papa's fishing boat."

Rebekah ignored her mother's last remark. Of course, she would stop by the wharf. Her dark auburn curls bounced under her gray head covering as she jumped from stone to stone toward the Galilean shoreline. As the aromas of the lake's sweet blue water, the wet sand, and the shoreline rocks mixed with the fishy odor of the boats, she imagined her life as a fisherman and laughed. *That would certainly cause the city busybodies to wag their tongues.*

"Papa! Andrew!" Rebekah waved to the men sorting their catch. Lifting her tunic above her ankles, Rebekah splashed through the shallows. She peered past her father's boat, hoping to see a certain fisherman in the next vessel.

I don't see James.

A momentary pucker quickly faded when she neared the boat's hull and heard her father's greeting.

"Ah," he thundered as he dropped his nets and held out arms of love. "There is my baby girl!"

Rebekah cringed. *Will he ever realize I am a woman?* She fingered a curl. *No matter, as long as James ...*

"Get back to work." Simon growled at his workers. "It's hard to sort the clean fish from the unclean when your eyes are not on your business."

Andrew chuckled as the men returned to the work at hand. "You know, Simon, my niece is much lovelier than any fish."

"Humph. I know that, but they don't need to know it. These men are too rough for the likes of my daughter."

With a teasing twinkle in his eye, Andrew replied. "Or perhaps she is too much woman for any of them?"

"A good catch, Papa?" Rebekah interrupted. A smile flirted with her lips. Her unusual deep blue eyes sparkled.

Simon ignored his brother's comment. "Ah, yes, a good catch. But here you are, and I don't see a morsel of bread or a bite of fruit for your starving papa."

"Oh, Papa, I didn't think. Dough and flour covered Gramma, Immah, and me. And Zebedee's servant summoned Gramma to Salome's bedside. My thoughts drove me to hurry, knowing you must already be to shore, and Immah needed me to go to market, and—"

"Salome?" called Zebedee from the other boat. "What's wrong? Is she ill?"

"Nothing serious. Your servant mentioned a slight fever," returned Rebekah. "But you know Gramma. She would trust no one else to tend to Salome."

"James, John," called Zebedee.

At the mention of the two brothers, Rebekah twisted a curl hanging on her shoulder and dared a sideways glance toward the other vessel. Her insides tickled her skin, and she hoped the tickling didn't show in a red face when both brothers appeared from the other end of their father's boat.

"I'm leaving this to you. I need to check on your mother. Make sure those men mend the nets well."

Zebedee's sons nodded and returned to their work, but not before James glanced in Rebekah's direction.

"Rebekah?" Simon leaned over the side of the boat and cradled her face in his rough hands. "All is forgiven."

"What, Papa? What's forgiven?"

"Not bringing any food?"

"Oh, that. Yes, Papa."

He patted her cheek. "Seeing you is enough for the moment. Now go. Finish your errand." He turned a steely stare toward James before finishing. "Your immah will be waiting."

"Yes, Papa." Rebekah trudged through the shallows like a soldier forced to keep eyes forward, instead of attempting a quick glance to see if anyone watched her go. She blew a wayward curl out of her face.

The mud caked on the bottom of her wet tunic made her steps cumbersome. She shrugged. It didn't bother her as much as the curl that pestered her like a persistent fly. A quick flick of her wrist and it fell back into place for the moment.

The smell of fresh baked goods in the marketplace would have been enticing if it hadn't been mixed with salted fish and sweaty merchants. Rebekah wrinkled her nose as she sprinted less than gracefully for Jacob's booth. She weaved between the other merchants' baskets, large pots, and produce littering the ground. She muscled her way through the growing crowd, keeping Jacob's canopy her focus. But in one move, it disappeared as she collided headlong into a pillar-like body carrying a basket of fruit.

The impact propelled Rebekah into a much less formidable figure who appeared beside the statuesque fruit bearer. Their flurry of arms and legs tangled together as both girls spiraled to the ground. Figs, grapes, and pomegranates splattered and rolled on the street. Trying to dodge the same fate, shoppers skipped over the produce and the girls.

The dark-skinned Nubian pillar grasped the hand of her charge.

"Miss Phoebe, are you hurt?" She dusted the girl's clothes as she turned her from side to side. Then she turned to Rebekah, who still sat on the ground, the pesky curl of hair dangling about her nose.

"And you, you—!" The Nubian, eyes glaring, spewed her venom. "You are worse than a runaway horse with no concern but getting home. It is a wonder you didn't hurt Miss Phoebe. And look at this ruined fruit. You will pay for it all."

Rebekah clenched her teeth against the words fighting to free themselves. She brushed the curl away as she tried to right herself and rise. As she did, someone offered her a hand.

"Miss, are you hurt? May I help you?"

"I am fine." She accentuated each word, then hesitated as she caught a glimpse of the face belonging to the voice. The light olive complexion revealed a life unaccustomed to outdoor labor. His clothes spoke of prosperity, but his youthful face, with its finely trimmed beard and eyes as black as the onyx on the high priest's breastplate, changed her rude attitude.

She amended her remarks but kept the edge in her voice. "Thank you for your concern. Forgive my bad temper." She stood, straightened her clothing, picked up her head covering, and turned to the offended pair.

"Pardon my clumsiness, Miss—was it Phoebe? Sometimes I go about like a goat ready to charge, head down and butting anything in my way."

The girl smiled wearily, but her brown eyes twinkled with hope not yet realized. Her small build and the dark circles under her eyes camouflaged her age and hinted at sickness.

Rebekah offered Phoebe a handful of coins. "I have some coins Immah sent with me. Instead of barley and salt, I will take home fruit. Papa will have fruit for breakfast today when he finishes with his nets. Will that amount be sufficient?" She laid the money in Phoebe's hand as she stooped to gather the salvageable fruit into her head covering.

"Sufficient? I think not," growled the servant. "What about the harm you have done to my mistress? Who will pay for that? Her father will—"

"Delilah." Phoebe's voice was firm. "You will not treat … uh, I don't know your name." She turned to Rebekah.

"I am Rebekah, daughter of Simon the fisherman, and Sarah." Rebekah held her head high as she spoke of her parents. "Are you hurt?"

"Not at all," Phoebe answered with a giggle. "And when I think about the tangled mess of our hair and clothes all piled together like dirty laundry …" She grabbed her side as her laughter exploded. It was contagious.

Shoppers gawked at Rebekah, Phoebe, and the young man who had offered help. Rebekah thought she might have seen a smile from the servant.

Suddenly, Phoebe's laughter turned into deep dry coughing spasms. Her face turned red, and she clasped her hands over her chest as she struggled to stay upright. She appeared to be suffocating even though she was surrounded by air. The young man rushed to her side as the servant grabbed a cloth from her belt and pushed him away. Curious bystanders stared.

Rebekah stood with her hand at her mouth and eyes wide as the servant placed the cloth to Phoebe's nose and mouth.

"Breathe slowly, Miss Phoebe, deeply," she instructed with unusual calmness.

Rebekah caught a whiff of eucalyptus oil. Within seconds the coughing began to subside. Phoebe's chest began rising and falling with slow rhythmic precision, as she took in precious scented air. The crisis over, the crowd dispersed. Merchants resumed hawking their wares.

Rebekah stepped toward Phoebe, but the pillar blocked her.

"Please forgive Delilah," said Phoebe haltingly, as she stepped around her servant. "She is much too protective." Her voice was no louder than a whisper. "Here are your coins. Buy whatever you need for your papa."

Rebekah blinked away fearful tears as she extended her hand. "You are well now?"

Phoebe smiled and nodded.

"Thank you for the coins. My papa does like cheese with his bread." Not knowing anything else to say, Rebekah asked, "Do you know my papa?"

"Everyone knows Simon," interjected the young man.

Rebekah shot him a disapproving glance. How did any of this concern him?

"Rebekah." Phoebe took control of the conversation. "I believe you are an answer to my prayers." She measured her words with her intake of air.

Rebekah crossed her arms. Then she wiggled her mouth side to side until a grin emerged.

"You asked the Lord to send someone to wrestle you to the ground?"

Phoebe grabbed her chest to ward off more laughter. "No, not at all. But if that's what it takes to find a friend, then yes."

Rebekah felt a warmth for the girl. "I'm sure you have plenty of friends without adding a clumsy one to the list. But if it's a friend you seek, I am up for the task."

"The Lord be praised." Phoebe enclosed Rebekah in her arms. Rebekah stood with arms full of fruit, unable to return the gesture or pull away until the girl released her hold.

"Do come by for a visit. My papa and immah worry over me more than Delilah, and I haven't many opportunities for getting out," Phoebe said. "They fear I will get sick, or hurt, or something," she added with a dismissive wave of her hand.

Delilah's scowl made it clear the "or something" was exactly what she thought had happened. Then she held out the basket so Rebekah could drop the fruit into it.

Before Rebekah could reply to Phoebe, the young man stepped to Phoebe's side and placed her arm on his.

"Come, Miss Phoebe, I'll walk with you and Delilah. I need to speak with your papa."

"Surely, Matthias." Before the trio made it through the crowd Phoebe glanced over her shoulder and called to Rebekah. "I do hope to see you soon. Shalom, Rebekah."

"Shalom," she replied, bothered more than a little by the young man's intrusion. But Phoebe's smile indicated she welcomed his attention. Rebekah tilted her head as she watched them go. His regal cloak swished with each step. She wondered if he was as important as he acted, but he was not her main concern. She would make her purchase and find out more about Phoebe from Jacob, her favorite among the merchants.

Matthias and Delilah may think I am beneath her, but Phoebe doesn't, and she needs a friend.

Rebekah made her way home past the grove of tall oaks behind the white limestone synagogue on the hill. The building stood in contrast to the black basalt homes dotting the hillside and plateaus. Her skirt whispered a song as she hurried around the blocks of houses butted one against another, creating the layout for the city roads. Moving east, she passed close enough to the synagogue to hear an elder teaching the young boys from the prophet Isaiah.

"For a child is born to us, a son is given to us; dominion will rest on his shoulders, and he will be given the name *Pele-Yo'etz El Gibbor Avi-'Ad Sar-Shalom* in order to extend the dominion and perpetuate the peace of the throne and kingdom of David, to secure it and sustain it through justice and righteousness henceforth and forever. The zeal of *Adonai-Tzva'ot* will accomplish this."

Rebekah's mind turned to the sea nestled in the valley. Its mist rose to welcome the late morning sun. *"Wonder of a Counselor, Mighty God, Father of Eternity, Prince of Peace, a child, a son, a kingdom."* The words swam in her mind and floated to her heart. Every virgin of Israel dreamed of being the mother of the Messiah. The Lord God would accomplish it. Her thoughts drifted to James, the oldest son of Zebedee.

One day, I hope he sees me as more than Simon's little girl.

She shifted the bag of produce slung over her shoulder. Its weight brought her out of her dreams of the Messiah, marriage, and a son.

"Immah!" Rebekah clasped both hands to her head, lifted her skirt, and quickened her pace. "Lord, you have blessed me with a friend today. Bless me also with an understanding immah."

CHAPTER 3

Simon stomped around the house. Rebekah followed him like a dog seeking a morsel of bread. "Papa, Magdala is not more than a Sabbath's day from here. You won't need much."

"If John and Andrew were here to help, perhaps. But no, they're off chasing rumors while James and I are left to manage hauling barrels of salted fish to the market."

"Will James go with you?"

"No. He will stay and oversee the workers until I return, hopefully with John and Andrew. I'm taking Jude."

Sarah entered the mix, carrying small round barley loaves. "This should last until you return."

Rebekah smiled at seeing her father's features soften at the sound of his wife's voice. He leaned towards Sarah and planted a gentle kiss on her lips.

"And here is some smoked fish Gramma prepared," offered Rebekah, with her cheek upturned and waiting for her kiss. Simon obliged. As he turned to leave, Rebekah took her last opportunity to beg. "Papa, can I not come with you? It's not a long journey."

"No," growled Simon. He threw on his cloak and secured his head covering. "I don't know how long I'll be, since I must find Andrew and John. They should not have followed the rumors about this one called the Baptizer. Every hand is needed when preparing for the coming Passover."

"They are young, Simon, and dream of the Messiah," Sarah said.

"Dreams do not feed the belly." Simon stuffed the food into the cloth bag and flung it over his shoulder. "Now I need to be on my way."

Simon made his way through the quiet twilight shadows of Capernaum, moving past the synagogue, across the deserted town square, and down the rocky hillside. James and his hired workers stood ready at the roadside, waiting beside a cart loaded with two large barrels of salted fish. The freshest fish had gone to the market in Capernaum. The cargo of salted fish would be sold in Magdala and sent all over Israel for the rich and the Romans. Simon spat at the thought before he examined the barrels and tossed his bag of food on the cart. He kept the wineskin slung over his shoulder.

James pulled on one of the ropes.

"They're tight. And Jude is ready to travel." He nodded towards the silent young man standing near the cart.

"That's good. You're an ox of a man, Jude, strong enough to pull two carts. We should make good time and get a fair price from this catch, if the tax collector doesn't take more than his share." Simon knew full well the tax would take a huge cut of their profits. Although Levi was one of the few honest tax collectors, he was still a tax collector working for the Romans.

But we always have enough. The Lord God's gracious provision keeps my family fed well.

Simon wrapped his arms around the two long handles of the loaded cart.

"Smart man, Simon," called James, "taking the morning to haul and leaving poor Jude to sweat it out in the heat of the day."

"He's young. He can manage it," answered Simon.

Jude slapped James on the back and followed Simon down the south road.

"May the Lord be with you and bless your travel with great profit," called James.

"And with you. Shalom," replied Simon.

Dawn's light outlined the distant landscape dotted with trees and boulders as the men traveled the dusty road away from the Sea of Galilee.

"Simon, aside from your frustration with Andrew and John, what are your thoughts about this John preaching repentance and the kingdom of God? Is he the one to announce the Messiah?" asked Jude.

"As far as this John the Baptizer, I have no thoughts. I don't know him and haven't heard him. Besides, my thoughts at this moment would burn the ears off a sailor ..."

"God be with you! Shalom!" The voice from behind interrupted the men's conversation. "Where are your travels taking you? How does this day find you?"

The voice did not stop Simon. He answered as he walked. "It finds us busy."

Matthias quickened his pace to come alongside. He gave no heed to Simon's ill mood and manners.

"I beg your forgiveness. But I have need to travel to Magdala and don't wish to travel alone. May I join your company?" His left hand rested against his cloak, where his dagger and a leather bag of coins were hidden. One never knew when either would be needed.

Simon snorted. "Do as you wish. The road is for all travelers."

"Including thieves," responded Matthias. "I am grateful for your company." With a clenched jaw, he stifled the words he wanted to use, knowing he needed Simon more than the older man needed him. "Perhaps I can be of help to you."

Simon shot him a sideways glance and kept walking.

"My name is Matthias. I am the son of ..."

"I know who you are." Simon's tone was a challenge.

Matthias stiffened his back as his grip on the leather pouch tightened.

"And I you, Simon." He hesitated the briefest moment. "And how is your daughter, Rebekah?"

Simon stopped. He rested his load on the ground and glared at Matthias. "My daughter is none of your affair. But do tell me how you know of her, before I teach you some manners."

"Would you want me to take the cart for a time?" Matthias offered.

"No. What I want is an explanation."

Matthias resumed walking. Simon took up his load and followed. All the while Jude trailed in silence.

"I can surely give you one," Matthias said. "Rebekah ran into a friend of mine in the market place a few days ago. She and Phoebe exchanged greetings. I learned of her then and there. She seems to have your temperament."

"And what is wrong with my temperament?" Simon's face burned red as he pulled harder on the cart.

"I was not implying anything was wrong with your temperament, sir. Only that your daughter seems to have inherited your grace."

Simon harrumphed.

The travelers continued their journey in awkward silence until the sun rose high in the sky. Beads of sweat formed on Simon's forehead. Jude came up alongside him.

"I'll take the load for a while."

Simon slowed his pace and drank from his wineskin. Matthias fell in step with Jude.

"You know my name, but I have not yet learned yours. It seemed ..."

"Jude."

Matthias stretched his curly sidelock of hair and tried again. "Do you wish to always be a fisherman, Jude?"

"It's a worthy profession. Simon is one of the best. I'm learning much from him." Jude glanced at Matthias. "It could provide well for a family if there weren't so many taxes, Romans, and rich people who buy for little and sell for much."

"And do you think I fit into one of those categories?"

"Don't know. I suspect time will tell. I must admit," continued Jude, glancing behind him. "I did admire how you handled Simon. Help me know where you fit."

"How?"

"What work do you do?"

"I manage my late father's grove of figs, as well as a vineyard," answered Matthias.

"That's where I know of you. Your father was an elder at the synagogue. Died about a year ago, yes?"

"Yes, he did," answered Matthias. "And now I am one of the rulers."

Jude gave him a cursory glance.

"Yes, Jude, I am young for the position. I received the appointment due to the respect all had for my father. It leaves me much to prove."

"What brings you to Magdala? Religion or business?"

Matthias chose his words with care. "A little of both, and some personal inquiries."

"You have heard the stories, then," Jude said.

Matthias frowned. "Stories?"

Jude answered his remark for what it was. "Stories, rumors, tales of the Messiah. Isn't that your true interest here?"

"You are quite discerning. What do you know?"

"Truth or tales?"

"Truth, Jude. Is this strange man wandering the wilderness—a man who claims to be the Messiah—is he the true Son of God? As a ruler, I need to know the truth of this matter."

I will not share the real need of my heart.

"Another seeker, no doubt," stormed Simon, surprising both young men.

"Sir?" inquired Matthias.

"You young men are all dreamers. You follow every whisper of the servants. When the Messiah comes, we will know."

"You have heard these rumors, Simon?"

"Heard them? My brother and partner are off somewhere looking for him now, when they should be here pulling a cart."

Matthias stroked his beard. "What do they tell you of this one crying out in the wilderness?"

"They call him John the Baptizer. And you are mistaken. He makes no claim to be the Messiah or the Son of God," Simon said. "I know no more than you. I will surely find out when I locate Andrew and John." He motioned with a jerk of his head toward a gruesome scene ahead of them. "I know enough to not speak openly of this matter unless I want a Roman cross to be my resting place."

Fear crowded into Matthias's heart as he stared at the side of the road before them, where three Roman crosses stood. The fear in his heart quivered through him.

I wonder if those are the prisoners that passed through Capernaum.

"Simon! Simon!"

The sudden shouts interrupted Matthias's thoughts. Two men ran towards the travelers as they called again, waving their arms.

"Simon, come! You must come!"

"Andrew, John, shalom." Simon rushed in their direction. "It's about time you came to work. I'm sure Jude would welcome your help."

"That I would," replied Jude, as he and Matthias approached the others.

Matthias noticed Andrew squinting in his direction.

"Simon," uttered Andrew, as he leaned closer to the big fisherman while glancing back and forth at Matthias. "You must come with us."

A crease formed across Simon's forehead. "The only thing I must do is get these fish to market."

Andrew took Simon aside. Matthias cocked his head, trying to catch their conversation.

"No, you must come. We have found the Messiah. We spent last evening with him. I've never heard a man speak like he does."

Simon considered Andrew's words, then studied John.

"I will deliver the fish. Then I'll come, to end this."

"No. We must go. Let Jude handle the fish," insisted Andrew.

Simon wiped the sweat from his face and turned to Jude. "When you're finished at the market, travel with any returning to Capernaum tomorrow. Tell Sarah of my delay. Let James know what is happening. Can you manage the rest of the journey on your own?"

"Yes, Simon. The cart will be lighter, and remember," he continued with a nod towards Matthias, "I am not alone."

Matthias watched the departing men walking briskly toward the answers he had hoped to find.

"Here," called Jude, offering the cart to Matthias. "We're not far from the city, and my throat is as dry as an old cow's udder."

Matthias glanced at Jude and then at the disappearing trio. He grasped the handles and pulled. An aching back and blistered hands would be his reward for nothing.

"I will travel back with you," he offered, with the hope of finishing their conversation. He tugged on the cart. At least it would be lighter on the return journey.

"What of your business?" asked Jude.

"My business? I am afraid most of it will remain unanswered." His heart ached as the trio vanished over the hill without him.

"You want to believe what you've heard," stated Jude.

"I want only the truth."

Matthias winced and kept his face forward as they passed the dead men. The stench burned his nostrils, threatening to turn his stomach inside out. He tightened his grip on the cart, set his face toward Magdala, and refused to show weakness.

"How badly do you want it?"

Matthias shrugged and tugged harder as sweat ran down his face.

CHAPTER 4

After settling herself for the evening, Gramma picked up the linen embroidered veil and examined its delicate stitching.

"It's beautiful," said Sarah. She fingered the fine threads of blues, yellows and greens intertwined into vines and flowers. "It brings to mind the veil you made for my wedding day."

"One day," the old woman whispered, "my spirited granddaughter will cover those beautiful curls for the man who dares to love her."

"I heard that, Gramma." Rebekah positioned a hand on her hip. "If and when the Lord finds me a husband, I'll be all I'm supposed to be. But I'm in no hurry."

Unless James chooses me for his bride.

She planted a kiss on her Gramma's leathery cheek, hoping to hide the telltale pink tinge on her own.

"Pray your papa does not frighten away the one who makes you blush," teased Gramma.

A knock at the door squelched Rebekah's need for a response she didn't have.

"Who would be coming after our door is shut?" asked Gramma.

Rebekah grabbed the oil lamp. She shuffled a few steps backward as she opened the door to the dark-skinned woman on the other side.

The unannounced guest squinted in the lamplight. "Miss Rebekah. My charge, Mistress Phoebe, has sent me."

Rebekah recognized the sharp disapproving tone. "Come in, Delilah. Is Phoebe well?"

Delilah stepped in far enough to clear the doorway but no further, as if the floor of the house might contaminate her sandals.

"Quite. Mistress Phoebe wishes me to issue you an invitation to travel with her and her family to Cana for the wedding of Lord Jairus's brother's daughter."

"I—when?"

"Two days," answered Delilah. "The journey takes a day's travel, but we will take two. Mistress Phoebe was permitted a guest." Delilah raised her nose so high, if it had been raining, she might have drowned. "She chose you. I will return tomorrow for your answer."

"Thank you. Would you like some refreshment before leaving?" Rebekah said, in an attempt at courtesy.

"No. My business is concluded," the woman answered. She turned to leave.

"Delilah, I need a moment of your time," commanded Sarah as she stepped into the conversation.

Delilah spun around, void of expression.

"What does Lord Jairus have to do with this invitation? And who is Phoebe?"

"Lord Jairus is the chief ruler of the synagogue and Mistress Phoebe's papa," answered Delilah. "If there is nothing else, I must be on my way." She left without waiting for permission, pulling the door shut behind her.

Sarah stared at the closed door.

"Impertinent," she said. "Quite impertinent. Rebekah, how do you know Phoebe?"

"She's the girl I—the one who had the coughing spasm."

"Ah, yes. I remember. And of course I know Jairus. A godly man. His wife Joanna cares for the poor whether they come to her door or she finds them on the streets. But wherever did they get such an uppity servant?"

"Haughty," agreed Gramma. "Most masters would drive the sass out of her."

"That's for certain," replied Rebekah. "I can assure you Phoebe is kind, as you described her mother. But I worry for her. She has no kiss of the sun or plump in her cheeks. And I know she's lonely for a friend. Would it be possible for me to accompany her, Immah?"

"In your papa's absence, Gramma and I will discuss it and pray for guidance. You will have your answer in the morning."

As dawn brushed away the shadows of night, Rebekah tossed off her woolen mantle covering. She paused on the flat roof to watch the first rays of sunlight tease the sea as it peeked over the Galilean hills. The variegated reds, oranges, purples, and midnight blues surrendered to the golden beams filling the valley below.

It's beautiful, Lord.

Rebekah lifted her palms to the heavens, embraced the warmth caressing her face, and abandoned her heart to the Lord in praise with a psalm sung on the Sabbath.

"Bless the Lord, O my soul. O Lord my God, you are very great; you are clothed with honor and majesty. You cover yourself with light as with a garment. You stretch out the heavens like a curtain." Rebekah whispered the closing refrain. "I will sing to the Lord as long as I live. I will sing praise to my God while I have my being. My meditation of him is sweet. I will be glad in the Lord."

The peaceful stillness filled Rebekah's mind with rumors of the Messiah.

What will he be like? How will the people know for sure?

Many had come claiming to be the Messiah. Would the whispers disappear as the night disappeared into day and day into night? She could only wait, as all Israel waited.

Rebekah cocked her head as a figure passed by on the shore below. She shrugged and hurried down the steps to the kitchen as she spoke into the air with a giggle.

"A wedding. What fun."

"Immah, Gramma, may the beauty of the Lord wrap you in his love." She greeted each with a kiss and grabbed a handful of flour to sprinkle on the kneading board. "The smell of fresh bread baking is like a warm hug." She wrapped her arms around herself and glanced at the two older ones. Their faces showed no hint of an answer. She tried to calm her nerves as she filled her hands with more flour.

Sarah shook her head and kept kneading dough without missing a beat. "You fidget like a little sparrow."

Rebekah turned a begging glance towards her mother.

"We decided to allow you to accompany Phoebe to Cana ..."

"Oh, Immah, thank you." Rebekah clapped and twirled around the small room.

"Rebekah," Sarah scolded. "Flour is flying everywhere. You must stop and listen. There is a condition."

The twirling stopped. Flour settled on Rebekah's hair and clothes. "What condition, Immah?"

"I go with you. I will help the servants at the wedding feast if I am allowed to accompany you."

"And if not?"

"Then you will remain here." Sarah grabbed the large wooden bucket hanging on the wall peg. "It's not right for a young lady to go unattended." She handed the bucket to Rebekah.

No amount of pleading would change anything. Her mother would give the response to Delilah. She resigned herself to leave it and do battle with their contrary old nanny goat.

"All right, Naomi, be good. Don't kick over the bucket. I'm in no mood." She sat on the three-legged stool and began coaxing the goat to give her milk.

The day's war of patience and impatience ended in victory. The next morning would send Rebekah and her mother on an exciting journey.

Preparations for travel passed the remaining hours of the day like a gust of wind. But now, in her rooftop room, Rebekah lay on her mat with eyes wide, rehearsing a mental list.

"We have bread, full wineskins, my best tunic." She snuggled under her cloak.

The twinkling stars sang a silent lullaby until she lost the fight with sleep.

"Dawn?' Rebekah sprang from her bed, splashed water on her face, ran fingers through her auburn curls, and draped her mantle over her shoulders. She grabbed her blue veil. "I mustn't forget this," she told herself, and raced down the steps.

"Slow down," called her mother as she opened the house door. "Falling down the stairs would end our journey before it begins. Gramma is packing the last of the dried fruit, bread, and pickled fish."

"But, Immah, we already—"

Sarah shushed her daughter.

"Gramma doesn't believe we can ever pack too much food. Come, let's get it and take our leave."

Rebekah and Sarah kissed Gramma and started down the path. Each carried a skin of weak wine, another of water, and bags of provisions.

Sarah called to Rebekah as she skipped ahead. "Slow down, daughter. We have a long way to go."

Rebekah turned to answer, but changed her answer to a question. "Did you forget something, Immah?"

Sara rifled through her provisions. "The honey, Rebekah, do you have the honey?"

Rebekah nodded. "Of course. Gramma wouldn't let us leave without it. She insists honey is the best medicine, should Phoebe have another coughing fit."

After passing the south side of the synagogue with its lone palm gently waving to them, Rebekah and Sarah walked southward to the pebbly knoll where Jairus's home stood.

"Rebekah! Shalom!" Phoebe ran to greet them as they approached the open door. "I've been watching for you," she exclaimed. She grabbed Rebekah's shoulders and kissed her cheeks.

"Shalom, Phoebe." Rebekah returned the greeting but pulled away when she heard her mother clearing her throat. "Forgive me, Phoebe. This is my immah, Sarah."

"Yes, and this is my immah, Joanna," the other responded, as Joanna joined the girls.

The two older women shared greetings and left the girls to chatter while they tended to the final preparations.

"Can't we help them?" asked Rebekah.

"I'm not to get too excited." Phoebe giggled. "Too late for that," she said, "and I am not to tire myself before we start."

"Then we'll do what we're told." The two stood watching, talking, and laughing as the servants tied leather pouches and cloth bags to the donkey patiently waiting nearby.

Once on their way, the company of travelers stopped at a stone house twice the size of Rebekah's, nestled behind the massive oaks on the synagogue's north side. The door was open, signaling all were up. Soon two men emerged.

"Matthias," called Jairus, raising a hand in greeting. "Shalom to you and Eliezer in the name of our Lord!"

"Shalom," returned Matthias.

Rebekah frowned. "Isn't that one the young man who helped you when I—um—we first met?"

"Yes, he is," replied Phoebe. "He and my papa serve together in the synagogue. Matthias is a ruler under him. Papa has helped him learn his duties. Haven't you seen him there?"

"I believe so." Rebekah regarded Matthias. "He's quite young to be a ruler."

"Some think so. But the elders chose him after his father's death."

Rebekah crossed her arms over her chest and cocked her head to one side. "I understand." Her tone was dry.

"No, Rebekah. It's not like that. I mean ..."

"Phoebe," called Jairus, interrupting her defense. "It's time I help you onto the donkey."

"Papa," pleaded Phoebe, "may I walk with Rebekah? When we get to the hill country I'll ride."

Jairus planted a kiss on his daughter's forehead. "For now, you may walk. Don't let yourself get tired." His caring smile betrayed his stern manner.

"I won't."

Jairus examined the belongings and turned to Matthias. "What do you say? Shall we continue?"

"We'd best, or the day will be too far gone to make any progress."

The smile on Matthias's face softened his features.

Makes him almost handsome. Rebekah skewed her mouth to one side and shook her head. *Where did that thought come from?*

Phoebe grabbed her arm, jolting her out of her pondering.

"The Lord God has blessed us with sunshine, a cloudless sky and"—Phoebe's high-pitched voice grew hushed—"with good company." She smiled and nodded toward Matthias. "I have seen him looking your way several times. Do you think he's handsome? You know Papa and he have spoken of the day, not far in the future, when I become old enough to be a bride. And you—are you anxious to marry?"

"When the Lord sends me a husband. Until then, this is the day the Lord has made. Let's rejoice and be glad," replied Rebekah, sidestepping Phoebe's questions. "Have you ever attended a wedding?"

"Do you feel it, Matthias?" asked Jairus. He wiped the sweat from his forehead. The day had passed quickly and soon the sun would be setting.

"Feel what?" Matthias shrugged. "If you're speaking about the heat, yes."

Jairus shook his head. "I haven't a name for it. But something—or someone—walks on the horizon of our lives."

"Perhaps. Possibly it is all this talk of the Messiah. I for one won't be one to follow the voice of just anyone, especially one wandering around in the wilderness."

"Be mindful, Matthias, not to speak against what you don't know. Many believe John the Baptizer to be a prophet of the Lord. It's been four hundred years since the Lord God has spoken to his children."

Rather than answer Jairus's chafing remark, Matthias slung his waterskin to his lips before they continued climbing the hill. He was thankful there wouldn't be many more before Cana, and the plateau with its shade lay just ahead. There they would rest the night.

"What do you know, Jairus? Have you learned more than when we last spoke?"

"I know the Lord God promised the Messiah would come. I know the word he spoke through the prophet Daniel, and I believe the time of the Messiah is near. I know he will perform his word exactly as he spoke it. Until I know more—I wait."

Matthias dropped his glance to the trail and remained silent.

"What do you question, Matthias? The truth of the Scriptures? The prophets' words you hear read each Sabbath? Or do you doubt our Lord God will bring it to pass now—in our lives? What causes you to doubt?"

This conversation wasn't going the direction Matthias imagined. He turned his stare on the other and stiffened his back.

"Of course I believe all of what the prophets have written. And haven't all before us believed the Messiah would appear in their day? Yet here we are. Besides, I value my life more than to believe every whisper in the wind."

Their journey continued with surface conversation, as the promises spoken to their fathers marched through Matthias's mind. Four hundred years. He would not soon believe this one who claimed to speak for God now. There was too much at stake.

CHAPTER 5

Rebekah grinned. "You look like a princess, Phoebe—surrounded by supplies and sitting on top of your donkey."

A smile as sweet as sugary dibs graced Phoebe's face. If it weren't for the dark circles framing her deep brown eyes, no one would guess this petite young lady was ill.

"How are you feeling this morning?" Phoebe had had another attack in the night. Rebekah rested her hand on the donkey's rump and listened as Joanna and Immah whispered behind them. Rebekah couldn't make out their words. They were probably rehashing Phoebe's attack.

Phoebe fought with the sky-blue veil covering her unusual blonde hair as both flew into her face.

"I wish Papa wouldn't make me wear this." She tugged at the veil, pulling her hair in the process. "Ouch!" She wrestled with the scarf and situated it in place before she continued.

"I shouldn't complain. He's only trying to take care of me. I'm doing fine now, thanks to the Lord God and your Gramma's honey. The oil usually helps, but not if the coughing won't stop. I'll be sure to carry honey with me any time we travel." Phoebe twisted on her crude throne, trying to work out the kinks in her back. "I would love to hop down and walk with you. Maybe once we're over the hill Papa will allow it."

Phoebe continued to chatter without a break. Rebekah shook her head, trying to free her thoughts from the picture of Phoebe struggling for air. Her strength of spirit certainly outshone any lack in her body.

The sun warmed their backs as they topped the last hill. The village of Cana lay before them, blanketed in green terraced hills of vineyards, gardens, and pomegranate orchards. People dotted the dirt roads as they made their way to the well in the middle of the village square. The well was the town's social center, where travelers and townspeople alike found refreshment along with the latest news.

"Do you see what they're doing?" asked Phoebe as they approached the village.

"Yes, but why are they carrying torches? It's nearing midday."

"The torches line the wedding route the groom travels to receive his bride," Phoebe explained. "They will light his path as he, his bride, and their friends—all arrayed in beautiful clothes—parade through the streets."

Phoebe hopped off the donkey and brushed dust from her arms.

"Hurry, the servants are drawing water. I'm ready for a drink of fresh water and a chance to wash away some grime." She brushed at her clothes. "What about you?" She pulled Rebekah towards the hub of activity and continued to rattle on. "Then we'll find our host and get ready for the wedding." Phoebe clapped her hands in front of her chin and giggled.

"Slow down, Phoebe," ordered her mother. "You must pace yourself."

"Yes, Immah."

Rebekah and Phoebe splashed cool water on their faces from the bucket Eliezer had drawn. Phoebe rambled on about the sights, the clothes the bride and groom would wear, the food, and the many guests gathering for the occasion, until without invitation an unexpected voice joined in.

"The village is overflowing with guests. The governor will need to be richer than I thought to provide enough food and wine for this crowd." The voice held an edge of doubt.

Phoebe playfully pushed Matthias and splashed him. "Don't be such an old man, Matthias. The governor will take care of everything. Our duty is to celebrate with the groom and his bride." Phoebe turned to Rebekah. "Let's find our host. Getting ready is half the fun." Phoebe shrugged as she and Rebekah promenaded arm-in-arm down the street.

"Phoebe."

Her father's voice halted their steps and put a slump in Phoebe's shoulders.

"Yes, Papa?"

"Keep your mother close," he ordered.

Sarah approached Rebekah. "And you, my lovely daughter, stay with Phoebe while I help serve."

"Yes, Immah," answered Rebekah.

"Sarah!"

Surprise lit Rebekah's and Sarah's faces at the thunderous voice echoing across the sea of people.

"Papa!" Rebekah called.

"Do you see him?" Sarah asked.

"He's there, over in that direction." Matthias pointed. "He is making his way ..." His words floated away on the air as the women moved toward Simon.

Simon caught his wife in his arms. Impropriety meant nothing in her presence. As he put her down, Rebekah heard him whisper. "I have much to tell you, my beloved. Our lives will never be the same."

A squeak escaped through Rebekah's lips as her father lifted her and planted a kiss on her forehead.

"What a wonderful blessing to see you both." Simon looked around momentarily. "But I can't stay with you." He gestured behind them. "The Lord is waiting. Once we leave the feast, I hope to walk with you back to Capernaum. Then I'll tell you about Yeshua the Nazarene and all that's happened."

"You call him Lord?" asked Sarah.

"Yes. Later, my beloved, but soon." He kissed her cheek and made his way back to the Nazarene.

"What did he mean, Immah? You're shaking." Rebekah gently rubbed her mother's arm.

"I'm not sure. But I know Simon wouldn't leave us or his fishing to follow wagging tongues."

Matthias, Phoebe, and Joanna pushed their way through the crowd to reach Sarah and Rebekah. Matthias stood beside the women, looking past them, following Simon's path. Rebekah watched him with a sideways glance.

What interest does he have in my papa? Or perhaps not my papa, but Yeshua?

"I must be on my way," said Matthias, moving past the women and through the crowd.

Joanna, Phoebe, and Rebekah accompanied Sarah to the groom's house, where the servants prepared platters of food and pitchers of wine. Others added garlands of flowers to the wedding canopy in the reception hall. An older woman approached the group as Rebekah hugged her mother before leaving with Joanna and Phoebe.

"We want to keep the trays filled with food. Would you care to oversee the servants traveling with your company?" she asked.

Rebekah turned at the woman's strange request. Servants were usually ordered to serve, not asked.

"Rebekah, hurry," called Phoebe.

Rebekah dismissed the woman's entreaty and followed Phoebe and her mother.

She's like the tiny hummingbirds that never sit still.

"Did you see all that food and wine?" asked Phoebe, wide-eyed.

"The whole of Capernaum's market doesn't offer so much to choose from." Rebekah tried to take in all the sights and sounds at once. "The noise is deafening."

"But filled with joy," exclaimed Phoebe as the trio entered their rooms off the great hall. "Now," she said, throwing off her veil and cloak. "Let's get ready for the celebration."

Rebekah watched Joanna braid Phoebe's long blonde hair, intertwining blue garlands of flowers into the strands.

"Would you like these yellow ones placed in your braids?" asked Joanna, as Rebekah wrestled with her unruly auburn curls.

"Would you? This stuff is impossible," replied Rebekah, tugging at an obnoxious curl.

Hair in place, the girls made their final pirouette, each surveying the other before making their entrance at the great hall of the governor's home. White columns stood at the hall's entryway like marble sentries, guarding the porches before the arrival of the wedding party. Songs from the street floated on the air as the groom, his bride, and their friends drew near. Phoebe and Rebekah clapped to the rhythm of the tinkling tambourines as they took their places in the hall.

The crowd hushed as the governor stood and raised his silver chalice. All eyes turned toward a room at the far end of the great hall. The groom in his finest linen mantle and gem-accentuated white turban ushered his bride, veiled and crowned with a garland of sparkling jewels, to the wedding canopy. Their guests oohed and aahed in hushed tones as they passed.

Once the wedding couple was seated like a king with his queen, one guest raised his goblet high and spoke the first blessing. "Blessed are you, Lord our God, King of the universe, who created all things for his glory."

The first blessing completed, the singing and dancing resumed. Servants entered and exited in a continuous parade, making sure all guests had sufficient wine and food. Rebekah stood mesmerized at the pomp and festivities, dreaming of the day she would sit under her own wedding canopy.

Matthias stood to recite the next of the seven blessings to be pronounced for the wedding couple. "Blessed are you, Lord our God, King of the universe ..."

Rebekah covered her gapping mouth. *Maybe Matthias is somebody.* She shook her head. "Not as much a somebody as he thinks," she muttered aloud.

Once the blessing ended, Phoebe clutched Rebekah's hand.

"Let's find some more of those cakes and honey." She pulled Rebekah in the direction of the long table, decorated with vases filled with lilacs and paper-white narcissus, and laden with meats, fish, cheeses, fruits, and various delicacies presented on platters with green herbs and ivy.

"I'm not sure I can eat any more," protested Rebekah.

"One more bite, then we dance it off with the other guests." Phoebe's long braid swayed as she kept time with the music.

The lamps and torches filled the outer courtyard with both light and shifting shadows as the sun set, and the time for the final blessing approached. Wine goblets were lifted to the God of the universe as another honored guest stood to bless the couple. A strange, reverent quiet fell over the celebration, swaddling the guests like a newborn baby.

"Blessed are you, Lord our God, King of the universe, who created joy and gladness ..."

The silence was palpable.

"... let there be heard in the cities of Judah and in the streets of Jerusalem the sound of joy..."

Chills rippled over Rebekah. The groom and bride sat transfixed, capturing every word. As the speaker finished, he took his seat ... next to her father!

"Phoebe?' whispered Rebekah. "Did the governor introduce him as ..."

"As Yeshua of Nazareth. I've heard rumors."

Maybe they're more truth than rumor.

The festivities resumed their previous gaiety except for the occasional cluster of tongue-waggers shooting curious glances at Yeshua. Rebekah watched him laughing and enjoying the company around him.

The couple in their bejeweled wedding garments pirouetted around the room with their guests. But all their finery could not distract Rebekah from the one called Yeshua, the Nazarene.

Servants carried more platters of cheese and fruit to the tables and reclining couches. Wine filled silver goblets. Rebekah's father, Andrew, James, and John stayed close to Yeshua. Her father called him Lord. Rebekah spotted two men with them she didn't recognize. And on the fringes stood Matthias.

"Rebekah?"

Phoebe's lighthearted call and gentle tug averted her wandering mind.

"Come, let's dance."

Rebekah saw through Phoebe's smile to the weariness in her eyes.

"It's been a long day. Let's sit and enjoy some more of this delicious food." Rebekah took Phoebe's arm in hers and led her to a corner across the hall.

"Doesn't the bride resemble a delicate butterfly?"

"And her groom a great stag ready to take his doe," added Rebekah.

"Rebekah!"

Rebekah turned her palms up and feigned an innocent expression. "What?"

Phoebe shook her head and changed the subject. "Isn't the wedding the most glorious thing you've ever seen?"

"It is glorious." answered Rebekah. *But I think there is even a greater glory among us.* "Thank you for inviting me." She drew her friend into her arms. The girl's frail body took Rebekah by surprise. Phoebe's clothes covered it quite well.

Phoebe smiled. "I'm glad you came. Did you know some wedding feasts last for days?" She pointed at a nearby platter. "Cheese?"

"Sure." Rebekah reached for an oblong piece of cheese but froze, as what appeared to be a self-conscious woman nervously approached Yeshua.

Phoebe frowned. "What are you watching? Why so serious?"

"Have you met Yeshua or the woman speaking to him? I saw her with the servants earlier." Rebekah took a piece of cheese and nodded in their direction. Phoebe glanced at the pair and shook her head.

"No, but we're not the only curious ones." She motioned toward the far side of the group. "Matthias has tried all day to get close to him. Maybe on the journey home he'll know something."

"Maybe." Rebekah preferred to speak with her father. "Look, Yeshua and those near him are following the woman. If Papa returns with us, I'll talk with him. And if he doesn't, Immah is with the servants. They always know everything and make up the rest." Both girls laughed.

Another servant entered wringing his hands. He whispered something to the governor, whose face turned crimson.

"Governor," shouted a wobbly guest. "More wine. Where are your lazy servants? They should be whipped."

Phoebe covered her gaping mouth. "Oh, no."

Rebekah looked from the governor to Phoebe and back again.

The governor stood, his head high, and forced a smile.

"My servant will bring more in a moment. Until then, everyone sing, dance, and celebrate our happy couple. And the Lord God of heaven and earth bless the fruit of the vine," he added with his hands clasped as if in prayer.

A grumbling moved through the guests like pebbles rolling down the hillside, gathering momentum as they went. Servants entered with more food. Insults were hurled in their direction.

"There is no more wine," whispered Phoebe to Rebekah. "The governor and the couple will be shamed."

"What will they do?"

Before Phoebe could answer, a tall servant, his face beaming, entered with a large pitcher, and filled the governor's goblet.

The governor set down his goblet and glowed with pleasure. "You will be glad for the wait, sir," he called to the outspoken guest. "The best wine is about to be served."

Rebekah pulled her braid over her shoulder. "What happened? Were they not out of wine?"

"I'm sure they were. And never is the best wine served last." Phoebe shrugged.

Yeshua returned and took his place. Servants entered and exited, their curious glances surveying him.

"Something's changed, Phoebe," Rebekah said, her eyes on Yeshua. "As surely as spring follows winter, there's more to come."

CHAPTER 6

Rebekah clasped her fingers around her father's large, rough hand.

"Papa, will we see you soon?" She searched her father's face in hope.

"Rebekah!" Phoebe's urgent call caught her attention. "Aren't you coming with us?" Phoebe's donkey shifted his weight, jostling her seat. "Come join me and my trusty steed." She patted the animal's soft grey neck.

"I won't be long," Rebekah called over her shoulder. "Papa, soon?"

"In a day or two. Remember—not a word," ordered Simon. He planted a kiss on her forehead, then turned to Sarah, embracing her with his eyes. "I will see you soon, but not soon enough. Now go, both of you, before Phoebe fidgets herself off that donkey."

Sarah smiled.

"Gramma will be worse than a little mouse scurrying around when she hears. Shalom, my love." Her hand lingered on his arm before turning to Rebekah. "Quickly, child, we're falling behind. If Phoebe twists around much further, she won't be all that comes off that donkey."

Rebekah and Sarah scurried to catch up with the company of travelers. Out of the corner of her eye Sarah caught a glimpse of Matthias and Eliezer rushing in the same direction.

"Rebekah, quickly," Sarah urged.

Once united with the travelers, Rebekah slowed her pace to walk alongside Phoebe. Sarah joined Joanna, and Matthias fell in step with Jairus.

"Wasn't the wedding the most beautiful celebration you've ever seen?" asked Phoebe.

Rebekah nodded without really catching Phoebe's words. Her thoughts were elsewhere. She concentrated on the talk behind her.

"Sarah, you were with the servants," said Joanna. "What happened with the wine? Tongues spread rumors like Samson's foxes in the Philistine cornfields. Are they true? Did Yeshua—" Her voice dropped to a murmur. "Did Yeshua perform a miracle?"

"I can tell you only what I saw. Mary, the mother of Yeshua, went to him for help. Then she told the servants to do whatever he said. They did, filling the water pots with water. They drew wine from them."

"Rebekah!" Phoebe's voice brought her back. "I don't believe you've heard a word I said. Oh." She nodded knowingly toward Matthias. "I see."

"Oh, no, I was eavesdropping on the conversation behind us. Not on the men up ahead."

Jairus walked with his head down and his hands in front of his chest. Matthias kept step with him, gesturing in one direction then the other, oblivious to those around him.

"Lord, you stayed close to the Nazarene's group," Matthias said. "What do you make of him? Is he who John the Baptizer said he is? He speaks with an authority that commands attention."

Jairus stared into the distance. "You just described a king."

Matthias stiffened. "Speak those words in the wrong ears and a cross will be your grave. Let me ask another way. Is he the Messiah?"

"Not sure. John the Baptizer declares he is the Lamb of God who takes away the sin of the world. John claims to be the voice preparing the way of the Lord. Based on his witness, many believe Yeshua is Messiah. His disciples, including Simon, say he *is* the Messiah, King of Israel."

"That echoes your first statement." Matthias walked a few steps in silence, remembering the three crosses on the road to Magdala. "Simon is an unlearned man, and so is Yeshua. How can he be the Messiah? What do you say?"

"I say Yeshua is like no other man I know."

The two walked on in silence until Matthias could hold his questions no longer. "What do you make of the rumors of this Nazarene turning water into wine? Why would the servants tell such tales?"

"Perhaps because it is true. The servants weren't alone in the telling."

Matthias squinted at the sun directly overhead and reached for the wineskin hanging from his shoulder. The sweet wine, the last wine of the wedding, caressed his lips. Jairus watched him and then called to the other travelers.

"Let's rest and refresh ourselves with a little wine and some of Cana's pomegranates."

Matthias rubbed his bearded chin and looked longingly at the trail ahead. He wanted to go on, but concern for Phoebe drew lines of worry on Jairus's face, and Matthias remained quiet. He watched the girl as she slid off the donkey.

"One day she can be your wife, Matthias," commented Jairus.

Matthias looked away from Phoebe's petite frame.

"Yes, I know you and Papa talked of those plans. But I want them to be her plans as well." Secretly he wondered if she would live to marry. If so, she would inherit her father's riches. Pushing those thoughts—and Rebekah's womanly figure alongside Phoebe's—from his mind, he changed the subject.

"We'll make it back to Capernaum by tomorrow evening, Jairus?"

"As long as all goes well."

The travelers found scant available shade in the huge boulders along the trail.

After eating his last bite of bread, Matthias rose, stretched his back, and took another drink. "It will be good to be home." His thoughts turned to time wasted resting, and the loss of profits.

Jairus rose and helped Phoebe back on the donkey.

"All set?" She nodded. "Then we will travel over these hills and be ready to stop before night falls. Then tomorrow, home."

Matthias quickened his pace as the company entered Capernaum's empty marketplace and drifted in different directions.

"Eliezer, go ahead of me. See that water is drawn and heated."

Eliezer closed his eyes as he bowed in obedience. "Yes, Master."

Matthias stopped as the tall figure with stooping shoulders and shuffling steps began to move away. "Eliezer."

The servant stopped, but before he could reply, Matthias continued. "Draw some water for yourself, and tell Deborah I can hardly wait to eat her sweet cakes and dibs. I will be along shortly, after I stop by the synagogue to tend to my duties."

Eliezer smiled and nodded.

Upon arriving home, Matthias removed the small scroll from the mezuzah.

"Hear, O Israel! The Lord is our God, the Lord is one!" His voice floated into the evening air as he recited the first scripture from Torah every schoolboy learned. He kissed the scroll and replaced it in its hiding place. He longed for the bath waiting for him and the cakes he knew Deborah had prepared. The business of finance, figs, and vineyards would wait until morning. The mysteries surrounding the Nazarene, the future with Phoebe, and the face of Rebekah, would be lost during a night of sleep.

Daylight stole its way into the darkness.

"Eliezer!" cried Matthias, springing from his bed and throwing his tunic over his head. "Why wasn't I awakened? The morning is half spent." He splashed water from the basin on his face. As he rubbed it with a dry cloth, he heard footsteps whispering across the floor outside his room. He threw the cloth down and stepped to his doorway to find Leah fidgeting with her apron.

"What is it, Leah?"

"Master, Eliezer has gone on an errand. He gave us strict orders not to disturb you," Leah explained , her eyes downcast and her voice tremulous. "But your morning meal is prepared, if you wish to be served now."

"Yes, yes, Leah. Leave it in the courtyard. What hour is it?" Matthias brushed his hand through his rumpled hair and tried to shake away the remnants of sleep.

"It is the third hour, Master. Is that all?"

Matthias shook his head at the sight of the thin housemaid seeking her escape from him.

Am I truly that frightening?

"Yes, you may go. But if Eliezer returns while I'm eating, have him join me."

"Surely, Master."

Matthias belted his tunic and washed his hands, cleansing them of any unclean thing, then wolfed down his breakfast.

"Deborah, Leah, somebody. I'm done with this meal. Where is Eliezer?" He rose from his seat and stomped across the courtyard as Deborah entered.

"Master."

Her calm reply told Matthias he was in for some sage discipline. He caressed the back of the bent-over frame before him.

"I know your eyes are scolding me even if I can't see them. So I will kiss the top of your head and ask if you know the whereabouts of Eliezer?"

Her gray hair, streaked with threads of the youthful black it once was, hung about her face where a few unruly strands had freed themselves from the bun atop her head.

"You're a good boy, Matthias."

He rolled his eyes and shook his head. "I am not a boy, Deborah."

She grabbed his hand and graced it with a kiss.

"You will always be my boy, but you are the master. So you are a good man, Matthias. Eliezer will return soon, though he did not say where he was going."

Matthias weighed his options. "I need to walk the vineyard, but that will have to wait until evening. For now, I'll work at my writing table, and hope the figures show some profit. Deborah, have Eliezer join me as soon as he returns."

"Yes, Master." After retrieving the meager bits left from his morning meal, she exited.

Matthias had meant for Leah to do that, but he knew full well Deborah spared her from his impatience. He reached for the papyrus and started checking his figures. He needed only a few workers during the hot summer months for harvesting the early figs and the midsummer grapes. Last year's profits supplied payment for the spring and summer workers. The grape harvest would pay the fall workers.

"Master?" Eliezer interrupted Matthias's work. "You wished to see me?"

"Yes. You were to wake me. Now I'm afraid the day won't be long enough to accomplish my tasks. And I desired to sit and speak with you about the wedding."

Eliezer stood in silence.

"You have nothing to say?"

"You have asked nothing of me until now, Master."

"Why didn't you wake me? And where have you been that was more important than my needs?" demanded Matthias.

"You needed the rest. And what you do not finish today, Master, can be finished tomorrow. I walked the hedge and found it in good order. The shepherds using your land are caring for the figs."

"I liked it better when you had nothing to say."

"Do you wish for me to stay and speak about the events of the wedding, or should that wait?"

"No. I mean, yes. Do sit. And no, that won't wait." Matthias put the papyrus aside. "You have taken care of most of my day, with my gratitude. Now would be a good time to hear what happened in Cana."

Eliezer set a small wooden stool near Matthias's writing table. His dark eyes focused on something beyond Matthias.

"The wine ran out." Eliezer shook his head and peered into the air as if searching for words. "Crispus, the governor's servant, served the last of it. He returned in a panic, fearing the governor's wrath."

"Rightly so," commented Matthias.

"After gathering his courage to report to the governor, he left us for whatever fate awaited him. Then Mary came in."

"Mary?" asked Matthias. "The Nazarene's mother?"

"Yes, Master. A woman full of grace."

"Yes, of course. Finish the story."

"Mary told us to do whatever her son commanded. We did not understand, but ours is to obey. Yeshua the Nazarene told us to fill the large purifying water pots with water. Our hands shook as we filled container after container. No one said a word. We just obeyed. Then Crispus came in and stormed at us about filling water pots when the governor needed wine."

"You stopped?" asked Matthias.

"Momentarily. Yeshua looked at Crispus, nodded to us, and we finished filling the six twenty-gallon pots. Crispus took the first pitcher to the governor as Yeshua instructed."

"The water! Did he want you all beaten?"

Eliezer stood. He laid his hand on Matthias's shoulder. "Do you remember the last wine served, Master?"

"Yes, of course. It was the best wine." Matthias stopped. He stood to face Eliezer. "Where did it come from?"

"The purifying water pots filled with water."

"No. It couldn't have been." He looked at Eliezer's expressionless face. "It was? How can that be?" demanded Matthias, waving his arms in frustration.

"Yeshua changed the water into wine. The best wine."

Matthias stared into Eliezer's dark eyes. "You saw it? You believe this?"

"I saw it. I do not know what I believe, for I don't understand what it means. But Yeshua's disciples were with him, and they saw it too."

"And what did they say?"

"They spoke to each other in excited whispers of Yeshua being the Son of God, the Messiah. They believed he performed a miracle." Eliezer paused.

"And you, Eliezer?"

His servant answered Matthias's question with one of his own. "You tasted the wine?"

Matthias nodded, remembering the smooth rich taste of the last wine.

"What I believe," Eliezer said, "is this will not be the last we hear of Yeshua the Nazarene. If you do not believe me, at least believe the work."

The two stood silently facing one another. Matthias folded his hands over his mouth as if in prayer. "I must think on these things, Eliezer. You may go."

Eliezer left Matthias alone with his papyrus. He dipped his quill in the ink, but the figures before him lost shape as Eliezer's words replayed in his mind. He set the quill in the ink, pushed his chair away from his table, and walked to the courtyard.

"Yeshua, why should I bother myself with you?" he muttered as he paced. "The Messiah? Hardly. Not from Nazareth. You're costing me peace and profit."

He returned to his table and the open papyrus filled with the figures that promised future riches. These things he understood. These things he believed in. These things held promise.

CHAPTER 7

"Immah" pleaded Rebekah as she pounded the bread dough. "I want to hear it all again. And I know Gramma wants it planted in her mind. Don't you, Gramma?"

Gramma looked up from chopping herbs and scallions. "My mind, yes, but more importantly my heart. The story remains the same. We choose to believe it, or we do not. Now we have much to do before your papa and our guests arrive."

Sarah nudged Rebekah from the table and placed the dough in a large wooden bowl. "I'm sure the Master will answer all your questions. At this moment, I need you to go to the marketplace and buy some carrots, potatoes, and a lamb shank."

"We have plenty of dried fish," offered Gramma with a smile. "A good fisherman's family never needs to go hungry."

"But tonight we eat lamb stew," answered Sarah. "Which reminds me—purchase some tahini. If Jacob doesn't have any with his produce, get the sesame seeds, and we will grind and roast our own."

Rebekah wiped her hands and fished a few copper coins from a small wooden box sitting on a shelf among the cooking supplies. "Is there flour on my face, Immah?"

"No. You're fine. Go. And remember, not a word about our guests."

Rebekah turned as she reached the door. "Not a word. Immah, could I hurry over to see how Phoebe is doing? She looked exhausted when we returned. I want to share all you've told me, and—"

"Stop, child." Sarah clapped the flour from her hands and approached her daughter. "Allow me to answer," she said with her hands on Rebekah's shoulders. "Yes, you may, but don't stay long. She needs rest. And I need food for our guests,"

"I won't."

Rebekah never considered her home small until she saw Phoebe's two-story stone home, complete with a covered entryway resting on white columns mirroring those standing guard at the synagogue. She hoped Hannah and not Delilah would meet her at the open door.

"Miss Rebekah," greeted Hannah. "Miss Phoebe will be glad you came."

"She is up to company, then?"

"You are always welcome. She is resting in the courtyard," answered Hannah, leading the way.

Phoebe rose and greeted her friend with a hug.

"What a great surprise." Loosening her grip, she wrapped Rebekah's arm in hers. "I prayed you would come soon. I can hardly wait to hear what you know about the wine at the wedding."

The girls sat on a bench underneath a large palm tree by the gurgling garden pool. Delilah stood guard not ten steps away.

"Delilah?"

"Yes, Miss Phoebe."

"Would you bring us some refreshment?"

Delilah glared at Rebekah. "Yes, Miss Phoebe. But remember not to tire yourself with too much company."

"I won't." Phoebe shook her head as the woman exited. "If she smiled, I believe her face would crack." The girls snickered. "But she is a most faithful servant," Phoebe said, "even if not the most pleasant."

"That's for certain," agreed Rebekah. "I can't stay long. There are—" Rebekah stopped before blurting out about their guests. "There is much to do since we returned from the wedding. Gramma kept most things in order, but she is older and tires easily these days. Immah wants me back to help her with daily chores."

Delilah reappeared in the doorway of the courtyard with a tray of dibs and sweet bread, and a pitcher containing a thinner version of dibs for the girls to drink.

"Miss Phoebe, the cook thought you would enjoy this with your guest."

"Thank her for me. Dibs is my favorite. What about you, Rebekah?"

Rebekah eyed the bowl of thick grape syrup. "Let's just say I ate more than my share at the wedding." Rebekah followed Phoebe's lead, dipping her bread in the sweet liquid.

"Mm. The grapes must have been especially sweet. This is good." Phoebe dabbed some syrup trailing down her chin.

Rebekah nodded agreement, since her own mouth was too full for words.

"Tell me, have you had an opportunity to speak with your papa or immah about the wedding? Papa has not spoken a word about it. When I ask him, he replies I am too young to understand. But I don't even know what I'm not supposed to understand."

"I'm older than you, and I don't understand it either," replied Rebekah. "Truth is, I don't believe anyone understands what it all means."

Rebekah hurried through the story, stopping only to answer Phoebe's many questions. Delilah stood like a sentry over the girls until the story ended. She scowled at Rebekah, then took the empty tray and left the courtyard.

"I believe Delilah wants me to go, Phoebe."

"Must you?" she begged. She moved a little closer to Rebekah. "Do you believe the whispers? Is he the Messiah?"

Rebekah shrugged. "I don't know. And yes, I must go, if I'm to keep Immah happy." She stood. "The men will soon leave for Passover in Jerusalem. I'll try to see you then and share anything new I've learned. I'm glad to see you looking rested."

Phoebe took Rebekah's hand and walked her to the door. "Don't worry over me. I'm in the Lord's care." The girls embraced. "May the Lord be with you. Shalom."

"Shalom, my friend."

Rebekah waved as she started down the hill, muttering to herself when she saw a smiling Delilah close beside Phoebe. "I know she doesn't like me. She smiles only when I leave."

She made her way through the marketplace, choosing the finest vegetables. Her family was not rich by any means—the tax collectors and Romans made sure of that—but they had sufficient to give their guests the best they could, and today's guests would be special.

"Jacob, I see you have tahini, and these grapes are beautiful," she exclaimed, holding up the largest bunch. The rotund man sitting behind the fruits and vegetables nodded in pride and handed her the hummus-like tahini.

"You are right. The grapes just arrived from the south."

"Then that means they are costly."

Jacob smiled again. "Not costly according to the flavor. Would you like a bunch?"

Rebekah considered the purchase for a moment before answering. "Yes. They would make wonderful dibs."

"Dibs?" The merchant's eyes widened in interest. "Someone special coming to your house?"

"Uh, Papa will be home. He is most special," she answered. As she handed him three of the coins, angry voices rose above the noise of merchants and customers.

"What do you mean, you brought in figs and wine from another?" The bellowed accusation rumbled through the marketplace. Startled, Rebekah stared in the direction of the uproar.

"Matthias?" The name escaped her lips without thinking, but not without notice.

Face reddened and chest heaving, he glanced at her before returning his glare to the merchant. He lowered his voice and with teeth clenched continued. "We have a *contract* ..."

Rebekah ducked her head and left. What little interest she'd felt for him began to wane. Then she remembered her father's bad temper and quick speech. She tugged on a loose curl. How many times had it gotten him into trouble? And hers could be just as stinging.

Instead of heading straight home, she let her feet take her on a detour to the lake, in case anyone interesting was there. Her instinct had been good—James was at lakeside, finishing up some work on his father's boat. The workers waded through the water, probably headed for their homes and a late morning meal.

"James!"

He waved a greeting and dropped his net.

"Andrew and Papa will be home today," she called. "Won't you come eat with us? John too, if he's home."

James stood taller than his brother John, and his beard made him appear older than his years. His straight black hair was shorter than most men's but long enough to tie in the back while he worked. He was Rebekah's choice of the two brothers.

Her choice now splashed through the shallow blue waters to shore. "By the looks of your load, you're expecting more than Simon and Andrew."

"I can't say." *He should already know who might be there.* "But I believe you will want to come."

James's laughter burst in the air like an old bag full of new wine as he playfully flipped a curl from her shoulder. "John is home and has already sent me word by Sarah. I'll be there."

Rebekah puzzled an instant about John being home, then responded to James's fun at her expense. "You just wanted to see if I would tell, didn't you?"

"But you didn't. A woman who can hold her tongue. What a treasure!" James chuckled as she left.

"Then I take it we'll see you this evening."

He may be laughing at me, but he called me a treasure.

Rebekah's steps were lighter as she tried to hurry with her mother's order across the loose pebbles on the path home.

"Rebekah! Rebekah!"

She turned to the beckoning call. Matthias was following her up the hill. She stopped and waited for him. "Matthias, shalom."

"Yes, shalom, Rebekah." He rubbed his hand across his beard before explaining. "My outburst in the marketplace may have seemed uncalled for."

"What's that to me? It's the merchants you have to deal with," she retorted.

"You are quite right, and we did work out our differences. But I didn't want you to think I behave that outrageously as a rule. I simply cannot abide a traitorous attitude, in business or otherwise."

"Again, what does it matter what I think? I need to be on my way." Rebekah turned to leave him and his explanations. He continued alongside her.

"You have quite a bundle. May I help you carry it?"

"I am quite capable. Thank you for your kindness," she replied, not missing a step.

Matthias took her arm and stopped her, causing her to sidestep. She glared at him.

"Matthias, remove your hand. I have guests to prepare for, and I must be on my way. I strongly suggest you be on yours."

Matthias smiled. "It seems I continue to make things worse each time we meet. But I will leave you to prepare for your guests. Does that mean your papa is returning soon?" He did not wait for her answer, but turned and moved back down the path.

She rolled her eyes and watched him go. Heat from within rose to her cheeks. Hopefully, she had not said too much.

Matthias sauntered away with a smirk. The morning had proved profitable in a couple of ways. He rattled the money bag hanging from his belt. His encounter with the merchant had gone better than his meeting with Rebekah, but he did learn she was preparing for guests. He smiled, wondering if the Nazarene would be among them. *Maybe I can question him concerning this so-called miracle.* Matthias would not be as easily taken in as some itinerant fishermen.

His smile faded. Hunger for truth gnawed at his heart, but fear of what it might expose threatened to swallow his appetite. The emptiness of his soul left room for nothing else.

CHAPTER 8

Rebekah stirred on her mat and curled into a tight ball as dreams and reality struggled for victory. A rat chewed on the wooden door. Rebekah opened her mouth to scream but nothing came out. The effort drew her into wakefulness.

She bolted upright and listened, one hand over her mouth, the other against her chest. She heard it, a scrunching of ... she cocked her head to one side. Someone walked on the rock path outside. Probably her father. He had stayed away from the sea as long as he could.

After all, we do have to eat, he'd said. She lay back and shut her eyes.

But not for long.

"Rebekah."

The whisper beckoned her, but her body rebelled.

"Rebekah." The harsh whisper's owner shook her shoulder. "Wake up. We need to start preparing a meal for our guests."

She rolled to her back and stretched out the night kinks. "Yes, Immah, I'm awake."

Rebekah braided her hair and rinsed her face before joining her mother and grandmother down in the inner court. Gramma patted down the unleavened dough into small cakes without breaking rhythm. Sarah and Mary, Yeshua's mother, smiled a greeting as they prepared fruit for breakfast.

"Rebekah, the nanny needs to be milked." Sarah motioned towards the bucket by the wall.

Rebekah grimaced at the notion of milking the contrary goat. To her way of thinking, the old nanny made a game of it, letting Rebekah get her bucket almost full before kicking it over. She could swear the nanny smiled in victory with each overturned bucket.

Rebekah headed for the door but stopped short as she overheard her mother and Mary talking.

"I'll have Rebekah take Simon and the other fishermen some food shortly," Sarah said. "They should be returning any time after being out all night. We should have fish this evening. If not, we'll have grumbling."

The two women's laughter would have lightened Rebekah's mood if not for having to face the stubborn old goat. She reached for the nanny's rope and patted her head.

"I wonder who was walking around so early this morning?"

The nanny bleated a reply.

"You're not much help."

On the other side of Capernaum, Matthias checked the area. No one was around this early. He slipped his feet from his sandals. The muddy sand squished between his toes as ripples washed the rest back out to sea. The cadence of gentle waves sloshing over his feet held hope of a peaceful cleansing he longed for in his heart. Eyes closed, he stretched his neck from side to side as his mind wandered to days long past.

A young boy walked in the early morning mist, hand in hand with his father.

"This is the Lord God's tabernacle." His father's voice washed through his mind, crisp and clear as the cool water.

"All creation," he would say, encircling the world with a wave of his arms, "speaks of the glory of its creator, the one true God, the God of Israel."

The young lad stood in awe as his father peered into the heavens. Then, just as the sun's rays peeked over the hills and burst into full view, his father would shout, "See, my boy, the glory of the Lord shining over the whole earth."

Matthias knew it was coming, but he never ceased to be caught off guard at that morning shout of praise.

Tears clouded Matthias's eyes as he waited for the sun. He had no memory of his mother. She had died shortly after his birth. It had always been him and his father, and Deborah, the oldest house servant he had ever known. And above all else for his father, this glorious God. The memory brought a mixture of sadness and joy. His peace faded.

Who is this God who had never let me know my mother, and took my father while I still needed him? Matthias lowered his head. Stinging tears reflected the burning anger of his heart. As a tear escaped down his face, he felt his father's hand slipping away from him, from the little boy's hand. The first rays of sunlight peeked over the distant hill, and his tears ran freely at the sight.

There would be no shout this morning. Not ever again.

A movement to his right caught his attention. Without hesitation, Matthias knelt at the water's edge, splashed the cold water on his face, then slipped on his sandals. He didn't recognize the intruder. As the stranger approached, a vaguely familiar voice called to him.

"May the Lord God who shows us his glory in the sun give you peace, Matthias. Shalom."

He returned the greeting as the figure came closer. "Forgive me for not remembering your name, as you have so easily recalled mine."

Before the visitor could answer, the sun burst over the hills, and Matthias saw clearly the one approaching him.

"I am Yeshua of Nazareth."

Pain seized Matthias's chest as he heard his father's words again.

See the glory of the Lord shining over all the earth.

He frowned. Before he could gather his thoughts and speak, the Nazarene continued.

"This is my favorite time of day, Matthias. I, like you, enjoy feeling the water washing the sand over my feet." Matthias then noticed the Nazarene carrying his sandals. "Let's walk together for a time."

"Surely." Matthias groped for words. His questions and skepticism faded in the presence of this man. His heart burned within him. Fear? Anger? He couldn't even glance in his direction, fearing what the Nazarene might see.

They walked along in silence until Yeshua's voice breached the quiet. "Many people have walked in darkness for so long they can't see the great light that's with them. They continue to walk in death's shadow, even though the light has come."

Matthias stopped and gazed at the man.

I don't understand, and I don't know how to ask him.

He struggled with how to address him. He did not hold him as his Master, nor could his tongue call his name.

"Master?"

Yeshua exposed his palm as he explained." There is glory here, now, among the people of Israel. It is a glory greater than the sun's, and his glory is the light shining on them. Those who are not blind and will come to the light of life, they will know the peace of God and live ... forever." He paused.

Matthias had neither question nor answer. The Nazarene kicked at the water, washing off bits of sand before donning his sandals. He laid his hand on Matthias's shoulder. "Be mindful. The light shines only for a short time." He turned and started back the way he came.

Matthias was still staring after him when the Nazarene stopped and called to him. "You know those walking in the light won't fall."

Then he walked away until Matthias could no longer see him. Now questions and his father's morning shout raced through his mind as he made his way home.

See the glory of the Lord shining over the whole earth.

What did it all mean?

"No," Matthias finally exclaimed into the air, waving a dismissive hand. "This is no more than what it is. I will not be led astray by emotions of the past, or by the fanciful dreams of the paupers who have no other hope but the Messiah. The most unlearned schoolboy knows no prophet ever comes from Nazareth. I'll have to hear more than I've heard, and see more than I've seen, before I risk everything to follow this Nazarene."

He stomped up to his door, took the small scroll from its hiding place, and spit out the oft-repeated words. "Hear, O Israel, the Lord our God, the Lord is one ... And you shall love the Lord your God with all your heart and with all your soul and with all your might ... I am the Lord, your God." He replaced the scroll and went inside, rumbling like thunder into the courtyard.

"Eliezer. Leah? Deborah! Anybody! Someone better be awake in this household."

"Master?"

Matthias turned abruptly. "Eliezer. Where's my morning meal? I've got business to attend to, but I can't do it on an empty stomach."

"Deborah is readying it for you now. I will bring it to you."

"Be quick about it." Matthias turned his back on Eliezer, who looked perplexed. Matthias didn't care. He shook his head trying to rid his mind of the image of the Nazarene walking back down the shore of the Galilee, probably straight to Simon's house.

Rebekah short-roped the nanny to the post, hoping for success. She sat carefully on the three-legged stool and spoke in gentle whispers, trying to convince the goat of their friendship. It appeared to work until ...

"Rebekah." The voice startled her from the stool, sending her sprawling on the ground. Her foot hit the bucket and knocked it over. Both her fists went up in the air and slammed down on the pebbly ground. Her jaw went tight and her chest heaved. Someone was about to pay dearly for surprising her.

She hoisted herself up at the same time a hand came into her line of sight, offering help.

"Rebekah, it's only spilled milk."

Yeshua kept his hand extended. A slight smile etched his bearded face.

"Yes, Master, it is, but ..." She stopped. Her eyes brimmed with angry tears.

"But?"

Rebekah took his hand and let her rage relax.

"But nothing." She brushed the dirt from her hands and skirt as she tried to keep her temper under control. "We shall have wine with our morning meal." Rebekah tended to the nanny, who wore her infuriating victory smile. She noticed the Master gazing somewhere far beyond the sea, then turned her attention to the knot in the nanny's rope.

"All who are thirsty are welcome to come."

Rebekah turned. Was he talking about the milk? The wine? "Master?"

He smiled. "Let's go in. I'm sure food is ready." Yeshua picked up the bucket and offered his free hand to her. "We'll walk together."

At the touch of his hand, she knew it was only spilled milk. Somewhere deep within, she also knew his invitation would take her farther than the home they entered together.

CHAPTER 9

"Eliezer." called Matthias, washing down the last bite of dried pomegranate seeds with a swallow of wine. Where was the man? "Eliezer!"

"Forgive me, Master."

Matthias whirled, his heart threatening to leap from his chest.

"I will be sure to announce my appearance next time," replied the servant with his bottom lip tucked under his teeth.

"You impertinent servant, you know if it was anyone but you …" Matthias ran his hand over his beard, hiding his own smile.

"Yes, Master, I understand." Eliezer bowed. "How may I serve you?"

"You've prepared my leather satchel, and has Leah prepared a pouch of food, my wineskin, and water?"

"Yes, Master, all is ready. Your clothes are bundled in this extra mantle." Eliezer laid each item at his master's feet. "And an array of dried fruits, unleavened bread, and parched grain fill your satchel."

Matthias grabbed Eliezer in a bear hug and kissed him on one cheek, then the other. Eliezer responded stiffly, eyes wide.

"What would I do without you, old friend?" Noticing his servant's sadness, Matthias added, "I know what Passover means to you, but you're more valuable to me here, seeing to my affairs."

Matthias quickly wrapped the dark turban around his head, secured his money pouch inside his belt, and grabbed the other bundles.

"I must be on my way. Jairus won't wait long." He turned one last time to Eliezer. "Next year for sure," he said, placing a hand on his shoulder.

Eliezer quickly brushed a tear from his face. "It's not that, Master. It's the many memories of times past when we all made this pilgrimage." He blinked and met Matthias's unwavering stare. "May the Lord God be with you as you travel."

"And with you while I'm gone. I will return soon." Matthias hurried down the path.

"May you return in peace."

"Soon, Eliezer, soon," called Matthias without turning, quickening his pace.

Pilgrims preparing their journey impeded his way as he neared the sea.

"Matthias! I'm here. Over here!" Jairus maneuvered around the crowd.

"Are all these traveling with us?"

"You know how this pilgrimage is. We begin as two, joined by two more. Soon we are a multitude. Some move a little faster, some of us a bit slower. But we all seem to arrive at the same time."

"Jairus!" A voice called from across a flock of other travelers. Both men followed the shout. "Walk with us. We're headed to Nain."

Matthias swallowed his disapproval.

"We would count it a blessing to walk with you, wouldn't we, Matthias?" Jairus landed a hardy pat on his companion's back.

Matthias's expression remained bland. He offered a conciliatory nod. He saw only trouble where this Nazarene was concerned. But if they traveled together, he would try to learn whether the supposed rabbi was a charlatan, a fool, or ... The idea of the Messiah was more than he could entertain.

Once on the road, Matthias lingered behind the rest without regard to the conversations around him.

Why do they attend to his every word?

He stared at the back of the Nazarene's head. What made him so different? He was plain and of ordinary build. Did everybody believe this man to be the Messiah, the one who would save Israel from the Romans? He had no army, no military training from what Matthias knew of him. In fact, he'd heard he was only a carpenter's son with a carpenter's skill. By their dress, his family certainly was not rich.

"He intrigues you."

Matthias shot a glance toward the unfamiliar voice. "James, isn't it?" he asked, trying to surmise if this was the Nazarene's brother.

"Yes." The other man cocked his head to one side. "And you? You don't know what to think of my brother, do you?"

"No, I don't. He commands attention verging on worship wherever he goes. He speaks with an air of authority, especially for an unlearned man." He hesitated.

"You're thinking it. Why not speak it? I'll answer honestly," offered James.

"You asked me what I think of your brother, rumored to be the Messiah. You were raised with him. What do you think? Is he the Messiah Israel waits for?"

"I don't know. Yes, he's my brother. Yet he speaks of another father." He lowered his voice. "He speaks of the Lord God as his father."

"But that's blasphemous, James. He could be stoned for such a claim." He spoke softly as a deep crease furrowed his forehead.

"Only if it's not true."

Matthias knew, true or not, the Sanhedrin would have the Nazarene stoned for such claims without proof. Maybe even with proof.

"I know about his miracle in Cana, at the wedding. And you?" asked James.

Matthias nodded.

"But of a truth, I don't know how to answer your question. It's like asking me if I am the Messiah."

Matthias studied James. Doubt—or was it fear?—etched the man's face.

"May our journey lead us both to find what we search for," concluded James.

"Where's he going? I believed we were to make it to Nain before nightfall." Matthias pointed down one road, then turned to another. "He's taking the road to Magdala."

A distant rumble caused both men to glance behind them. Ominous clouds rolled across the western plain as winter and spring collided in their clash for dominion.

"He's headed for shelter." The men climbed around the larger white stones dotting the hillside until James hurried ahead. "I'm going to see where Yeshua plans to stay."

Matthias shook away the fear creeping up his back, as he gazed at the stone structure standing sentry at the top of the hill. The brownish-white watchtower stood guard over the wealth and populace of the city below. The town sat on a lush green carpet of grass, dotted with groves of trees that couldn't seem to decide whether or not the time for budding had arrived. The twin towers of the textile and fish industries proclaimed the city's wealth for every boat that anchored on its Galilean shore.

A sudden shudder coursed through Matthias to the very marrow of his bones. A darkness greater than the approaching thunderheads threatened to steal his legs' strength. Three crosses stood silhouetted against the sky, empty but full of gruesome reminders of the price a man would pay for following the promises of a false Messiah.

"Stopping here doesn't sit well with you?' asked Jairus as he came alongside Matthias.

"No. For all its beauty and wealth, the city is dark with harlotry, drunkenness, and demons. I come here to do business, but never to stay longer than necessary."

The travelers entered the city square. Merchants struggled to get one last sale while packing baskets and produce away from the impending storm. A scream from a distant world pierced the din of noise. Activity halted. Every head turned. A servant girl raced down a path away from a stone home as large as Matthias's and Jairus's homes put together. The Nazarene ran toward her, reaching the girl before she entered the marketplace. Pilgrims, merchants, and buyers swarmed Yeshua and the shaking servant. Her ashen face resembled every man's idea of the visage of death. Another shriek emanated from the stone house, filling the air with its terror.

Once his frozen body could move, Matthias craned his neck and pushed closer to the inner circle to hear the Nazarene's words.

Yeshua placed his hands on the servant's shoulders. Her shaking calmed and her terror-stricken eyes focused on the Nazarene's face as he spoke.

"What's happening in the home of your mistress?"

"It's Lady Susanna, Master." Her eyes pleaded the message she spoke. "I fear she will hurt herself or my lady."

Without hesitation the Nazarene followed the servant through the gate of the rock wall. Matthias and the rest of the town pushed their way after them.

"Who are these women, Jairus?" Both men strained against the frenzied crowd.

"The servant's mistress is Mary, a weaver of fine purple cloth." Jairus struggled to keep pace with those around him. "The Master healed her the last time he was here."

"Of what?"

"Demons."

Matthias twisted toward Jairus. His eyes narrowed and the hair on his neck bristled. He would have stopped had he not feared being trampled by the throng. As the door to the house began to close, Jairus elbowed his way inside, dragging Matthias with him.

"Let no one else enter," called the Master as he headed down the large corridor.

Jairus barred the door just as a guttural cry coursed through the hall from the room at its end, followed by the crash of shattering pottery. A woman with dark, tangled hair surged down the hall with the force of the sea's crashing waves against the northern white cliffs. Fury filled her painted eyes. Her ripped tunic hung off one shoulder. She ran with a pottery shard toward the Nazarene, her bracelets and wrist bells clanging. The words she uttered were not her own.

"Yeshua, Son of God!" The woman's eyes rolled wildly.

Yeshua stood firmly planted in her path. His eyes never moved from her face. As she drew back to strike him with the jagged shard, he spoke a quiet, firm command.

"Keep quiet."

She collapsed at his feet.

Silence hung in the air, interrupted only by the brushing sound of steps scurrying down the hall. A well-kept woman knelt beside the broken body at the Nazarene's feet.

"Master, Susanna came to me ready to destroy herself. She begged for help, desperate to flee the darkness in her soul. Without pause these demons torment her, sending her into convulsions and fits of rage. They are set on her damnation."

The Nazarene took the pleading woman's hands from his garment, raised her to her feet, and placed her next to him. He turned and knelt by the first woman, and caressed her hair from her face.

"Loose her," he commanded.

At his words, the woman's body contorted. Guttural groans from somewhere within her disrupted the quiet. The sounds and sights made Matthias's flesh crawl with the sensation of death. One last scream emanated from the tormented body, and then there was only lifeless silence. Matthias scanned the room without moving his head. All seemed to have the same thought—was she dead or alive?

The Master took her hand in his and lifted her to her feet. Whispers of "Praise the Lord God" spread like a current from person to person, as the woman stood, her eyes clear, her rage gone.

He laid his hand upon her head. "You are made whole."

Tears streamed down her cheeks. "Truly you are the Messiah, the Son of God."

The Nazarene smiled and turned to the other woman. "Mary, see to her needs, and then I hope you will welcome us for the night."

Matthias wondered at what he had witnessed. The Nazarene behaved as if this was an ordinary occurrence.

Mary's face glowed. "Of course, Master. We'll celebrate the mercies of our God for his visitation upon his people."

Throughout the evening, praise permeated the home of Mary Magdalene as her own story and Susannah's were told and retold. Matthias could no longer deny there was a power at work in the Nazarene. But what power?

"You're not yourself, Matthias," said Jairus as the servants showed them their sleeping quarters.

"Weary from the journey."

"Which journey?"

Matthias squirmed on his bed. "What's your meaning?'

"You seek to know, yet you refuse knowledge."

Matthias sat cross-legged on his makeshift bed. "I'm tired, Jairus. Speak plainly or this conversation is ended."

"You seek truth," answered Jairus, "yet you refuse it when it stands before you. You have seen and heard truth, but you don't believe what you see or hear. You walk on the edge, but never close enough to experience truth. What are you afraid of?"

"I'm not afraid of anything." Matthias lay back down, pulling his cloak over him.

"Sleep well, my friend."

Matthias stared into the darkness. He lied. He did fear. But what? He turned to one side. His money pouch made an uncomfortable bulge in his side. He moved it slightly and slipped into restless slumber.

CHAPTER 10

True to Jairus's word, Magdala overflowed with pilgrims headed for Jerusalem. A restless night left Matthias in no mood to deal with the influx of people, but deal he must if he planned on leaving with his company of travelers. Sarah and Mary, the Nazarene's mother, were among the latest arrivals. He pursed his mouth, surprised Rebekah was nowhere in sight. At least her presence would have made the journey more interesting.

"Mary!"

Matthias whirled around at the sound of Susanna's voice. Bracelets adorned the woman's bare arms, and a silver comb glistened in her auburn hair. But her lips no longer bore the remnants of the red they had been bathed in the night before. Her beauty was no longer hidden behind a mask of painted eyes.

"Shalom. Peace adorns you with its beauty," Mary responded. Her outstretched arms welcomed and embraced the young woman. "You have decided to travel with us?"

Travel with us!

Matthias's mouth would have gaped if others hadn't been around. Instead, he watched and waited. Surely the Nazarene would stop this unholy engagement. No matter how Susanna appeared today, he knew what she was.

Susanna shifted her gaze downward.

"I cannot. You've been so kind. I want to give this for your journey." She handed Mary a handful of coins and slipped the bracelets from her arms.

Matthias stretched his neck to glimpse the number of coins, but they disappeared into Mary's hand. He did know the bracelets were not cheap. *I'm beginning to understand.* Was it possible the Nazarene made money in miracles?

The unfolding scene would tell the story. Matthias cradled his elbow and pinched his mouth. A true prophet wouldn't accept anything from this woman.

The Nazarene covered the harlot's hand with his own. Surely the man knew what kind of woman he touched. Contact with her made him unclean. Matthias noticed the others watching, some curiously, others with kind smiles, and some with the same horrified expression he was sure appeared on his own face.

"When we return," said Yeshua, looking deep into the woman's brown eyes, "be ready to join us. Until then, walk in the light."

Susanna offered a faint smile. "Yes, Master, I'll be ready. Darkness has engulfed my soul far too long. My heart yearns for more of this light."

"Keep walking in the light. There's an abundant supply. The Lord God be with you and bless the offering of your heart. Shalom." Yeshua turned from Susanna to his mother. He lifted her onto the donkey and led them toward the way westward and south to Nain.

"I will, and I'll join you when you return," Susanna called.

"As will I," called Mary Magdalene.

What is this Nazarene doing? Matthias twisted sideways to view the woman, Susanna, still standing and watching the pilgrims. *She would be an attractive woman if not for...*

"She is quite beautiful, isn't she?" whispered the Nazarene's brother with a sly smile.

"Who?" asked Matthias, scowling.

James laughed.

The band of travelers stayed on the eastern side of the hills overlooking the Jezreel Valley, to take advantage of the shade when the sun burned the hottest. By sunset, Nain would be in view.

Matthias moved forward through the group as they walked along the edge of the valley. Philip, another follower of the Nazarene, and Andrew walked a few paces behind Yeshua. Matthias grew curious about what motivated these men to befriend a woman like Susanna. He fingered his money pouch.

Only one way to find out.

Matthias approached the two disciples.

"The Lord God has blessed our day with the light of his glory. It's a great contrast to the darkness we left in Magdala. My father loved the morning when the sun peeked over the hills. Its light, he would say, scared away the hidden things of the dark."

Philip nodded in agreement. "It is beautiful how the hills frame the valley," he said. "But I'm just as thankful for the evening with its blues, oranges, and yellows creating shadows and light together. But it's truly the shade I'm most thankful for as we approach this hill to Nain. It gets longer each year. But that's something a young man like you wouldn't understand."

"Look to the north," said Andrew. "Mt. Hermon's peaks embrace the last rays of the Lord's glory shining over all the earth."

Hearing his father's words gave Matthias pause.

"Have you ever wondered what stories these hills would tell if they could speak?" asked Philip. "Wouldn't it be great to hear their tale of Gideon?"

"Gideon? He was a coward." Matthias rejoined the conversation. "I prefer hearing of Elijah outrunning Ahab as the rain began to set in." He turned around so that he walked backward up the slope to Nain. "Do you believe almighty God actually caused fire to devour the sacrifice of Elijah?" he asked, as they followed the skyline to Mt. Carmel's peak. He envisioned the fire bursting from the heavens to consume the bull and altar drenched in water.

"How can I not believe it?"

As if in response to Andrew's question, a dark cloud rolled across the evening sun, creating an eerie shadow over Carmel. The three stood in silence. A distant rumbling made the earth tremble. A streak of lightning cracked the silence and lit up the shadowed face of the mountain. A sheet of rain fell over its heights.

Matthias had just asked, "And what do you believe about Yeshua and the miracle we witnessed?" when the Nazarene's voice boomed from behind them and through the valley as he reminded them of Elijah's words.

"How long will it take you to make up your mind? If the Lord be God, follow him ... Hear me, O Lord, hear me, that the people may know you are the Lord God ..."

The pilgrims stood transfixed by the Lord who gazed steadfastly into the heavens. Thunder pursued the approaching lightning. Matthias shivered.

"If we take much longer," spoke Yeshua, breaking their trance, "we'll all be soaked. Early spring rains are chasing us." All followed him without hesitation, as they discussed among themselves where they might find shelter.

Matthias and Jairus decided to seek shelter in a lean-to built off one of the houses along the main city road. Here they could tie the donkey and sleep in quiet, as the clouds and rain had passed to the north and east. They would stay dry tonight without seeking another's hospitality. A few of the travelers would join them. Philip and Andrew chose to stay with one from the city called Nathanael. Others headed for shelter in the common inn with Yeshua, his mother, Sarah, and Simon.

The more Matthias watched the Nazarene, the more perplexed he became.

"Your thoughts run deep, Matthias," commented Jairus, as he took some dried fruit, salted fish, and a cake of bread from his bundle.

"I don't understand this Nazarene. His own brother couldn't answer my questions, for mine are also his. What of you, Jairus? Has your opinion of the Nazarene changed after seeing him with the harlot?" Matthias took some food from his pack and drank a long drink from his wineskin. "Well?"

Jairus chewed on the question as he chewed and swallowed a bit of dried fruit.

"I believe we each are on a journey of faith. There are two opinions. Yeshua is either the promised Messiah, or he is not. Each one must find his answer. I know the Lord is God. Yeshua—he is from God. This I believe. What more there is to believe will be revealed as faith brings faith." Jairus washed down his bread with a drink from his wineskin. "I'll know the truth. I believe this one is truth. If you desire to know truth, then you must hear him, not me. And now," he continued, with an encompassing wave of his arm, "O Lord, God of the universe, who blesses us with food from your earth and drink from your vine, we give you glory, honor, and praise as we seek your rest for the night."

Matthias stared long at Jairus as he prepared bedding for the night. "You did not answer my question."

"Ah, but I answered mine. I can't answer yours. Only you can find that answer." Jairus pulled his cloak over his shoulder and settled on the bed of hay. "And as far as the harlot goes—she no longer exists. She is a new person. May the Lord God bless you with rest. And peace," he added, almost as an afterthought.

Matthias rested his head on his rolled-up cloak. Tomorrow would begin the longest part of the journey to the Jordan River and down its banks. The only shelter would be the night sky.

Several more pilgrims joined their company as they followed the Jordan. Matthias preferred the smaller group and sought solitude as he walked closer to the swollen river's bank. He eyed the Jordan's swift current caused by the recent rains and melting snows of Mt. Hermon. The ensuing night wrapped the rushing river in ominous sounds and eerie shapes.

Matthias glanced back over his shoulder. The campfires cast shadows that danced across the pilgrims' faces. He turned, slipped his sandals off, and gingerly placed one foot in the moving water. "Aah!" He huffed, yanked his foot from the cold water, and replaced his sandals.

"It deepens rapidly."

Startled by the voice, Matthias flinched, and the leather straps of his sandals knotted around his ankles, sending him sprawling into the river. He flailed his arms against the river's flow as the frigid water squeezed the air from his chest. He feared the current would sweep him away as he struggled to right himself, when a hand grabbed his arm and lifted him from the churning water's grasp.

Matthias shook uncontrollably from the night breeze blowing over his soaked mantle.

"Here," offered his rescuer, taking Matthias's cloak and replacing it with his own. "Mine's a little drier. We need to get you back to the fire."

Angry words formed in Matthias's throat, but his chattering teeth cut them off. None of this would have happened had this one not come uninvited. He turned angry eyes on his offender and rescuer.

"Yeshua?"

Yeshua wrapped his own cloak tighter around Matthias's shoulders and held him close, radiating warmth from his own body to Matthias. The cloak was as dry as a bone scorched by the sun. Matthias couldn't think as his mind tried to process exactly what had just happened. When his shivering stopped, the Nazarene loosed his hold on Matthias, and together they walked to the fire.

"Dangers lurk in the darkness," whispered Yeshua. "It's best to walk where there is light."

Matthias gritted his teeth, tightening his jaw. Did the Nazarene have the gall to chide him for something he caused?

As the two approached the closest fire, others made space for Matthias to warm himself. Sarah took his soaked cloak and spread it on a boulder.

"Did you bring a second mantle, Matthias?" asked Jairus, offering him his own. "And what about shoes?" he added, noticing his bare feet.

"They're in the basket on the donkey, along with a dry tunic." Matthias clutched his belt, feeling for the money pouch. It was there. His turban was probably already in Jericho. He tossed his head back, trying to free his face from the tangled mess of wet hair.

Once he was in dry clothes and wrapped in the fire's warmth, the chill subsided from his bones. With the excitement past, the company of pilgrims settled down for the night amidst whispers Matthias was certain centered around him.

"Here's your cloak." Matthias handed the damp garment to the Nazarene. "You may need it, albeit still damp. May the Lord bless your kindness." His offering was less than sincere as a new wave of irritation swept through his mind. He wondered if his rescuer might expect payment for his good deed as he had received from the harlot. That hope would be disappointed.

"The night air is cool. Come close to the fire, and try to find rest wrapped in your Father's arms." Yeshua took his cloak and made himself a place for the night.

Matthias walked closer to the fire without responding. His heart screamed blasphemy. To his amazement, he found a place prepared for him. He glanced at Yeshua resting peacefully. Matthias's exhaustion drained his anger, as wonder about what really happened at the river tumbled through his mind. He felt the touch of the Nazarene as if his arms still held him wrapped in his own dry cloak. Matthias's body and heart began to warm as the dancing flames played with one another. He laid down and found rest for the first time in his journey.

CHAPTER 11

The lone morning star took center stage among the wispy gray clouds lined with dawn's opalescent blue, pink, and purple shades. In the quiet, Matthias stole away to Elisha's Spring. Memories of his father recounting Elisha's healing of the bitter waters with a handful of salt brought a calm to his spirit.

Miracles, signs, and wonders occupied the scrolls of the prophets and Scriptures, as almighty God revealed himself to his chosen people. The memory of the Nazarene's dry cloak clung to Matthias's thoughts and threatened his peace. He splashed the sweet water on his face and wrung the trickling stream from his beard. He glanced over his shoulder toward Jericho, as he wiped clinging curls from his forehead.

"Yeshua." The whisper of the Nazarene's name slipped through his lips.

Are you a prophet? The Prophet?

Matthias turned to the pool and raised a handful of water to his mouth. Its purity caressed his tongue. A stream trickled through his fingers. Hard to believe it was ever bitter.

Almost as hard as believing the Prophet of Moses could be walking among us.

Matthias didn't look forward to the steep slope leading to Bethany, or the scorching heat of midday. He covered his head with a rag, tied it in place with a narrow band, and made a mental note to purchase a turban in Jerusalem. The idea of an overnight stay in Bethany equaled his disdain of staying in Magdala. Bethany didn't harbor demons, but it did harbor fevers and sicknesses which were almost as bad.

The leper's warning call—"Unclean! Unclean!"—had sent fear coursing through him as a child. His father had tossed the beggar a few coins, but the thought of the wretch in his filthy rags calling out his misery made Matthias shudder. No, he would not stay in Bethany unless he had to.

Elisha's Spring faded from view but not from his mind as the sun grew hotter and the hill steeper. Sweat ran down Matthias's face into his beard. He licked his sunbaked lips and hoisted the water skin to his mouth. Nothing but a trickle.

"Here," offered Jairus, handing him his skin. "I have enough to share. We'll be in Bethany soon, and we'll be able to replenish our supplies."

Matthias took his offer, drinking only enough to ease the pain in his throat. "Bless you, my friend. The journey is harder each year."

Jairus smiled. "Your elders have outdone you today?"

"The proof's before you. What can I say?"

Silence ruled, mainly to conserve the travelers' energy as they continued the climb. Matthias's legs burned. He kept telling himself rest waited in Bethany, and after his rest, then on to Jerusalem. He grabbed a slender limb lying along the path, slowed his pace, and hoped to steady his heartrate.

"Are you able to go on?" asked Jairus.

Matthias nodded. "We'll rest in Bethany before continuing to Jerusalem. That'll suffice. We should be there by nightfall."

"I overheard Yeshua speaking to Simon about staying the night in Bethany. I believe he's concerned for the women," Jairus said. "And he has friends there."

"Will you be staying as well?"

"As long as there's room."

Matthias scowled.

"There are others going on. There's no need for you to remain. But consider this," Jairus challenged. "Yeshua's words and works ring true to his life. I want to hear him. And you say you're searching for truth." Jairus paused and smiled as he twisted from side to side stretching tired muscles. "Not to mention my body needs a rest, as does yours."

Matthias twisted his sidelock.

"Rest would be good."

But doubtful to be found in a place full of the sick.

A pause in the group's progress caught his attention. Matthias silently watched an interchange between Yeshua and Simon, not peculiar in itself except for Simon's odd response. He nodded to Yeshua and ran up the rest of the hill in the heat, carrying his water skin. The group of travelers moved on behind him.

As the pilgrims arrived, they saw Simon posted at the city gate, his face beaming with the success of whatever errand Yeshua had sent him on. Together, he and Yeshua led the travelers through the village and up a path to the right. Several pilgrims took their leave to travel on to Jerusalem. Matthias watched them go, hesitating for a moment before following Jairus up the trail behind the Nazarene.

A massive stone wall with an arched entry stood on the hillside, inviting the travelers in. The Nazarene rang the bell hanging to the right of the entryway to announce their arrival.

The inner courtyard welcomed the company with its colorful arrays of flowering bushes. Roofed galleries lined the walls. At the end of the courtyard two stairways lead to a second level of rooms. One stairway continued to the roof, which was enclosed in a small wall and held another large room. A vibrant green ivy climbed its way up the sides of the stone structure.

Plenty of room. Matthias resigned himself to staying the night. The couches lining the galleries promised a night of comfortable sleep. He examined the gate as he walked through the opening. Why would one with a home like this be so foolish as to not have a door to lock at night?

"Shalom, Lazarus, my friend."

A man responded to Yeshua's greeting with a kiss on each cheek. He stood a head taller than the others. Matthias grinned. The scene reminded him of Israel's first king. *Saul, similar only in height but not build. A warrior such as Saul would have been more muscled.*

Two women appeared from the house and stood at the host's side.

"My sisters and I have been preparing for you. We have room for all. Martha," Lazarus said as he gestured to the taller of the two women. She stood with her back straight and head held high. No smile or frown. To Matthias, she seemed uncertain of so many guests.

"And this is Mary," continued the owner of the home. "They have a meal prepared for you. My servant will take your beasts and tend to them, while my house servants wash the dust from your feet."

Martha retreated to the house. Mary lingered in the Nazarene's presence, then followed her sister's lead.

Yeshua put his arm around Lazarus's shoulder as they made their way inside. "May you be blessed of my Father for your kindness."

Matthias cringed. *Why does he continually address the Lord God as Father?* He shook his head as he took note of the heavy door to the home. The host at least used wisdom in protecting his home, if not his courtyard.

Servants began removing the travelers' sandals as each one found a cushion or couch along the wall to recline upon. Matthias relaxed as one washed his tired feet and another massaged a fragrant oil over them. He assessed his surroundings. For all the home's outward appearance of wealth, the inside showed no sign of extravagance. Yet all were treated as royal guests.

After everyone had been refreshed, servants appeared and disappeared like a finely orchestrated symphony, moving around Matthias and the other guests as they carried platters filled with fruit, cheese, unleavened bread, baked fish, mutton stew, and wine. After overseeing the servants, Martha and Mary joined Mary, the mother of Yeshua, and Sarah at their places. Lazarus stood.

"Rabbi, you grace our table. Would you speak the blessing on the food and drink?" Yeshua nodded his assent, and Lazarus reclined on his seat.

As the rabbi concluded the usual blessing, a rapid knocking caught the guests' attention. As a servant hurried to the door, Matthias stared toward the interrupting racket. *Who would come at this hour, knowing families would be sitting down to their evening meal?* The servant returned and whispered to Lazarus, who nodded and sent him away.

"Enjoy the bountiful blessings of our Lord," said Lazarus as he uplifted a cup of wine.

Stories of the pilgrims' journey buzzed around the room like so many bees around a hive. While the guests enjoyed their host's hospitality, Matthias noticed Lazarus's servant reappear with a bulging bag tied at the top. He slipped around the edge of the gathering and handed the bag to a man covered in filthy rags and lacking a mantle or head covering.

The curious scene continued to unfold as Lazarus motioned to his servant, who disappeared and reappeared as before. This time he carried a cloak, which he handed to the beggar. Then both disappeared.

Shortly, the servant returned and reported to Lazarus in low tones.

"He is staying the night in the courtyard. He will be quite comfortable." Lazarus nodded his assent. All the while the other guests continued to enjoy their meal and one another's companionship.

Matthias watched the oblivious travelers, shifting his glance from person to person. The hair on the back of his neck raised. He looked past Lazarus. Yeshua's deep brown eyes held him with the love and tenderness Matthias had so often seen in his father's eyes. He lowered his gaze, fearing what the Nazarene might see behind the mask he wore over his soul. His heart pounded. Tears were forming in his eyes, threatening to fall. But why? Matthias chewed on a dried fig and washed it down with a gulp of wine as he worked to hold back the tears seeking their escape.

Before the guests finished the meal, three more interruptions took place. Each time the same activity was repeated, except not all needed a cloak. But each needed something. No one left empty-handed.

When stomachs were full, and the chatter began to fade, Lazarus spoke the final blessing on the meal and his guests. Afterward, the servants led each to their sleeping quarters. Each room bordered a courtyard filled with several fruit trees and beautiful flowers of blue and white, watered by a pool in the center. A single bench bespoke of the quiet solitude someone found in this place, not unlike Matthias's own courtyard with its fig tree canopy.

Jairus entered the room with Matthias.

"Comfortable bedding, a good meal, and tired bodies make for sound sleep." Jairus removed his mantle and threw it over the floor mat. There would be no need to sleep under it tonight. "You studied our host most of the evening. What do you think?"

"He is either richer than I imagine, or soon he'll be the pauper begging at another's door," answered Matthias curtly.

"Or maybe he chooses to bless others as he has been blessed, would you not agree?"

"Most certainly," answered Matthias, with his jaw set and his hands on his hips. "I'll say it again, he will need that same generosity if he's not careful."

"You know," said Jairus as he made himself comfortable, "you must beware that what you hold dearest doesn't become what holds you."

Matthias stared at Jairus's back and tossed his cloak down. His hand instinctively went to his belt. You would not find him parting with his coins as freely as this Lazarus. Money meant power.

When the money is gone, so is the power, the influence, the friends.

He chest felt like it was caught in a carpenter's vise. He didn't understand this heaviness, nor why Yeshua's eyes peering into his soul still filled the darkness. Unspoken words of love floated in the recesses of his mind. He was certain this Nazarene approved of the benevolent host, which meant he would disapprove of him.

Sheer weariness of body carried him from his discomfited thoughts into a restless sleep.

The morning light ushered in a flurry of activity. Pilgrims gathered their belongings.

"You mustn't leave without this," called Lazarus as he and his sisters approached the travelers with a bag of food for each. "I know it's not far, but you will be glad for a bite after climbing Mount Olivet's summit."

"May you know the blessing of the Almighty," called Yeshua as the refreshed wayfarers followed him through the gate toward their destination.

Today the group would enter Jerusalem, the city of God. Matthias would purchase his lamb to be confined for the week before Passover, to prove its worthiness for sacrifice. What was said of John the Baptizer? Matthias tried to think.

"I know," he said aloud. "It was not what was said of John the Baptizer but what he said of the Nazarene."

"What are you rambling about?" asked Jairus.

"Yeshua," answered Matthias. "I heard John, the son of Zebedee, say the Baptizer called Yeshua the Lamb of God who takes away the sins of the world."

"Do you believe this?"

"Don't you understand, Jairus? If it's true, if he *is* God's Lamb, he would have to die. He would have to prove himself worthy for sacrifice, without spot or blemish. The Messiah cannot be a Messiah if he dies. He cannot be both."

Jairus made no comment. Both fell silent as they continued up the Mount.

The other pilgrims exchanged excited chatter until they reached the summit. Once over the top, a worshipful hush united the band of travelers in a cloud of wonder at their first sight of the temple wrapped in a golden halo of sunlight. Awestruck praises sought to capture the moment.

"Surely the glory of the Lord God almighty is enthroned in this place."

"Our Lord is clothed in radiant light."

Another pilgrim lay prostrate proclaiming, "Holy is his name. There is no God like Israel's God."

Matthias stood transfixed by the magnificence as the others ended their worship and continued on in silence. This he could see. This he could believe.

Yeshua no longer led the pilgrims, but stood in a circle of light. With his arms extended to Matthias, he welcomed him to come.

"My son, what you see on Jerusalem's hill is a shell of my Father's glory. I'm here to reveal the Father's full glory. I am the light of the world. If you follow me you won't live in darkness, but in the light of life."

Matthias worked his jaw. The Nazarene's compassionate call wrapped him in a warmth greater than the cloak he wore when the river wanted to claim him.

No.

With his back as rigid as stone, he stood his full height, with his hands balled into fists hanging at his side. Blood pumped through his body stronger than the river's current. Words of reprimand rose and stuck in his throat. How could this Nazarene make such claims? Matthias wanted to deny, to run from the brilliance before him, but couldn't command his muscles to move.

Yeshua pointed toward the distant temple. "True glory isn't found in buildings made by men, but in the light of eternal life. Come. See. Believe."

Matthias felt naked under his gaze. His shoulders relaxed as his defiance attempted to melt. His heart yearned to move forward. But his mind waged a war against his heart. In his moment of hesitation, Yeshua turned. Matthias lowered his head.

Had the Nazarene known his thoughts? His heart? Matthias mechanically made his feet follow the others. *A Messiah who is a lamb? A lamb would die.*

Israel needed a lion to free them from Rome's rule.

His questions left him with answers too difficult for him to believe, and a price he couldn't pay.

CHAPTER 12

Ananias clucked his tongue in a series of high-pitched tones, coaxing his lambs to follow. The poor creatures bleated innocently, unaware of impending doom.

"Sapphira," the lean man called to his wife. If only she were a sheep to follow his voice. "We must hurry to find a place out of the sun." He set his jaw and frowned. The greedy money changers would set up their tables before dawn, taking the best shady spots. This left him and his lambs standing in the sunlight reflecting off the marble paved courtyard. At best, a small shady spot might wait along the outer wall.

Sapphira groaned. "Badger, badger, badger," she muttered. "I'm coming. Always you are in such a hurry." The round, cherry-faced matron huffed as she urged her feet to move faster.

Ananias handed her the donkey's rope. "You lead him. But be careful the cages of doves don't work loose. I'll tend the lambs. You'll be glad we hurried when we return home with my bag full of the pilgrims' money."

The river of wayfarers flowed into the courtyard, hoping to find at least one honest money changer or merchant. Those without temple coins in the exact half shekel found themselves at the merchants' mercy—or lack thereof—before purchasing their animals for sacrifice.

Matthias clutched the money bag secured inside his belt. He narrowed his eyes, searching the crowd for Gentiles, zealots, and thieves, believing them to be one and the same. He didn't let his hand drift far from his waist.

He glanced around the courtyard looking for the best lambs, but other animals held his curiosity. Wolves disguised as zealots, men with unkempt beards and dressed in plain country clothes skulking around the perimeter of the court of Gentiles. Their hands, hidden beneath cloaks, clutched small daggers instead of moneybags.

A shiver surged through Matthias. *If any could cause the wrath of Rome to rain down on thousands of pilgrims, these could.* He glanced towards the high fortress at the far edge of the temple wall. Roman soldiers stood watch.

"Young man!" Ananias's shrill voice wafted over the din of noise. "Come, my lambs have been inspected and found worthy. I am a fair man, wanting only to honor the Lord God with the finest."

Matthias followed the man's voice.

"Fine, yes, and at an even finer price, I'm sure," answered Matthias, as he looked over the flock.

"Sir, you insult me." Ananias bowed his head. "For one dressed as elegantly as you, I would think money would be no object in choosing the very best to offer to the Lord God for your freedom from death's long fingers."

"I'll take this one." Matthias indicated one in the middle of the flock. He ran his hands up and down its body, inspecting it for sores and blemishes in the flesh or wool.

"You have my word," Ananias said. "You will find no blemish on my fine lambs."

Matthias spared a momentary glance toward the merchant before continuing his inspection. When satisfied, he counted out his coins, and led the lamb toward the temple fold for safekeeping and final approval until Passover. It must remain unblemished until it gave its blood for him to live. Matthias stopped and took the lamb's head in his hands.

How could an animal's blood over the doorposts keep death at bay? Any more than the thousands of sacrifices since that time could pay the price sin demanded?

He squinted against the morning sun as he surveyed the crowd for Jairus. He wanted to find a place in the city to stay, a place where he could share the Passover meal with another. Jairus's family would be joining him if Phoebe stayed well, and they could join a caravan coming this way. A sudden cacophony of screeching birds, bleating lambs and coins clanking against the marble floor interrupted his thoughts, causing Matthias to tighten his grip on the lamb's tether. He changed directions to investigate the uproar.

A pulsating wave of pilgrims pursued him, some pulling their lambs in haste, others holding tight to their pigeon cages. Caught in the middle of the pandemonium, Matthias found himself pummeled by others moving through the mayhem. Knocked to his knees, he covered his head with his hands, losing his grip on the lamb. He wrestled his way upright against the onslaught of stampeding feet to keep from being trampled.

The crack of a whip split the air. Matthias spun around just as another whirl of the whip found its mark on a moneychanger's table, sending more coins rolling across the marble floor. The whip cracked again and again. Some dared to crawl across the courtyard to collect their coins. Others in the crowd began to cheer as those who had long burdened pilgrims with their greed received their just due.

Matthias halted his retreat and gaped as he stood planted like one of the many columns surrounding the temple courtyard. The Nazarene wielded the whip, driving out the sheep, oxen, and goats. He shoved and overturned tables, causing cages of frightened doves to break open. His eyes burned like relentless flames of fire.

Now the whip hung silently at his side as he stood regal as a king. His chest heaving, he descended the temple steps. His cry carried across the marble courtyard and bounced off the pillars, echoing throughout Jerusalem. With outstretched arm, he used the whip as an extension to aim his words at the guilty.

"Don't make my Father's house one to hawk your wares and burden your brothers for gain. My Father's house is one of prayer. You have made it a den of thieves."

The open courtyard cleared of all its visitors until only a few were left—several curious gawkers, some indignant Pharisees—puffed up like clouds of greasy smoke, and the Nazarene with his men. Many of the pilgrims peeked anxiously from behind the massive columns lining the open area.

Matthias moved through the hiding crowd like a wolf after a lamb as he pursued Jairus. *My lamb!* Might as well forget an impossible situation. The lamb was lost, and the threat of Roman boots thumping on the marble floor compelled him to move faster and farther from the Nazarene. Impending death hung in the air. He didn't want it to be his.

"Jairus," shouted Matthias, waving both arms over his head. "Over here by the eastern gate." No response. He hesitated before thrusting himself forward in pursuit of his target, who was headed straight for the Nazarene and the Pharisees still facing off against him. At least no whips split the air as Matthias caught up to Jairus and grabbed his arm.

"Where are you going? You can't be going back in there."

Jairus jerked his arm from Matthias and turned back toward Yeshua, as he spoke through gritted teeth. "I planned on it, yes. Do you have a problem with that?"

"Quite," Matthias nodded, "I don't plan on dying today or anytime in the near future."

Jairus lowered his head and rubbed the back of his neck before answering Matthias's objection. "There will be no death today. Look around. Already the people are emerging from their hiding places."

Matthias surveyed the scene. A few brave souls wandered in, not daring to get too close. Merchants made themselves small as they gathered lambs, pigeons, doves, and money boxes.

"You may be right, for today." Matthias nodded in the direction of the small group that had confronted the Nazarene. "It seems the Pharisees have had their fill of him. Whatever he said to them, they aren't happy."

Jairus didn't reply. He watched as Yeshua and his followers walked away.

"Jairus, were you able to secure a lamb before this all started?" asked Matthias, hoping this whole scene would soon be forgotten.

"No," the other responded blankly. "You?"

Matthias flapped his arms like the wings of an angry rooster as he related his tale. "I did have one, but in all the ruckus I lost him. I'm sure the merchant—Ananias, it was—would sell him to me again at an even higher price, if by chance he found him."

A smile played on Jairus's lips as he did a once-over of his young friend. "Apparently you weren't hurt."

"No. But that's not the point. I could have been trampled to death. I did lose my lamb and"— he reached for his money bag—"I was robbed!" The vein in his neck protruded and beat wildly. He slammed his fist into his palm. "Now someone will die." He turned every direction searching for someone, anyone remaining who looked the part of a thief.

Jairus laid a strong firm hand on Matthias's shoulder.

"Matthias, look at me. Did you see who knocked you down?"

Matthias lowered his eyes. His shoulders sagged under his companion's grip. "No, no, I did not. I was in the middle of a mob."

Jairus freed his captive. "Then you know it's lost."

Matthias raised his chin. His eyes showed the agony of his soul.

"What will I do? I have no money. I'll have to be at the mercy of another even to share in the Passover meal and the law requires ..." His words, strength, and confidence melted in his loss. He knew the law commanded all males to appear with a sacrifice. He had never appeared with less than the finest lamb, never a poor man's sacrifice of doves or pigeons. Now he had nothing.

Jairus pulled him to his side. "You're not alone," he whispered. Then he held him at arm's length. Matthias's pain eased at the love Jairus expressed.

"My family is coming," Jairus said. "They should arrive today. We planned to meet in Bethany and come to Jerusalem together. But Lazarus offered us room at his home that we might enjoy Passover with him and his sisters. We'll stay there. You're to be his guest, too, if you desire."

It sounded good until Jairus mentioned Lazarus and Bethany. Matthias feigned a smile of gratitude. He had no choice but to accept. Foreboding, not of Bethany but of the Nazarene, filled his heart. Yeshua would surely be among the guests. The words of worry stuck in his throat as he accepted Jairus's offer. "You're a true friend. May the Lord's blessing be yours for giving me a family."

Jairus gave him a hearty pat on the back.

"Come, then. Let's go to the temple flock and find a lamb, one to celebrate our escape from slavery and death."

The two men left with Jairus doing most of the talking. "Simon's mother-in-law and daughter are arriving today along with my family. The older one and Phoebe had to travel by cart, none too comfortably, but neither could make the long trip on foot."

Matthias's spirit lifted hearing Simon's daughter would join them.

But why should that make any difference? She was a high-spirited, disrespectful young woman, not at all like Phoebe. She definitely would not fit into his plans for rising to importance in the city. Still, the idea did brighten the moment. And tomorrow would be another day. He could secure money from the bank on his name alone.

The week of preparation finally reached its climax as families gathered around their tables of special Passover foods. Homes filled with the aromas of succulent roasted lamb and bitter herbs along with matzo and steamed vegetables. Each food, with its significance, would be explained throughout the celebration to wide-eyed children and adults, who never tired of hearing about the first Passover.

Tonight, Lazarus sat at the head of his table with Yeshua seated on one side and a young boy clothed in rags on the other. Matthias sat somewhere in the middle, no place of importance. But Rebekah seated across the table provided a pleasant view. The candles' dancing flames lent to the festivity of light and life. Matthias turned toward Lazarus as he called for the Kiddush, to bless the fruit of the vine.

"Blessed are you, O Lord our God ... who has created the fruit of the vine ... Blessed are you, O Lord our God, who has kept us alive, sustained us, and enabled us to enjoy this season."

As one, all raised their cups of red wine toasting the life given through the sacrifice of the lamb.

Yeshua spoke next. "I am the Lord, and I will bring you out from under the yoke of the Egyptians." As he put the cup to his lips all followed his lead.

Matthias drank, but his attention fixed on this man whose words said more than he dared to hear. As the celebration resumed, he set his cup on the table, shifted on his cushion, and propped his bearded chin in his hand.

Before the evening ended, the events of the first Passover would be commemorated, told now to be retold forever.

All stood with Lazarus as he ended the joyous occasion with the final *hallel* from the Psalms. "Not to us, O Lord, not to us but to your name be the glory because of your love and faithfulness ..." With each line the voices rose with glad expectation. As his words came to an end, the room rang with praise.

"This is the day the Lord has made; let us rejoice and be glad in it. O Lord, save us; O Lord grant us success. Blessed is he who comes in the name of the Lord. From the house of the Lord we bless you. The Lord ..." Matthias recited the words, but watched Lazarus, Simon, and Jairus. Their eyes saw only one—the Rabbi, the Nazarene—as if the words spoke of him. "The Lord is God, and he has made his light shine upon us ... You are my God ... his love endures forever."

Matthias lost all concern for anyone in the room but the Nazarene. What did others know that he did not?

Or did others not understand—the lamb was the price paid for life?

PART TWO

A prophet is not without honor but in his own country, and among his own kin, and in his own house.

—Mark 6:4b (KJV)

CHAPTER 13

"Did you hear ...?"

"No, but I saw with my own eyes ..."

Rebekah and Phoebe walked arm in arm along the rocky shore of the Galilee. The first rays of sunlight played across the landscape as the curtain of fog draping the distant hills drew back. The girls chattered endlessly about the one subject on everyone's lips—Yeshua.

Rebekah swung one arm high in the air as her voice reached a fevered pitch.

"Before Immah and I left Jerusalem, Papa spoke far into the night about the miraculous works of Yeshua." The faster she talked, the faster her feet carried her while she continued to pummel the air and pull Phoebe along.

"Wait," cried Phoebe. Her feet barely touched the ground as she tried to keep pace with Rebekah. "Let's sit a minute." Her chest heaved in a heavy rhythm.

"Oh, Phoebe, forgive me." Rebekah rested Phoebe's arm against hers and leaned her against a boulder. "My mind races in circles like chariots when I try to sort out all the miracles, teachings, and stories. When it does, I forget everything else." Rebekah grew concerned. Phoebe's face was pale and her skin clammy. "This may not have been the best idea," she added, shaking out her damp skirt.

"We'll dry." Phoebe exhaled slowly.

"You're as pale as a white lamb. Will you be all right?"

"I only need a moment to rest."

"Let's return through the marketplace," suggested Rebekah. "The walk is easier."

In moments, the color seeped into Phoebe's face, and her breathing returned to normal. "Easier is good." A weak smile played across her blue-tinged lips. Holding her hands to her chest, she inhaled deeply, hesitantly exhaled, then continued their conversation. "What more did your papa say about Yeshua?"

"The more he told, the more we wanted to hear." Rebekah retold the many wonders her father had witnessed and related to her.

Phoebe's eyes widened with each revelation, as if wider eyes might help her see the panorama of events. "Not only did they see his works but heard his words ... the words—"

"Of the Lord God himself."

"Rebekah, did I hear you right?" Phoebe grabbed her friend's arm. "Be careful what you say and where. Papa says there are ears everywhere, and the Lord is losing favor among the leaders. You could very well be put out of the synagogue for voicing such thoughts."

"We're alone." Rebekah shrugged, dismissing Phoebe's reaction. "You know John the Baptizer declared him to be the Lamb of God. Some even say a voice from heaven declared him to be the Son of God."

Phoebe covered her mouth as color began to drain once again from her face.

"I do know. I also heard Papa saying the Baptizer is now in Herod's prison."

Rebekah twisted a loose curl as she tucked her bottom lip between her teeth. Phoebe gave her a look of astonishment. "You didn't know this?"

"No," answered Rebekah. "I didn't. And what of Yeshua? Is there any word from him?"

"Papa was walking through the marketplace when he spoke with one of the merchants from Jerusalem. He told Papa of the Baptizer and reported that Yeshua and his followers left Judea when they heard the news."

Rebekah's heart pounded. "Were they safe? Where were they going? Did he say?"

"Rebekah." Phoebe's mouth gaped as she raised her hand to her chin. "Your papa is with Yeshua?"

Rebekah nodded as tears pooled in her blue eyes. She blinked hard, trying to dam them up and keep them from spilling out.

"Papa did say they were to return to Galilee. There was no word of Yeshua or any of his followers being harmed in any way." Phoebe wrapped her arms around her friend.

Rebekah closed her eyes and mouthed a silent prayer of thanksgiving.

"May the Lord protect them on their way," she whispered in Phoebe's ear. "I think it's time we both go home."

Phoebe nodded . "Maybe there will be word from your papa. As for me, Immah will send servants to hunt me down if I don't return soon." Phoebe patted her stomach. "Besides, my stomach is starting to rumble. I could eat a camel." Both girls chuckled.

"That might be lumpy," Rebekah added. Their laughter eased the unspoken roiling tension, as they locked arms and headed toward the marketplace.

Rebekah tried to set a steady pace even as her feet urged her to move faster. She wanted to get home.

The sea sparkled like precious gems in the sun's light. An occasional fish leaped from its home in praise to Rebekah's creator. Her heart pulled her to the shore, but her mind pushed her home. She stopped and planted her feet at the edge of the sea. Surely the creator of heaven and earth could take care of her father. She raised her hands to the Lord God of heaven.

"Who in heaven have I but you! You alone are God! All praise, glory, and honor belong to you who shines your glory upon us!" Her song sailed on the wings of the wind, carrying with it the worry that had filled her heart.

"Rebekah?"

She turned red-faced toward the sound of her name.

Matthias approached. His eyes appeared softer than she remembered. But her mouth spoke her embarrassment. "How do you dare impose yourself on someone in such a private moment?"

Matthias halted his steps. "I heard a woman's voice calling out. I thought someone might be in trouble."

"Did you hear calls for help? I was singing."

"Not that I need explain, but I did not hear your words. The breeze carried them away from me," replied Matthias as he turned without waiting for a reply. Not looking back, he called over his shoulder. "Know this. You will not be bothered by my offer of help again."

Rebekah stared at his back as he walked away. Her shoulders slumped. *How could one's tongue go from praising God one moment to berating another of his own?*

"Matthias, wait." She ran to catch up with him. "Forgive my brash tongue?" The words were hard for her to speak, but if she would have peace in her heart, they had to be said.

"Forgiven," answered Matthias. "But it's doubtful this will be the last exchange for either of us." He bowed his head and continued walking.

With a tilt of her head and a quick smile, Rebekah agreed as she watched him go.

The sun's warmth beckoned her to return to meditating on the Lord. Head bowed, and her voice a whisper, she prayed, "O Lord God, who reigns above all, your mercy endures forever. I need your mercy, your forgiveness. I have no animal to sacrifice, only a broken heart. Put a lock on my tongue that I might learn to use it only to express your praise." She lifted her eyes in search of a hidden face. An unexplainable love filled her soul.

He forgives. Always he forgives.

She continued home in peace. Concern for her father couldn't steal that, but it did quicken her pace.

A figure large enough to be her father stood silhouetted in the doorway of her stone house. She lifted her skirt in both hands and ran.

"Papa." She loosened her grip on her skirt and waved a hand wildly. "Papa, you're home!"

Simon's long strides met Rebekah on the path. She threw herself into his arms, wrapping hers around his neck, as he enclosed her in his embrace.

"My beautiful daughter." Simon held her at arm's length and shook his head. "Your beauty rivals that of the legendary Queen of Sheba. One day I'll return, and there will be a man waiting here to see me."

"Papa, you know no man would dare want me for fear of facing you first." Rebekah took his rough hand in hers. She beamed in her father's attention as they walked. "Did Immah know you were coming? If she did, she didn't let me know, not a word. And I was worried after hearing about John the Baptizer."

"Yes, she knew. I sent her word by Salome. But in her defense," added Simon, "I asked her not to say anything. I wanted to surprise you if we arrived today and not disappoint you if we didn't."

"What a wonderful surprise! And I want to hear all about everything that happened." Rebekah rambled without waiting for answers. "Has John the Baptizer been arrested? Were you or Yeshua or any others in danger? Did Yeshua do any other mighty works? I want to hear everything."

Simon opened the door.

"You'll have the answers to all your questions." He nodded for her to enter. "Yeshua is here, as well as all of us who have been with him these last several weeks." Before entering, he stopped her and added, "But the Master needs rest. His cousin, John the Baptizer, was beheaded while we were on our way here."

"Papa, no!" Rebekah's hand flew to her chest. "Are you all in danger?" She searched Simon's face for reassurance. His reply supplied none.

"There is danger only for those who speak the truth. But come, there is much good to tell. Let's dwell on those things." Simon nodded and pointed Rebekah toward the courtyard.

She scanned the room and what she could see of the courtyard.

"James and John traveled on to see their parents. They'll meet us tomorrow at the synagogue."

"And Yeshua, he is here, you said?" Rebekah asked impatiently.

"He will be back shortly," answered Simon. "He often goes out alone to pray. His immah, Mary, is with Sarah and Gramma preparing for the Sabbath meal. Several will be joining us."

Rebekah dashed through the room towards the courtyard, calling back as she went.

"I forgot again. Immah will be wondering where I've been." Nearing the center of the courtyard, she stopped and turned to her father. "I love you, Papa. It is so good to have you home and safe."

"I love you, Daughter."

Her father's size matched his tenderness, but today it sent a wave of apprehension through her mind as the future's uncertainties tugged at the joy of the moment. She tossed her hair back in an effort to free her mind of all the endless tomorrows. Today, she would rejoice.

CHAPTER 14

Matthias slipped the linen tunic over his head, girded it around his waist, and pulled on his linen cloak. He caressed the colorful fabric, remembering his father's special gift to him. He imagined the love Joseph must have felt, wrapped in his father's gift of the coat of many colors. Matthias ran a hand over the sleeve. Jacob's love for Joseph could not compare with the love his own father had for him, of that he was certain.

Memories. Methodically he placed the fringed tallit over his shoulders.

"Master?" Eliezer interrupted Matthias's dreaming. "Your servants wait for your word to leave for the synagogue."

"Yes, they may go. I have no need of them today. It is the Sabbath. But—" Matthias paused.

"Yes, Master?"

"Eliezer, walk with me." Matthias's words mirrored the apprehension in his heart.

"Of course, as you desire, Master." Eliezer bowed his head in compliance. "I will send the others ahead." He slipped away on silent feet.

Matthias swallowed the emotion swelling in his chest. He had heard the Nazarene was in Capernaum and staying at Simon's house. As ruler of the synagogue, the duty of selecting someone for the reading and teaching of the

Scripture fell on him. His heart raced at the thought. He grabbed his head cover and wound it into a turban.

"Master?" Eliezer's voice held concern. "Are you well? You look pale."

The two alone in the house, Matthias placed his hands on Eliezer's shoulders. Their eyes met. Matthias blinked back the apprehension surging through him.

"Eliezer, my dear friend, you know me too well. What would I do without you?" He let his hands drop to his sides before feelings overruled good sense. "Let's be on our way. I'm sure we have a special Sabbath ahead of us."

People from the town and surrounding countryside packed the synagogue. Many stood on the perimeter. Matthias scanned the congregation from his seat on the platform. What he saw confirmed what he already knew. The people heard, and they came. The elders sat in the front for all to see.

Jairus stood behind the *bema*, the lectern on the elevated platform, his arms outstretched to the heavens, eyes lifted to the Creator God. The congregation stood as he raised his arms to begin the blessing.

"Bless the Lord, O my soul. O Lord my God, you are very great: you are clothed with honor and majesty. Who covers yourself with light as with a garment ..." Jairus's melodic voice swelled with each mention of the Lord God. "Who laid the foundations of the earth, that it should not be removed for ever ... I will sing of the Lord as long as I live. I will sing praise to my God while I have breath ... Bless the Lord, O my soul. Praise the Lord." Jairus turned his eyes upon the congregation, then to the cantor, who immediately proceeded to the bema and began to sing.

Hands clapped as joyful voices joined in the Psalm of praise. "It is a good thing to give thanks to the Lord, and to sing praises to your name. O most High: to show your lovingkindness in the morning, and your faithfulness every night ..."

Matthias clapped but could not make himself sing from the heart as he watched Yeshua and his followers twirl and clap above their heads as if caught up into another realm. His chest heaved in a panic. He struggled for control, knowing as the Psalm ended, he would introduce the speaker. His mouth moved, but no song of joy or praise sprang from his lips.

"Those who are planted in the house of the Lord shall flourish in the courts of our God. They shall still bring forth fruit in old age; they shall be fat and flourishing; to show that the Lord is upright: he is my rock, and there is no unrighteousness in him."

The Psalm ended, and the congregants sat on the hard stone benches in rows surrounding the platform or stood along the walls. Matthias took his place behind the bema where the scrolls awaited a minister to read and explain them. The congregation once again stood as Matthias read the *Shema*. The words strangled his throat.

"Hear, O Israel, the Lord is our God, the Lord is One."

In unison the somber tones of the people recited, "Blessed be the name of his glorious kingdom for ever and ever" each time the creed of Israel was spoken.

Beads of sweat pooled on Matthias's forehead. It would be disastrous if his sweat fell on the scroll. His muscles grew taut. All eyes were one him as the congregants waited for the next lines.

"And you shall love the Lord your God with all your heart." He glanced at Jairus with begging eyes. Jairus stepped forward, rescuing his young colleague. Matthias gave Jairus a nod toward the Nazarene before taking his place next to the bema. He fought the urge to take flight.

"And you shall love the Lord your God with all your heart and with all your soul and with all your might."

Jairus's voice resounded through the synagogue. "And these words that I command you today shall be in your heart. And you shall teach them diligently to your children, and you shall speak of them when you sit at home, and when you walk along the way, and when you lie down and when you rise up. And you shall bind them as a sign on your hand, and they shall be for frontlets between your eyes. And you shall write them on the doorposts of your house and on your gates." He bowed his head as he laid his hands on the wooden canister containing the scroll of the prophets. With measured movements, he removed the inspired words written hundreds of years ago.

Jairus held the treasure in his arms and spoke before returning it to the bema.

"Yeshua of Nazareth will read from the prophets and teach us what our Lord would have us know."

The people sat as Yeshua made his way to the central platform. Jairus sat near Matthias. As Yeshua stood behind the bema, the congregation rose. According to his obligations, Matthias stood directly beside and behind the Nazarene to insure the reading of the Scriptures did not deviate from what was written. He stood emotionless, his expression deliberately empty as the Nazarene read from Isaiah.

"Yet now hear, O Jacob my servant; and Israel, whom I have chosen: Thus says the Lord that made you ..." Matthias sneaked a look at the Nazarene, then turned his eyes back to the Scriptures and scowled.

Yeshua did not once scan the scroll. He quoted it as though the words were his own.

"... which will help you. Fear not, O Jacob, my servant ..." Another quick glance confirmed Matthias's suspicions. He forgot his own discomfort as he listened.

"For I will pour water upon him that is thirsty, and floods upon the dry ground: I will pour my spirit upon your seed, and my blessing upon your offspring ..."

The Nazarene had captivated his listeners. Always the people stood in respect to the reading, but this was different. No feet shuffled. No mothers whispered to their children. No babies cried.

Yeshua continued. "Thus says the Lord the King of Israel, and his redeemer the Lord of hosts; I am ..." A muffled gasp escaped a hearer's spirit.

"I am the first, and I am the last." The intensity and authority with which he spoke declared truth. As he continued, he extended his arms and returned them to his chest as if to gather the people to himself with his words. "... and beside me there is no God. And who, as I, shall call, and shall declare it, and set it in order for me, since I appointed the ancient people?" He paused and scanned the sea of listeners.

Matthias looked from the scroll.

The Nazarene's voice neared a whisper. "... and the things that are coming, and shall come, let them show unto them." With one hand raised to the heavens, he cried aloud, "Fear not!" People straightened their backs at the sudden proclamation. "Neither be afraid: have not I told you from that time, and have declared it? You are even my witnesses. Is there a God beside me? Yea, there is no God; I know not any." The Nazarene finished and took his seat on the platform as he prepared to expound on the words he read.

Matthias feared to touch the Holy Scriptures with his sweaty palms. He pulled the linen cloth from his girdle and picked the scroll up with the cloth, carrying it to the ark. There it would remain until the next reading.

A shrill cry exploded from the back of the synagogue, Matthias startled, and had to scramble to save the scroll from falling to the floor. With one quick motion, he placed it in the ark. Every head turned to examine the source of anguish. Jairus's hurried footsteps took him off the platform toward the commotion, with Matthias close behind.

They stopped as suddenly as they had started.

"Let us alone!" The guttural scream caused Matthias's flesh to crawl. All eyes were wide with fear and fixed on the man rushing toward the platform and Yeshua.

"What have we to do with you, Yeshua of Nazareth?" howled the intruder. "Are you come to destroy us? We know who you are. The Holy One of God." The cries emanated from the pits of hell.

As the man reached the platform, Yeshua stood, arm outstretched, pointing at the possessed. He spoke with unquestionable authority and command.

"Hold your peace and come out of him."

One last tormented scream sprang from the depths of the man's soul as the evil spirit fled, shaking the man like a dog would a rat, and flinging him to the floor. Yeshua knelt, took the man by the hand and lifted him to his feet, only to have him drop to his knees in worship.

Matthias surveyed the crowd. Some whispered. Others stood frozen with their hands over their mouths. Matthias's gaze returned to the Nazarene, remembering the words of the prophet. "Fear not ... you are my witnesses ... Is there a God beside me?"

Witnesses to what, to whom?

His knees threatened to buckle beneath him.

The Nazarene nodded to Jairus, who proceeded to the bema. With arms outstretched, Jairus recited each phrase of the ending blessing, punctuating each phrase with the strength of his voice.

"The Lord bless you, and keep you; The Lord make his face shine on you, and be gracious to you; The Lord lift up his countenance on you"—he paused as he glanced at the man kneeling, his face to the floor, before the Nazarene—"and give you peace."

Matthias stood mesmerized. Others hesitated to move, while several made haste to leave. Puzzled faces hurried to spread their version of this Sabbath day. Matthias, following behind the Nazarene and the rescued soul, caught the glint in the rabbi's eyes and the glow of his face as Yeshua wrapped his arm around the man's shoulders and spoke in hushed tones.

On the synagogue steps, Eliezer, faithful Eliezer, waited. He would wait from now until eternity. This Matthias could believe, unlike the events of this day. He wondered what stories would travel from ear to ear among the servants.

For me—I will not speak of what I don't understand. Besides, didn't this Nazarene know the commandments and traditions of the elders? Some would take offense at his performing this work on the Sabbath. Matthias straightened his back and held his head high. *He* took offense. With his resolve strengthened, he and Eliezer walked home in silence.

Matthias could not help but notice that Eliezer's gait reminded him of a much younger man, and his countenance shouted life and glory. So why did he feel so dead?

CHAPTER 15

Rebekah pressed her way down the balcony steps through the other women and away from the crowd. She raised her skirt and ran for home.

"Forgive my insolence, Lord God, but I do believe you understand," she huffed, as she slowed down to maneuver around a particularly rocky stretch of the path. The scenes, words, and ultimate glory involving Yeshua rolled around her mind like the pebbles under her feet. *How can I describe all that has taken place?* Immah waited at home with Gramma, who lay sick in bed with a fever. Rebekah believed the rabbi to be all Gramma needed.

She flung open the big wooden door with a force that surprised even her.

"Immah? Gramma, Immah!" Not finding them inside, Rebekah continued to call as she sprinted up the steps. Her mother stopped her at the top.

"Rebekah, I'm glad you're home."

"Immah," interrupted Rebekah. "You'll not believe—"

"Rebekah."

Her mother's stern tone halted Rebekah's excitement.

"I haven't time for stories. I need you to go to the cistern and draw some water. Bring it to the room on the roof. Gramma isn't well. Her body is full of fever. Hurry, child, hurry." Her mother turned and vanished in a swirl of robes.

"But—" Rebekah stood deflated. She hurried to the courtyard, and soon wrestled the full bucket of cold water up the steps.

"Immah?"

Gramma's drenched hair lay plastered around her flushed face. Her mouth gaped, pleading for air like a fish dying on the shore—not unlike Phoebe's when her lungs were robbed of precious air. Rebekah sucked in her bottom lip, as she twirled a strand of loose hair.

Sarah took the bucket, dunked a cloth, wrung it out, and laid it on the old woman's forehead in one flowing motion. Gramma groaned.

"I hear the men on the path," said Sarah. "Go tell your papa Gramma's condition worsens."

Rebekah took the steps two at a time, holding her skirt high enough to keep from stumbling. Her father, James, John, Andrew, and yes, she saw *him*, Yeshua, all climbed the path. Their laughter and joyous chatter reminded her of the morning's events. Surely this one who cast out a demon could calm a raging fever.

"Rebekah," called Simon. "What's your hurry?"

"Papa," Rebekah's eyes pleaded with Yeshua as she spoke to her father. "Gramma is sick with fever, and there's a gurgling sound in her throat." She tugged at her father's hand. "Come quickly."

"Take me to her." Yeshua answered Rebekah's plea before Simon could respond. Rebekah fought to hold back tears.

"She's in her room on the roof, Master. Thank you."

She followed as Yeshua and his small band made their way upstairs. Rebekah waited outside. Minutes passed like hours, until finally she detected the sound of voices and shuffles of movement behind the door. She reached to open it at the same moment it opened from inside.

Gramma's smile greeted her. Her face was pink as a desert sunset, her eyes bright as evening stars, and her hair neat and combed into a gray braid, twisted into a bun, and perched on top of her head.

"Rebekah, don't dawdle. These men are hungry. Go." Gramma pointed toward the kitchen area. "Don't stand there gawking. I'm not dead or addled. I'll be down to serve our guests, our family."

Yeshua kissed Gramma's cheek. "I'm as hungry as a lion on the prowl, so don't be long," he said with a wink.

"It'll be a meal fit for a king," replied Gramma, full of renewed vitality.

Rebekah stood gaping, until Gramma commanded her once more to go.

While the women tore bread, chopped onions, and placed dried fish and cheese on a wooden tray, Rebekah wanted to ask what had happened, but Gramma would have none of it until her guests were served. "We'll talk of all the day's happenings as we enjoy one another's company."

With the greater portion of the meal prepared before Sabbath, it wasn't long before Mary filled cups with sweet wine, while Gramma, Sarah, and Rebekah took the platters of food to the hungry men reclined around the table.

"Gramma, can I tell you and Immah about today while we serve?" Rebekah shivered, thinking about all she'd witnessed in the synagogue—and what she didn't see concerning Gramma. "There's so much to understand …"

"First, we serve," answered Gramma.

Rebekah grimaced. She could hear bits and pieces of the men's conversation, the excitement in their voices. She longed to sit, to listen, to learn. She tossed the vegetables on the plate, taking no time to arrange anything for appearance. It would be eaten as soon as she placed it on the table and the blessing of the wine was given. After

Sarah and Gramma finished with the roasted lamb, Simon asked Yeshua to bless the wine.

"Father, Lord God of the universe ..." Rebekah stole a glance around the room as Yeshua continued the blessing. The others didn't seem bothered that he called God his Father. As Yeshua ended, a hush fell across the room. The Nazarene reached for the platter of vegetables.

"Gramma, you kept your promise. This is food fit for a king." His smile filled the room with warmth. The others chuckled nervously and between mouthfuls, continued sharing their own version of the day's events.

As the meal and the talk waned, Yeshua stood. All stood with him. He raised his cup once more and began the blessing to the Lord for his provision of food, friends, and family. As he ended, all drank the last of their wine. He set his cup down and with a sweep of his arm began his praise.

"Bless the Lord ... who forgives your sins and heals all your diseases ... who redeems your life and crowns you with lovingkindness."

Rebekah leaned her ear toward a clamor of voices outside. She scanned the room. None of the others were moved by the noise. An insistent knock hammered against the door. The company turned as Rebekah jumped to answer the pounding.

"Wait," ordered Simon. "Our door was closed. Someone coming this late can only mean trouble somewhere. It sounds like there's a mob out there." Simon flung open the door to a man with a crutch under one arm, and his hand pressing against his rapidly rising and falling chest as if trying to hold back a tidal wave. A horde of broken people pressed in around the lame man clamoring for attention. Simon was speechless.

"Sir, I seek the rabbi, the one from the synagogue. He healed the possessed one. I was told he was here. I must see him." Without giving Simon opportunity to answer, he tried to push his way inside. Simon's massive frame stiffened, obstructing his path.

"I'm here," called Yeshua as he approached the man. Simon moved to one side, giving the Nazarene full view of the crowd gathering in his courtyard. "What do you want?"

At the sight of Yeshua, the crippled man dropped his crutch, falling to his knees. "My Lord," he begged. "My leg has no strength to carry me. If you say the word, I would be healed."

Yeshua lifted the young man, holding him under his shoulders.

"Your faith has made you whole. Stand and walk." Yeshua released him, and immediately the young man stood. He jumped up and down. He laughed. Then once again he dropped to his knees.

"Blessing, honor, and glory belong to the Lord God, and to the One who comes in his name."

"Go," commanded Yeshua, as the man stood. "Go, and praise the name of the Lord."

The man ran, leaping his way down the path as he went. "Praise to our God Most High, who has visited his people, Israel." His shouts resounded across the valley below.

Meanwhile in the house, Simon, James, John, and Andrew moved the table out of the room to make a place for the masses to come in. As many as came, Yeshua healed. They arrived lame, sick, diseased, and in pain. They left whole, healed, elated by the touch of the Master.

Rebekah's head reeled with the flood of people pouring into her home pleading for mercy and leaving rejoicing. The image was dream-like, until a clear idea burst its way into Rebekah's whirling mind.

Why isn't Jairus here with Phoebe? Certainly the Master can heal her, whatever her malady.

She pushed her way to the door and up to the rooftop, bounding up the steps to the room where a few hours earlier Gramma lay dying. Now the old woman greeted the sick coming to her door. Rebekah grabbed a shawl, hurtled down the steps, and waded through the crowd to the path through town. The sun would soon sleep. Already the night hues of blue blended with the sun's deep oranges and violets, creating shadows. She had to hurry.

"Rebekah."

She heard the loud whisper, knowing if she hesitated her opportunity might be lost.

"Rebekah."

She turned, but could only make out an unrecognizable shadow.

"Rebekah, it's me, Matthias." He stepped away from the boulder.

"Matthias, I can't stop. I must go to Phoebe." Rebekah recoiled at the sharpness in her own voice.

"Then I'll go with you." He stepped closer to Rebekah.

She took pause at his words.

"I mean you no harm. The hour is late. You'll be safer in my company than apart from it."

She wrestled with the truth of his statement, but knew it was so. "Come then, but we must hurry."

Matthias did most of the talking, as they made their way down the rocky path.

"Why would you run through the night alone?" he asked, his tone one of admonition as they approached the shoreline and turned in the direction of Jairus's house. "What happened that's so important it couldn't wait until morning?"

Without looking his direction or slowing her gait, Rebekah answered his rebuke with her own.

"What were you doing outside my house among the crowd, cowering behind a boulder? If you hadn't been too frightened to come closer, you wouldn't have to ask such a foolish question. You would know."

"I wasn't frightened." Matthias defended himself. "I saw the crowd of infirm folk finding their way to your place by any means possible, and my curiosity overtook my good judgment."

"You saw the sick leaving healed, then. How do you explain what's happening?"

"I have no explanation. I don't even know if they were really sick or had anything wrong with them."

"You do know what happened at the synagogue, though. Explain that."

Matthias's silence found him guilty in Rebekah's eyes.

"Well?" asked Rebekah.

"I won't judge any man before I know the truth," he replied. "I know this Nazarene speaks as no man ever spoke. He's not a handsome man for the masses to be drawn to, nor rich that they should desire him, yet they come."

"Listen to his words." Rebekah grew impatient. "Look at his life. Believe the works and you'll know."

Matthias raised his chin. "I hear his words, and I see him transgress the traditions of the elders. He doesn't wash his hands, and picks grain on the Sabbath. Can he be a prophet, a man from God if he does not keep the Lord's Sabbath?"

"Ugh!" Rebekah stopped the conversation and the walk. She stood staring at the top of the hill.

Matthias followed her gaze. "What's wrong?"

"You, for one," she answered. She nodded her head to the top of the hill. "No lamps burn in the windows, and the door is shut. They have retired."

"Can your errand not wait until morning?"

"I suppose it will have to." Rebekah's shoulders sagged in defeat. "Tomorrow. Tomorrow, I'll bring Phoebe to

Yeshua. He'll heal her weakness." She turned to start back the way they had come. Matthias followed without a word.

"You know you don't have to accompany me," she said. "I'm perfectly capable of taking care of myself."

"I am sure any man would run the other direction if he once tried to harm you," Matthias muttered from behind her.

Rebekah did an immediate about-face, her hands on her hips.

"What does *that* mean?"

Matthias bowed his head slightly.

"I meant," he answered, "you are a most capable young woman. Any man's equal."

Rebekah tilted her head to one side. Her mouth pinched.

"And," he continued, "knowing this, I will leave you here." He pointed up the path to her house. "You haven't far to go." Before she could retort, he moved off.

Rebekah watched him momentarily before trudging up the path. If the crowd dispersed and her father missed her, a scolding would be waiting for her.

Rebekah approached the dark house which stood like a sentry guarding those inside. She smiled. Gramma's rhythmic snoring beckoned her up the stairs. As she stepped inside, Rebekah's mother fidgeted on her mat.

Settling on her own mat, she relaxed. *This has been a day of wonders, disappointment, and renewed hope for Phoebe.* She slipped into a sleep filled with dreams of what might come—tomorrow.

CHAPTER 16

In the cool of the morning, Matthias walked among the ancient fig trees. Their gnarled trunks twisted the branches upward and outward. The words of the prophet Micah brought a smile to Matthias.

"They shall sit every man under his vine and under his fig tree; and none shall make them afraid ... the kingdom shall come to the daughter of Jerusalem." He caressed the rough bark as he spoke the words.

He scanned the rustling leaves filtering the sunlight and spoke his thoughts to the prophet.

"Micah, what would you tell us about these incredulous days of signs and wonders among all of Israel? ... They've all gone mad after the Nazarene. All except the chief priests and elders."

Would Micah believe the kingdom had come to Jerusalem?

Matthias headed home with an image in his mind of the unlearned and needy seeking the Nazarene. He hesitated mid-step and cocked his head at the sound of a muffled voice. He took measured steps toward the sound, as he scanned the hillside.

There.

The Nazarene sat alone, his hands tucked under his chin, staring into the sky. Matthias backed away, but not before the Nazarene called to him.

"Matthias, come sit with me."

As Matthias drew near, the Nazarene gestured toward the field of flowers. "The gentle swaying of the white lilies reminds me of my Father's beauty and grace."

Matthias fidgeted at his mention of the Father but more so at the longing in the Nazarene's dark eyes. He recognized the yearning.

"I ... I didn't mean to intrude. I was on my way home."

"Intrude? Nonsense. Shalom," said Yeshua, as he grabbed Matthias's shoulders and kissed his cheeks. "This is the best part of the day. It's never an intrusion to walk with the Father. He welcomes all who will come to him in spirit and in truth."

"I really must be on my way," stammered Matthias. "Time calls me to my work at home, and my servant Eliezer will wonder at my absence." Even as he spoke the words, Matthias's heart pounded with desire to stay.

"Which way are you going, Matthias?"

Matthias opened his mouth to speak, but not knowing how to answer, he closed it without a word.

"You don't know your way?" Yeshua smiled and pointed to where the path split. "There are only two ways. One leads to your eternal home, the other to a world of darkness. Follow me and I'll lead you home."

"There! On the hill!"

The shout averted Matthias's attention. His eyes widened at the crowd advancing toward them. Simon led the pack. None seemed to notice the lilies.

"Master, we've been looking for you," called Simon with a wave of his arms, "as you can see. The people want to hear more of the kingdom of God."

"They come only to see the miracles."

The sadness in the Nazarene's comment caught Matthias off guard, but he didn't care why they came. He was glad for the interruption. It gave him a chance to leave. Matthias glanced over his shoulder at those seeking the Nazarene's miracles but not the man.

"They want you to return and tell them more," explained Simon.

"I can't stay," Yeshua said. "We must go into all Galilee and preach the kingdom of God. Others might hear and believe."

Yeshua's voice carried to Matthias's ears.

Believe? Believe what, exactly?

Matthias paused at the bottom of the hill and searched the multitude. Someone shouted his name. He paused.

Rebekah?

"Matthias, over here." Rebekah stood on the edge of the crowd, waving her arms wildly above her head.

He nodded and raised a cautious hand. He could not imagine why she would be hailing him. By all signs she didn't think highly of him, of that he was certain.

"Rebekah, what is it? I'm in a hurry."

"Begging your pardon," she said with a slight bow of her head. "Be on your way, then."

"Excuse my abruptness. How may I help you?" He had begun to suspect this journey home might never end.

"You were with Yeshua?"

"Yes, but—"

"Is he leaving? Did he say something? Did you say something?"

He crossed his arms and glared at her. "Yes, I heard him say he's leaving. No, I said nothing. And if I did, I don't believe he's one to be swayed by another's words."

Rebekah grimaced.

"I did it again. If ever I learn to think before I speak, now that will be a miracle." Her shoulders sagged along with her usual exuberance.

With a look of surprise, Matthias nodded and acknowledged his agreement. "Will Simon follow him again?"

"I haven't spoken to him or Immah about it, but I'm sure he will. I believe Yeshua asked him and John, James, and my uncle Andrew to leave their nets behind and follow him, to become—how did he say?—fishers of men. I'm not sure what that means. With so many conversations at our table I can't be sure who said what. But I do believe Papa will go with a deeper commitment. What they are going toward, I don't know."

"You're very close to your papa?"

"Yes, but that's not why I'm sorry to see them go so soon."

"Ah, is it Phoebe?"

"Yes. I hoped Yeshua could see her, but I didn't have a chance to speak to him before he left."

"Knowing Jairus, I'm sure he will seek Yeshua's help if Phoebe is in need. And now I will take my leave. May the Lord God shine his face upon you. Shalom."

"And you. Shalom," returned Rebekah, as she headed up the shoreline.

Matthias watched her walk away. She didn't head home. Maybe she was going to Phoebe's. He smiled. Their conversation was the most pleasant one shared thus far. But what did that really matter? She was of little interest to him, and he was certain he didn't interest her.

Matthias reached for the mezuzah hidden in its encasement on the doorpost. After kissing the scroll, he recited the Shema written upon it. "Hear, O Israel: The Lord our God is one Lord: And you shall love the Lord your God with all your heart, and with all your soul, and with all your might ..."

How many times had he repeated these words without considering their meaning? He continued until he ran across the same words again. "... love the Lord your God, and to serve him with all your heart and with all your soul ... lay up these my words in your heart and in your soul ..." He finished Israel's theme song perfectly, kissed the tiny scroll, and returned it to its hiding place. Yeshua's words rang in his ears.

Follow me and I will lead you home.

He shoved open the wooden door. "Eliezer."

No one answered. "Eliezer!"

He heard footsteps.

"No, Master. It is I, Deborah."

"I know who you are. Where are Eliezer and Leah?" This behavior was not at all like them.

"Master, I have your morning meal prepared." She kept her eyes lowered and her chin down, making it hard to hear her faint voice.

"I did not ask about a meal. I asked for Eliezer and Leah. Where are they?"

"Matthias," began Deborah with a strength of tone she didn't use often. It was one she slipped into to gain his full attention, like a mother scolding her child.

He crisscrossed his fingers in front of his chest and waited.

The ancient little woman stood before him wiping her wrinkled hands on her apron. "They followed the townspeople to the hill."

"After the Nazarene? I didn't see them." Matthias dropped his hands to his side. "I cannot believe the audacity of those two."

Deborah raised her chin and met Matthias's eyes with her own glare.

"After Yeshua, yes."

"Whatever for? Do I not provide all of you with your every need? Why would they go seeking after him? At least you had the good sense not to go after him, too."

"You," began Deborah, accenting each word with care, "you credit me with more wisdom than I have. For I *would* have followed after Yeshua if my worn-out legs had the strength to carry me up and down the hills of Galilee."

Matthias's shoulders slumped as his spirit deflated. "You would leave me, Deborah?" Images of her cradling him as a child and singing him to sleep played in his mind.

The wrinkled old woman with a crooked back could barely reach Matthias's face as she embraced his chin in her loving hands.

"I am here, Matthias." He could feel the love of her heart in her touch. Tears filled his eyes.

"Forgive a young fool, Deborah."

"Before you even ask," she answered with a twinkle in her eyes. And before she could continue, Matthias chuckled as he lifted the old woman off her feet in a tight embrace.

"Put me down before you break me," she commanded.

Matthias gently set her down.

"Come," she said as she sat on the couch along the wall. She patted a place beside her. "We must talk for a moment."

Matthias obeyed without question.

"I will leave you only when the Lord God calls me to his side."

Matthias puckered his lips. "It won't happen. You will live forever." He smiled.

"You are right. I will, but not in this old worn-out shell. You asked earlier if you did not provide all we have need of."

"What is it, Deborah? Ask and you shall have it."

Without hesitation, Deborah replied, "Eternal life."

Matthias pulled away from the frail woman. Her hand fell away from his arm. "What you ask I can't give. Only the Lord God Almighty can give life."

"That Matthias, is why I would follow Yeshua."

Matthias could see the conviction of her soul reflected in her eyes.

"And," she continued, "I will follow him from afar, for he has the words of life. He *is* life."

They sat in a moment of deafening silence. Matthias pondered the words of this woman who loved him as her own.

With a pat on his arm Deborah rose.

"I will take your morning meal into the courtyard. It is a beautiful day, shining with the sun's glory and hope of the Eternal. You can sit under the shade of the fig tree."

Matthias watched the old woman hobble away.

Always away.

His heart ached with a weight of loneliness and uncertainty. Would they all leave him to find his way alone?

CHAPTER 17

Rebekah weaved through the maze of merchants, searching for the items on her mother's want list. She skewed her mouth to one side, her thoughts a tumbled mess. Her distraction obscured the things her mother expected her to procure.

"Why the gloomy scowl, Miss Rebekah?" Jacob's jovial tone could lighten any cloudy day. "Do I not have what you need?" The merchant's smile filled his round face. "Ask and I am sure to find it for you, and at the lowest price in the marketplace."

Rebekah returned a faint half-smile. "I'm sure you would, but I must remember it before you can find it." Her smile faded.

"I think that is not all filling your mind." Jacob nodded sagely, then pinched his lips together and waited for Rebekah's answer.

She nodded. "You're right. The summer heat has not been easy for Phoebe. We've missed our morning walks for several days. I left her moments ago, and her fading color chases away all other concerns. Maybe now that summer is past …"

Rebekah didn't finish her thought but started examining the fruit Jacob had spread across the table. She shook her head as she struggled to dismiss the image of her friend's face and regain her memory. "For now, I need to get Immah's things and return home. She says I dawdle worse than a carefree little donkey."

Jacob's laugh sent his belly into ripples like the waves of the sea. Then, growing serious, he waved his hand across the display of produce. "Then let me help you find what you need. I have some fine grapes and figs, and ..."

"And all at the lowest price." She finished his sentence with a smile. "I'll take these." She reached for the dried figs. "And I need a bag of flour, and—" She hesitated. "I think that completes my order. I know there's more, but my cares have carried it away"—she waved her hands over her head—"like wheat chaff in the wind."

"Look a little more," invited Jacob. "And while you look tell me what you hear from your papa and the lord they follow. Are they returning soon?"

"Looking more won't help." Rebekah dug coins from the pouch tied to her sash. "We haven't heard any word of late. But I'm hoping to hear soon," she said as she turned and moved away.

"Me too," he called after her. "The Nazarene prophet brings many people. Many people increase business. And I grow rich!"

Both laughed as she added, "By selling at the lowest prices. And I'll return as soon as I remember what I forgot."

She headed toward the Galilee with a prayer filling her heart for the merchant Jacob and his wife.

Lord of Israel, may your face shine upon them. They long for a child with the ache only parents losing one could know.

The breeze floating from the sea held a promise of cooler weather. She closed her eyes and raised her face to the sky. The air flowed through her hair, and she enjoyed the moment without heeding the price of later combing out her tangled curls. For now she savored the peace as the wind whispered its promise ... and hope, hope for Phoebe when the Lord returned.

As she stepped towards the water's edge, Rebekah let the bag filled with fruits and flour slip from her shoulder to the rocky beach. Peace washed through her as the sea's therapeutic wash swept over her feet. The Galilee stretched across the horizon with small whitecaps playing hide-and-seek across its expanse. The sun shared its glory with the water's surface, and she squinted at the brilliant reflection.

Soon her father would return. Yeshua, too, she hoped, more for Phoebe's sake than her own. She stared across the sea, willing a ship to appear.

"Many others will come, too," she said to the breeze, "if what I've been hearing is true."

The limited information she knew of their return felt like a dam in her soul about to burst. She refrained from sharing that knowledge with others, because it would bring a wave of people flooding those seeking rest.

Rebekah turned from her reverie, slung her bag over her shoulder and started homeward. As she walked up the hill, she smacked the side of her head as the forgotten item was jarred loose from her mind. "Immah's salt."

Rebekah did an about-face to return to the market, and noticed a figure in the distance ambling down the shoreline. Apparently she wasn't the only one needing the solace of the sea. She hesitated only a moment before hurrying on.

Matthias picked up a small, smooth, flat stone. He smiled and placed it between his thumb and forefinger like his father had taught him, then flicked his wrist and sent it sailing across the water. Six times the stone skipped across the surface before plunging to the sea's depths.

That's my best yet. Papa would be proud.

He stared at the rippling water. A cloud of doubt overshadowed his memory. Would his father be proud of him, his only son?

"Why wouldn't he?" said Matthias aloud. "I keep the commandments of the Lord God. I serve in the synagogue. I treat my servants well, and I'm making money." He patted the leather money pouch hidden in his belt as he looked above. "All you have left me, Papa, I have increased." He paused. In a whisper he added, "Why then do I doubt your approval?

He glanced at the rocky ground. Another stone just the right size and shape lay waiting to fulfill its purpose in his hand. He gave it a toss. It plunked into the sea and dropped to the bottom without skipping. His shoulders sagged.

I'm like that stone. Sinking. Why?

The gentle waves gave no wisdom. The heavens' silence allowed his thoughts to be engulfed with the face of the Nazarene.

He invades my life at every turn. After the Nazarene left to travel Galilee, Eliezer and Leah came home and constantly spoke in whispers with Deborah. Even the field hands couldn't work without mention of the latest news from whatever city he visited. Fantastic tales of lame ones walking, lepers cleansed, and demons fleeing their long-held captives kept every tongue talking and every ear itching for more.

Everyone's ear but mine.

"Enough," he said to the open air. Matthias turned and marched toward the synagogue, determined to find peace. Someone—maybe Jairus—would be there. He would hear what they had to say about this Nazarene turning the world upside down with his presence. While there, he would make sure all was in readiness for Sabbath. He did not look forward to a repeat of the Nazarene's reading in the meeting.

His heart pounded in his ears the closer he came to the synagogue. A battle grew in his soul ... but against what?

Matthias took the synagogue steps two at a time. He could hear Samuel, the teacher who was old when Matthias sat under his tutelage, instructing the children in the connecting courtyard. At the top step, his feet felt like heavy stones. He placed a hand on the door and gave it a push. Surely this would be the place to find relief from the weight in his chest. But no. As he stepped into the sanctuary, his skin crawled as if it was covered with small serpents. Scriptures, prophecies, and psalms of the Promised One washed into his mind.

"The Lord your God will raise up a prophet like me from your midst, from your brethren. Him you shall hear ... I will declare the decree: The Lord has said to me, 'You are my Son, Today I have begotten you ...

"Therefore the Lord himself will give you a sign: Behold, the virgin shall conceive and bear a Son, and shall call his name Immanuel ...

"Nevertheless the gloom will not be upon her who is distressed ... By the way of the sea, beyond the Jordan, in Galilee of the Gentiles. The people who walked in darkness have seen a great light; those who dwelt in the land of the shadow of death, upon them a light has shined ...

"Behold! My servant whom I uphold, my elect one in whom my soul delights ... Who has believed our report? And to whom has the arm of the Lord been revealed?"

He clasped his hands over his ears, as a scream lodged itself in his throat. He closed his eyes against an onslaught of confusing thoughts. The darkness and shadows of death swirled through his mind.

"Matthias?"

He flinched as a hand touched his shoulder. Like a child seeking refuge, he found sanctuary in the eyes and compassionate touch of his mentor and friend.

"Jairus," he whispered. He clung to his friend and sobbed.

Jairus held his young friend until the sobs subsided.

"What has happened to cause such grief? Is it Eliezer? Deborah?"

Matthias took a step back, wiping his face with the corner of his cloak. He offered Jairus a weak smile.

"No. No, they are fine. It is me, my dear friend. I think I shall lose my mind if I cannot find answers." He lowered his eyes and shook his head. Then he returned his gaze to Jairus, as he regained his composure. *I must remember my station in life.* He was a ruler of the synagogue, not a small schoolboy.

"What are your questions?"

"There is really only one. The same one I have asked you many times. Always your answer is the same. Does it remain the same?" Matthias searched his friend's face, seeing the answer in the confidence of his eyes and strong set of his mouth.

"Yeshua, the Nazarene?" asked Jairus.

Matthias nodded.

I have to hear the truth. To know the truth.

"My answer is the same."

Matthias considered his friend's words. "Then you believe he is the Messiah, possessing life eternal?"

"I pray for faith to believe." Jairus placed his hands on Matthias's shoulders and continued. "I do believe he is sent from God."

Matthias removed Jairus's hands. He tilted his head inquiringly. "Then you aren't sure. Is that why you haven't taken Phoebe to him?"

Jairus glanced around the room and ducked his head as he spoke.

"Now that the summer's scorching heat is past, Phoebe is doing better. And," Jairus lowered his voice as he continued,

"I fear the elders. I hear the Pharisees are none too happy with the Master's popularity. Until I'm certain of what I do believe, I don't want to cause trouble in the synagogue."

"So neither the elders nor the Pharisees believe this Nazarene is from God?"

"They don't speak openly for fear of the masses following him. They don't speak of him at all except behind closed doors or to challenge and accuse."

Matthias repeatedly rubbed his beard before answering.

"You have said the price for believing may be too high. But what keeps drawing you to him?"

"He speaks with authority and truth. His words are life. They speak of life. Eternal life."

"But we know and believe in the final resurrection. That's nothing new to us."

"But he says those who believe in him shall never die but have eternal life. As if we can have it now."

Matthias rubbed the back of his neck as he considered Jairus's words. "Do you understand this?"

"Not yet, but I'm ready to understand and risk the cost of believing."

Matthias studied the resolution reflected in his eyes.

Jairus must believe. His daughter may die an early death without this hope.

Shouts from outside the synagogue interrupted their conversation as the schoolboys hurried down the hill.

"We can talk later, if you desire," offered Jairus. "I've finished my work here and need to return home. Do you want to accompany me?"

Each clasped a hand around the other's arm.

"No, I'm fine, or will be," Matthias said. "Perhaps another time."

He watched as his friend exited the synagogue. Wisdom said for him never to speak of this again, but only listen. For now, he couldn't believe the reports, but he wasn't ready to shut the door on them either. He wanted to be free of this shadow of death, this darkness and turmoil threatening to swallow his soul. He wanted to find the light that could give life. He set his mind and energy to preparing the synagogue for Sabbath.

CHAPTER 18

"Eliezer." Matthias's tone sliced through the morning like a rooster's cocky crow. "I need my heavy cloak. Where is it?" Scurrying footsteps responded.

"Master, I have it here." The servant placed the cloak around Matthias's shoulders. "Will you be checking the groves and vineyard this morning?"

"Yes," Matthias irritably pulled at his cloak. "The wind last night may have done some damage."

"Spring may be near, Master, but the north wind isn't ready to surrender."

A slight grin creased Matthias's lips. "That's a truth we can all accept."

"Did you not find it strange how suddenly it died, and peace regained rule?"

"I thought nothing of it," retorted Matthias, trying to believe his own lie. He made another unnecessary adjustment to his cloak. "I'll return as soon as I survey any possible damage to the vineyard. I don't expect much with the fig trees. Those trees have stood and lived for more years than you and I together." Matthias walked out the door, barking orders as he went. "Be sure Leah and Deborah have my breakfast ready when I return. I need to check my ledgers, and then I will tend to my duties at the synagogue."

"It will be done, Master."

Matthias pulled his cloak tight around his shoulders. The warmth of the sun on his back belied the crisp air slapping his face as he headed across the meadow and up the hill. When he reached the vineyard tower, he paused to view the Galilee stretching out before him. From here the fishermen's boats looked like toys rocking in a shallow pool. No doubt the men would be tired, with little to gain for their trouble following last night's fury.

As he started to turn back to his task, a gathering crowd below caught his attention. The merchants wouldn't be set up yet. What would cause this mob to rush around like so many ants after a pot of honey? He shook his head, turned to his field, and began walking the perimeter of the vineyard.

Matthias mentally calculated the wind damage, figuring the cost in profits. He would have to hire workers earlier than usual to repair the breaches in the fence. The young fig trees had some branches broken and would need to be pruned. This early in the year there would be no loss of fruit. He smiled and nodded. The sun shining on his face warmed him.

It could be worse.

His work completed, Matthias headed home. The road into town was deserted. Maybe the ants had gone home to enjoy their breakfast. At the thought of breakfast, his stomach rumbled, and he hastened his steps. Leah and Deborah would have something good waiting for him.

Matthias made quick work of reciting the mezuzah's contents. One whiff told him the cakes he'd hoped for would fill his empty stomach.

"Eliezer," he called into the vacant room where a small fire chased the chill out of the air. "Tell Leah to bring my breakfast in here." His shoes off and his cloak tossed to one side, he reclined at the table waiting for the delectable source of the fragrance to be served. "Eliezer!"

Matthias frowned. No one came. Then he heard faint, slow footsteps approaching. The scent of the cakes and dibs grew stronger. He twisted to see who approached.

"Deborah? Where are Leah and Eliezer?" He rose to take the tray from her, but Deborah stiffened her crooked back and pulled the tray closer to her body.

"Sit down, young man. I am not dead yet. There is still some strength in these arms."

Matthias bowed his head, kissed the top of hers. and returned to his place. "You know I could have you beaten for such insolence."

"Not if you want these cakes."

Matthias raised his hands in surrender as Deborah placed the tray before him.

"Won't you join me?"

Deborah's eyes widened. "You want my company, Master?"

"I have no other choice. It seems you are the only one here. And," he said with a tilt of his head and a pitiful look in his eyes, "it's better than eating alone."

Deborah gave him a playful slap on the shoulder. "I will sit with you as you desire. But with your permission, only for a moment."

Matthias didn't say it, but he wondered when she had begun waiting for his permission. "Tell me, where have the others gone?"

"To the synagogue," she answered, settling gingerly onto the bench opposite him, "and by your uncommon good humor, you must have found the grove and vineyard in fair condition."

"Some damage," replied Matthias. "But nothing that will cut into my profits if we have a good harvest." He dipped a piece of the cake into the thick grape syrup and pushed it into his mouth, licking his lips to get each sweet drop. He swallowed it down with a mouthful of wine.

"Why didn't Eliezer and Leah wait for my return before going for morning prayers?' He took another bite of the flat cake.

"They did not go for morning prayers," answered Deborah, working her weight to one side as she lifted herself up with both arms.

Matthias quickly stood, reached for her hands, and helped her to her feet. "Then why did they go?" He towered over the frail figure. Her unruly hair that could not decide whether to be black or gray sat in a knot on the top of her head, with strands escaping all around.

Deborah avoided looking at him. "They went to hear the rabbi. He is teaching in the synagogue."

Matthias dropped her hands and sat back down without an answer. He tore at a piece of cake and drowned it in syrup before attacking it with his mouth. He swallowed hard and gulped more wine. Deborah waited.

"Again. I should have known. Here," he said, shoving the platter towards the old woman. "Take this and go. That's what you want, isn't it?"

Deborah turned to face Matthias. With him sitting, their eyes met. "Master, I will take my leave when my task is done, if you allow it."

Matthias flinched at the pained look in her eyes. He reached a hand to her wrinkled face. "You know I will allow it, Deborah. Tell me again. What draws you to this Nazarene?"

Deborah took his hand between her two calloused hands and brought it to her lips with a gentle kiss. "I am old, Matthias. Soon I will be buried with our ancestors." Her wrinkled face and weak smile told the story of a life lived well. "Yeshua has the words of eternal life."

Matthias longed to understand, but the fierce battle within him tore at his heart. Plainly his dear Deborah believed what she said. What chain bound him in unbelief?

"Walk with me, Matthias. Let's go to the synagogue together and hear his words, words of life."

Matthias rose and grabbed his cloak.

"Get your shawl, and I'll walk with you and help you find Leah. She can walk home with you. While there, I'll attend to my duties."

Holding Deborah's arm, Matthias guided her to the slope of the hill where the synagogue sat above all other structures. "With this mass of people, it will be impossible to find Leah." Matthias blinked back the sunlight as he peered toward the steps.

The Nazarene stood above the crowd on the top step, calling to the people. His followers sat huddled at his feet below him. Mothers sat on the grass. Men stood. Circles of Pharisees gathered and whispered among themselves, watching like vultures waiting for their prey to die.

"If you have ears, hear this," called the Nazarene. "My Father sent me from heaven to do his will. His will is for anyone who sees the Son and believes in him to have everlasting life, and on the last day, I will raise him up."

Matthias's chest pushed air out quicker than he could take it in. He wanted to escape but didn't dare leave Deborah. This Nazarene said he would raise believers up. Only God could do that. The whispers of the Pharisees echoed his concern as they argued about how Yeshua, a carpenter's son, could have come down from heaven. Matthias searched for Eliezer or Leah, anyone who could help Deborah and free him so he might flee.

The Nazarene continued to speak. "Stop your murmuring." His eyes locked with the Pharisees. "On the last day, I will raise up those whom the Father gives me."

The Pharisees raised defiant chins as the crowd furtively watched their reactions.

"I'm telling you with absolute certainty, anyone who believes in me has everlasting life." The Nazarene paused.

"I ... am ... the bread ... of life ... If anyone eats of this bread, he will live forever; and the bread I'm going to give is my flesh. I will give my flesh for the world to have life."

The Pharisees' faces grew red, and the arguments amongst them became more than loud whispers. Matthias waited for the Nazarene's response. His eyes widened with hope at the sight of Jairus standing at the outer edge of the Pharisees, his hands twisting together in knots. Jairus wanted to find an escape route. Matthias was certain of it.

The Nazarene's appearance illuminated the darkness of those around him, including that of Matthias's soul. His next forceful words sliced through Matthias's bones and into his heart.

"Believe me when I tell you, unless you eat the flesh of the Son of man and drink his blood, you don't have life in you."

Eating his flesh? Drinking his blood? No life?

The Pharisees began making their way through the crowd, shoving aside any who stood in their path. Matthias saw others shaking their heads, muttering of this being more than they could understand. Jairus fidgeted where he stood.

The Nazarene's words made no sense. Matthias would not stay and hear any more.

"I'm leaving, Deborah. You can come or you can stay."

"I'll stay. Eliezer or Leah will help me home."

She'd made her choice. As Matthias and many others began to leave, the Nazarene continued to plead with them. His voice grew in intensity, urgency.

"Whoever eats my flesh and drinks my blood has eternal life, and I will raise him up at the last day. For my flesh is food indeed, and my blood is drink indeed. The one who eats my flesh and drinks my blood has life in me, and I live in him. As the living Father sent me, and I live because of the Father, the one who feeds on me will live because of me. This is the bread which came down from heaven—living bread, and not the manna your fathers ate and are dead. The one who eats this bread will live forever."

Matthias walked away from the synagogue, making his way past the throng of afflicted masses waiting for the Nazarene's healing touch. One caught his attention as the man ran up the hill toward the synagogue, showing no consideration for those unable to move from his path. He thought he recognized the servant but dismissed the thought, believing it to be just another weak soul in search of a miracle.

CHAPTER 19

Matthias locked his jaw. His focus paused on a few fishermen mending their nets.

Everyone needs to eat real food, not the nonsensical prattle the Nazarene spoke of.

He would not entertain the Nazarene's words any longer. But he found it an impossible task as he plodded through the marketplace toward home.

Pockets of people talked to each other of only one thing. Matthias started to make his way around one group when, without warning, someone from behind him shoved past him.

"Watch where you're going!" he snapped. No sooner were the words spoken than another man rammed him. He kept his balance but not his temper.

"You! Do you have no thought but for yourself?" Matthias grabbed the man's cloak and whirled him around.

"Forgive me, sir, but you can see my master," pleaded the man, as he twisted his arm to free it and pointed in the direction of the first offender. Matthias recognized the man, a servant, as the one racing up the hill to the synagogue earlier. He looked in the direction the servant pointed. His mouth dropped open. His heart pounded as he caught sight of the figure running full speed ahead.

"Man, what is wrong?" Matthias demanded. "What has happened with Jairus?" When the servant hesitated, Matthias shook him by the shoulders. "Speak, man. What is happening in the home of Jairus?"

"My master's daughter." The servant wrung his hands and stared at his feet. "She, she—" He covered his mouth and swallowed hard as if words were stuck in his throat.

Matthias loosened his grip. "What? What is happening?"

"She is very ill. I plead with you, let me go."

Matthias released the servant and watched as he ran to catch Jairus.

"Matthias." A familiar voice spoke from behind him. He wanted to ignore it and pursue the servant and Jairus.

"I beg you, Matthias. I must talk with you," Rebekah touched his arm as she caught up to him and wiped her unruly hair from her face. "Wasn't that Jairus's servant you were talking with?"

Matthias nodded.

"What did he say? Is something wrong with Phoebe? Has she grown ill again? Please tell me." Her grip tightened on his arm.

Matthias took her hand. The softness surprised him.

"Something is wrong," he said. "Phoebe is very ill."

Rebekah pulled her hand away from him and covered her face. Her shoulders began to quiver with her muffled sobs. A fire burned inside him for her sorrow, compelling him to pull her close, but he stood frozen.

"Rebekah?" He barely recognized the sound of his own hoarse whisper. "We'll do no one any good here. Come," he said, taking her hands from her face. "Phoebe may want to see you."

"Yes." She sniffled and used the end of her shawl to wipe her face. "Let's go, quickly."

Matthias recognized an unfamiliar resignation in her voice. He put his arm around her shoulder as they hurried to Phoebe's home. Their steps halted at the bottom of the hill leading to Jairus's house. Rebekah pulled away from Matthias.

"No." She lifted her skirt and ran. "*No!*"

Matthias followed with measured steps. The wail from the gathered mourners at Jairus's home meant only one thing. Death had claimed the life of one too young to travel its path. Before they reached the house, Jairus came running back down the trail, his cloak flapping in the wind as if he might take flight. He ran by them as one possessed. When Matthias and Rebekah reached the house, they were met by servants and neighbors wailing the shrill message of death.

Rebekah dropped to the bench in front of the house. She stared into nothingness. She didn't wail. She sat with her hands folded in her lap. Tears flowed over her cheeks like a gentle brook. Matthias started to sit next to her when he saw the servant who had collided with him.

"Where has Jairus gone?" he asked.

The servant stood facing the door, his chin raised, not acknowledging Matthias other than to answer him. "He has gone for the Rabbi."

Matthias studied the servant as if something in his answer would suddenly make sense. He walked back to Rebekah. She sat silently, in contrast to the mournful wails around her. Her tears had left her face blotched and her eyes swollen.

"What did Micah say?" she asked, still staring off in the direction Jairus had run.

"Micah?"

She turned her head toward Matthias. "The servant you spoke with." She blinked back more tears. "His name is Micah."

Her voice remained a monotone that unnerved Matthias. He covered his mouth, pinching his lips together, as he looked away from her.

"What is it? What did he say?"

He swallowed emotion as he faced her. "He said Jairus went for the Rabbi."

Rebekah jerked her head to the side, and her eyes grew bright as if life had suddenly pushed death away. "Yeshua?"

"Yes, but Rebekah, *it is too late*. What can he possibly do now but offer comfort?"

"I'm not sure," she whispered, looking around at those continuing the death wail. "But when I asked him to heal Phoebe, he said her time was not yet." Rebekah moistened her lips and rubbed her temples. "Yeshua told me to believe and see the glory of God." She sat straighter on the bench. "He'll come."

The wailing mourners could not drown out the words of Yeshua, the ones Matthias had heard at the synagogue. They flashed in fragments through his mind.

Believe. Eternal life. Everlasting life. The living Father.

What was it Deborah had said about him? Matthias turned his eyes towards the sun-filled blue sky. Its brightness belied death's visit upon this family.

"Life," he whispered. "He has the words of life."

The sudden intensity of the mourners brought Matthias back to reality, to the certainty of death within the house. He glanced toward the path, seeing what had caused the outburst. The Nazarene, his followers, and Jairus marched resolutely up the hill. When they came to the door, Yeshua glanced at Rebekah. His nod seemed to speak to her heart. Matthias could see peace cover her like a warm blanket.

The Nazarene opened the door and told those within to come out. He raised his hands to quiet the mourners and spoke loud enough for all to hear.

"What is all this weeping and wailing you're doing? The child is not dead. She only sleeps."

Matthias gaped and shook his head. Surely this Nazarene would not give Jairus hope when death had already stolen his daughter. He watched the crowd as those inside came out. Some laughed at the Nazarene's words. Others derided him without mercy.

"Peter, James, John, come with me, and the child's mother and father," he commanded, with no comment to the ridicule. The door shut behind them.

Many of the mourners murmured among themselves, while others stood silently. Some began the death wail again. Matthias watched Rebekah wait at the door.

In a span of moments, the door opened. Phoebe stood before them, her cheeks full of color, a broad smile on her face, the sunlight shining around her and encasing her in its brightness. Matthias saw Rebekah reach for the wall to steady herself. He would have helped her but hesitated, fearing they might both go down.

Phoebe came to Rebekah first. Tears streamed down Rebekah's cheeks as she cupped the living girl's face in her hands. Some of the mourners' ridicule turned to shouts of praise. Others gawked. Those who had shouted the loudest now turned and ran toward the city. Matthias imagined their tongues would report all to the Pharisees.

"Get the child something to eat," called the rabbi. His voice was hearty, but Matthias recognized pain in his eyes as he watched those running away.

"That sounds good," said Phoebe. "I am hungry." As she and her parents returned inside, the people drifted away, waving their hands and marveling, telling and retelling the miracle of life's victory.

Matthias meant to wait for Rebekah, but when he saw her accompany Phoebe, he left to walk home alone. Deborah's words of eternal life swam through his thoughts.

But this is not eternal life. Life, yes. But even Elijah and Elisha brought the dead to life. He continued to argue with himself as he walked. This Nazarene surely had power, but from where? He claimed to be more than a prophet. He claimed to be the source of eternal life. Matthias knew his claim made him equal with God. He shook his head.

There is only one God.

He dared not to speak the holy name of Jehovah. His heart was divided by what his knowledge had taught him and his eyes saw.

CHAPTER 20

Matthias cocked his head as he listened to a crescendo of voices pouring from his house. Rejoicing? His lengthy stride carried him toward an uncertain discovery. He laid a hand on the mezuzah and raced through the holy words. A chorus of praise greeted him from his courtyard. Eliezer's rich voice accompanied by Leah's and Deborah's harmony danced on the air, filling the house with glory. Their psalm of praise beckoned him to the music.

"Praise ... the Lord. Sing unto the Lord a new song, and his praise in the congregation of saints. Let Israel rejoice in him that made him: let the children of Zion be joyful in their king. Let them praise his name in the dance: let them sing praises unto him with the timbrel and harp. For the Lord takes pleasure in his people: he will beautify the meek with salvation."

The sight before him arrested his steps. Eliezer, Leah, and Deborah weaved in and out among the benches and budding bushes. They twirled with their hands above their heads, clapping out a rhythmic beat as they sang. How could they have heard the news so soon? Matthias gaped—Phoebe wasn't the reason for their celebration.

Words exploded from his mouth.

"This can't be!" Matthias ran into the middle of their rejoicing. The music ceased. The dancing stopped. He lifted

Deborah off her feet and whirled her around. "What has happened? How?" He asked as he put the old woman down.

"Master," Eliezer bowed slightly. "We, we ... didn't hear ... we didn't expect ... forgive—" he stammered.

"Eliezer," said Matthias as he put a hand on his servant's shoulder, "no forgiveness is necessary." His eyes grew to the size of a platter. Deborah—poor aging bent-over Deborah—stood steady before him, her back and shoulders straight. He waved a hand up and down as if measuring her height. "How did this happen?"

Deborah's face glowed. "Yeshua."

Matthias blinked. He could not deny the proof before him, nor would he steal the rapture from his beloved Deborah. He smiled. "We will praise the Lord God Almighty who has healed you."

"Yes," agreed Deborah. "The Lord God is mighty to save and mighty to heal. He has sent us his salvation."

Before she could speak more of the Nazarene, Matthias interrupted. "Deborah, tell me how this happened."

"It is as I said, Matthias." She looked into his eyes and graced his face with a hand that earlier could not have reached his chin. "Yeshua," she whispered with a smile, leaning her face closer to his. Matthias saw the light of life in her eyes. Her radiance erased the long years of her pain.

"He saw Leah and Eliezer helping me down the hill. He came to me and asked if I would be healed."

Matthias's mouth grew dry. His heart beat like the hooves of a runaway stallion as she continued without averting her attention from his face.

"I could not see into his face as I now can see into yours. I dropped to my knees and could only answer with two words. 'Yes, Lord.'"

Matthias took her hands between his own. "Then what?"

"Yeshua did exactly as you did."

Matthias's hands suddenly felt as if a fire burned within them. He wanted to look away, release her, and stop this tale, but the truth stood before him.

Deborah continued, "He held my hands even as you do now as he raised me to my feet. But when he raised me, I stood straight." Deborah flung her hands from Matthias, clapped them above her head, and twirled to the music in her heart.

Matthias's mouth curved in a smile as his heart pondered her words.

"Strange things," he murmured, "things beyond the natural, saturate this day as a gale does on the Galilee."

"Besides what we saw at the synagogue?" inquired Eliezer.

"Yes," nodded Matthias, patting Eliezer's shoulder. "But for now, we will set aside our lack of understanding, and celebrate the wonders weaving into our lives." He could not bring himself to say of God, but who else could do these miracles?

Who else has the power of life ... and death?

Leah and Deborah hurried to the kitchen to make ready a platter of dried figs, cheese, bread, and smoked fish. Soon it sat on the table along with sweet wine.

Matthias lifted his glass above his head.

"All praise, glory, and honor to the Lord God of the universe, who gives us fruit of the vine to gladden our hearts." Then he added with tenderness as he looked at Deborah, "And for the wondrous works he has done this day."

Each drank a sip in thanksgiving to begin the meal. As they sat, Matthias related Phoebe's story. He recounted the rush to the house of Jairus, the death wails, and the entry of the Nazarene and his men into the house.

"And then she stood in the doorway, alive, smiling, and hungry," he added, concluding the event.

The three servants sat wide-eyed. Leah placed her fingertips over her mouth. Deborah raised a hand over her head and whispered, "Praise the Lord God, for he has visited his people. Those who believe will never die."

"Certainly," added Eliezer with a nod of his head.

Silence settled over the group. Matthias shifted on his pillow as the quiet screamed at his heart.

Eliezer broke the stillness.

"Master, it has been a long day. You must be weary. May we clear the table so all may retire?"

Matthias pushed himself up from his seat on the floor.

"Yes, Eliezer, I believe we could all use some rest." He reached for Deborah's hand. She offered it willingly and used the other to get her old bones, now made new, headed in the right direction. Matthias leaned over and planted a kiss on her wrinkled brow. He released his hold on her and smiled. This morning that kiss would have been on the top of her thinning hair. "Good night, Deborah. May the Lord God give you rest such as you have never had."

Deborah returned his smile. "He already has, and most assuredly he will." She picked up a tray to take to the kitchen. Leah followed.

"I'm going for a walk before calling it a day, Eliezer. No need to wait for my return."

"Are you sure, Master?"

"Yes. Get some rest, dear friend." Matthias shut the door behind him, thinking of how much love these servants had given him over the years. He remembered, as he walked the path, the times they had returned kindness for his insults, and the days following his father's death, when each chose to put an ear to the doorpost and stay with him forever. His father's death freed them, but they remained. Matthias tilted his head to one side and watched the stars speaking to one another in their twinkling code. "Surely, Lord God, you have shown me love in these three."

Matthias walked past the sleeping city to the fishermen's wharf. All the boats floated at anchor. Even the fishermen were caught in the day's excitement.

"Is that you, Matthias?"

He jerked around.

"I didn't mean to startle you," said Rebekah, covering her mouth to hide the grin that crept across her lips and into her eyes.

"You think a late-night's heart-stopping is funny?"

Rebekah licked her lips and tucked them in her mouth to control her reaction. "Not exactly, I suppose."

"Now you're not being truthful."

"You're right. I'm not being truthful." A chuckle seeped out of her parted lips. "I am sorry for startling you."

Matthias wasn't convinced.

"Why are you here so late?" she asked.

"The better question is why are *you* out alone at night?" Before she could answer, he continued to scold her. "You know it's not proper for you to be unescorted."

"You're here," she retorted, "so I'm not alone. And concerning my propriety, I will be the judge of my actions."

"And Simon?"

Rebekah twisted her mouth, turning it into a pucker. Her eyes grew rounder than normal. "Papa isn't home," she stated. "Immah has gone with him. And Gramma is sleeping."

"So you sneaked out?" Matthias lowered his chin and turned a palm up in her direction.

"No, I didn't. I walked out of the house, and if you are going to continue examining my actions, I will simply leave." She tilted her chin up and turned as if to go.

Matthias took her arm. "You needn't leave."

Rebekah looked at his hand on her arm, then looked at him with a hard stare. Instantly he withdrew his grasp. "I— maybe you—"

"What?" She raised her hands. A frown shadowed her face in the moonlight.

Matthias lowered his head, closed his eyes, and considered his words before speaking.

"I don't know. So many strange things have happened that I don't understand." He raised his eyes to meet hers. "You, you seem to—well, to understand the things the rabbi says. Who do you say he is?"

He rubbed his hand over his mouth and down his beard. "Please forgive me." He shook his head, rebuking himself. "I shouldn't be confiding in you in this way. After all, I am a ruler in the synagogue. I should be answering your questions. Our being here is not proper." He did not wait for a response but started to walk past Rebekah and off the wharf.

"Matthias." The tenderness in her voice halted his steps. He turned to her so they stood face to face. "You asked me a question."

He nodded, and she placed a hand on his sleeve. "I wish to answer. He is Yeshua, the Nazarene, the Lamb of God who takes away the sin of the world. He is the Messiah." She let her hand drop.

Matthias peered at her through narrowed eyes. They stood in the silence under the witness of the night sky and the breeze that played with Rebekah's curls. He twisted his sidelock. "You simply believe the things others have told you. You're a child easily influenced." He spoke in a monotone.

"Yes, I believe the things I've heard. But," she continued, "I believe the witness of the works that follow the man. The works testify to who Yeshua is and where he is from. You only need to look to them, and you will understand."

Matthias searched her face for a hint of doubt, but found only steadfast conviction.

"It's not mine to convince you of the truth, Matthias. You must be convinced in your heart of what you already know."

He acknowledged her words with a slight dip of his head.

"I think I should leave these words with you, Matthias, and return home. It's getting late." She glanced down at the wharf.

Matthias knew she was waiting for him to answer, but he had no answer. He simply offered, "Yes, it is late. Do you want me to walk you home?"

Rebekah blinked and her mouth gently curved. "No, but thank you."

Matthias stood in the moonlight, the only sound being the gentle splash of the sea against the wooden dock and the crunching gravel under Rebekah's feet as she made her way to the top of the hill. When she reached the top, he saw the silhouette of her hand as she waved. He responded in kind. Then she disappeared.

"I could almost believe," he said, as he looked at the reflection of the moon swimming on the sea.

He turned and followed his path home.

CHAPTER 21

"Eliezer! Eliezer!" Leah's scream pierced the air like a hawk's war cry.

Matthias sprang from a deep sleep and rubbed his hands over his face, trying to wipe away any remaining stupor.

What is that noise? Footsteps?

He pressed both hands against his pounding forehead and closed his eyes to hide from the morning light. Quiet reigned. He let his body fall back on the mattress, blinked a couple of times, and convinced himself he had been dreaming. Sleep began to push consciousness into oblivion.

"Master."

Matthias lowered his chin to his chest, hesitated, then slung both feet over the edge of his bed and ambled to his door. If Eliezer chose to disturb him, there must be something that couldn't wait. Opening his door, he found his servant standing before him pale, tears pouring down his face.

Matthias put a hand on Eliezer's shoulder.

"Eliezer?" He waited for an answer as tremors coursed through his insides.

Eliezer pulled Matthias against his chest and sobbed unashamedly.

Matthias shoved away from his servant's grasp and glared into his eyes. His chest rose and fell to the measure of his rapid heartbeat, his dread mounting until it exploded from his chest in a bellow of pain.

"*No!*"

Pushing Eliezer aside, he fled into the courtyard.

"This cannot be happening." He ran to Leah cowering in a corner, eyes wide, her face blotched and wet from crying. He grabbed her by the shoulders and shouted at her. "Is it true? Certain?" She could not lift her eyes to face him but only nodded.

Matthias spun around. "Eliezer, my mantle and my shoes."

Eliezer moved in obedience without hesitation. In a single action, Matthias threw his mantle over his shoulders and slid his feet into his sandals. Eliezer knelt to tie them, barely finishing before Matthias moved toward the door. He flung it open and fled down the path without turban or belt … without touching the mezuzah.

Rebekah listened to the sounds of Gramma in the kitchen below. She closed her eyes and rested in the morning peace. Her conversation with Matthias replayed in her mind. She prayed.

"Lord God of heaven and earth, our creator and redeemer, our strong and mighty tower, you have visited your people, Israel. Open Matthias's eyes to see, his mind to understand, his heart to believe. So be it, Lord." Ending her prayer, she ran her hands through her curls and washed her hands before going down to help Gramma with the morning chores.

Rebekah planted a solid kiss on her Gramma's cheek. "May the Lord God bless your day with beauty and joy, Gramma."

Gramma looked up from pounding her dough and smiled. "He has allowed me to look into your face, and I behold his beauty and hear your voice, and I feel joy."

Rebekah smiled as Gramma flipped the dough over and tore it into pieces.

"Now," said Gramma. "Bless me more with some help." The old woman laughed and tossed a lump of dough in Rebekah's direction.

Rebekah joined in her laughter and began pounding out the dough. The *slap-thump* of dough striking the wooden table kept a steady rhythm. A distant hawk could be heard calling its mate. "His call sounds lonely, Gramma."

"Child," Gramma started to scold her granddaughter, but the sudden pounding on their door changed her mind. "Who would be hammering on ..."

Rebekah wiped the flour from her hands and left the old woman in mid-sentence. She peered out the small window and jerked back.

"Matthias?" She greeted him with a smile as their eyes met, but he did not wait for an invitation to enter. She stared at him, her mouth open and ready with a rebuke.

"Where is he?" he demanded, scanning every corner of the house. "I demand to know where he is."

"He who?" Rebekah challenged, scowling at him.

"The Nazarene," Matthias spit out. "You call him Yeshua."

Rebekah shivered. The eyes of death looked at her from within his own. "He's not here, Matthias."

"I see that," he answered. "I want to know where he can be found." He worked his jaw. His teeth clenched.

Rebekah fought the urge to throw him out, but the pain in his face cautioned her to proceed with care.

"Matthias." She forced calm into her voice. "Yeshua left last night for Jerusalem. He and several following him ..."

"If he left just last night, then I can surely catch up to him," interrupted Matthias. He darted for the door.

"No, Matthias, you cannot catch him." Rebekah followed on his heels, as she tried to explain. "They traveled by boat, going across the sea. Yeshua wanted to preach on the other side as he made his way to Jerusalem for Passover."

Matthias turned and glared. Rebekah attempted to put a comforting hand on his arm, but he jerked away.

"Deborah is dead."

Matthias's flat statement of fact sent chills rippling across her skin. "Deborah?"

"My servant," he answered. He turned his lifeless eyes from Rebekah to her Gramma, who stood across the room, watching the scene unfold. He lowered his head.

"I must go. Mourners will be gathering. I'll have to bury her." He stopped, faced Rebekah. "Since the Nazarene isn't here, that's all I can do."

"Matthias, I am so sorry for your pain."

"Sorry?" His tone sounded accusatory. "Did you know your Messiah, this Yeshua, this one who raises the dead, did you know he healed Deborah only yesterday?" He peered at her as he continued. "Why? Can you tell me why? Are these the works I am supposed to believe? And now that I truly need him, he's nowhere to be found."

Rebekah had no answer for one who already had his answers. She watched him walk away, his shoulders slumped.

"Lord, comfort this one that seems so lost," she whispered.

Gramma slipped an arm around her granddaughter's slender waist and pulled her close. "Deborah," she explained, "was more than his servant. She raised Matthias after his mother died."

Rebekah watched him with a new understanding as he plodded his way down the path.

Matthias's legs were heavy, as though iron chains shackled them. He wasn't sure how long he had wandered through Capernaum or even how he got to where he was. All he knew was the chains grew heavier with each step— and he knew what waited for him when he got home. Eliezer would have helped Leah gather women to prepare Deborah for burial, and the mourners would be arriving. Had he been gone long enough for this all to be done? Nearing the house, the death wail pierced his heart as clean and painful as if a Roman javelin had run him through. Was it only yesterday that cry pierced the hearts of Jairus's house? He replayed the scene in his mind. *She only sleeps,* Yeshua had said. Phoebe's face full of life appeared before him. Tears pooled in his eyes as the mourning wails moved the winds of heaven. He walked past those standing outside his door, oblivious to who was there. He glanced at the mezuzah and proceeded inside.

"Master," Eliezer met him as he came in. "We must proceed with preparations for Deborah's burial."

"Take me to her, Eliezer." Matthias, his face hard as flint, followed as Eliezer silently led the way to where Leah and the other women had been preparing Deborah's body.

There before Matthias lay his beloved Deborah. Her frail body wrapped in cloth, she looked like a gift being offered back to her Creator, a perfect gift, straight and whole. He fell on his knees before the bier that held the small package, laid his head on her chest, and wept.

When his tears would no longer flow, Matthias stood. His stiffened joints did not want to hold him, and Eliezer helped steady him.

"Master." Eliezer's voice, raspy and almost unfamiliar, interrupted Matthias's grief. "Those who would carry

Deborah to her final place of rest are ready when you wish to begin."

Matthias turned to him. "You, my friend, my father, you and I will carry her. I will be at her head and you at her feet. We will carry her to my family's tomb. There she will rest."

Eliezer nodded. The procession began, and the mourners followed the two men. Two barrel-chested field workers rolled the stone from the tomb's entrance. Matthias and Eliezer entered the cool darkness with their precious cargo, while a field worker lit a torch to guide them to one of several small rooms. Here the dead would be housed until their resurrection.

After placing Deborah on the stone bed, Matthias took the face cloth, kissed it, and laid it upon the wrinkled, expressionless visage.

Will I ever see her face again?

Eternal life? How does one know of its truth?

He wanted to believe for Deborah. What of himself?

"Master." Eliezer spoke into Matthias's ear. "The mourners wait. Do you need more time? Should I send them back?"

Matthias gazed at the shell of the old woman who had loved him as no other. The mixture of dank air and spices caused his eyes to burn, threatening more tears.

"No." He turned from the form lying on its rock bed. "No, we will return. Leah will have wine and bread to offer them."

They walked together from the tomb, passing the room holding his father, mother, and the brother he never knew. Before leading the mourners back to the house, Matthias and Eliezer waited for the workers to return the stone to its place, guarding the bodies within. Then Matthias, head sunk onto his chest, turned to begin the long walk home.

Finally the house emptied of mourners, leaving Matthias alone with only Leah and Eliezer. Both busied themselves putting the house back in order. Matthias walked to the courtyard and sat on the bench under the shade of the fig tree. He covered his face with his hands and closed his eyes, but quickly opened them when his mind returned to the night before. Deborah had stood before him whole, singing praises to her God. He sat straight and rubbed the back of his neck.

"Eliezer," he called as he walked toward the dining area. Eliezer met him as he entered. "Come with me." The servant obeyed without question. Matthias sat at his desk and wrote furiously.

"This," he said, "gives you authority over my business. You will take care of the workers and all that needs to be done. They are good men who know their jobs. You are a faithful servant aware of all my dealings. You'll handle my affairs well. I'm leaving in the morning. Have Leah prepare food for my journey to Jerusalem. If she needs help while I'm gone, hire a servant to help her."

Matthias saw Eliezer's look of confusion as he handed him the instructions. "I mean to know the truth, Eliezer. I *will* know the truth."

"Master?"

"Many think the Nazarene holds the words of truth, of life, eternal life. I want to know the truth. I want to know the way to eternal life, if indeed it does exist."

Eliezer listened without reply.

"I've lost too many to death's reign." Matthias stood before Eliezer, searching the servant's face for answers. "I want to know I will see them again. I don't want to miss the way, if indeed eternal life awaits those who are God's. Those whom I have laid in that tomb believed. I will know the truth no matter the cost."

CHAPTER 22

Rebekah's unruly curls bounced against her shoulders as she skipped down the hill toward the Galilee. She scanned the horizon, searching for a ship she knew would not come. Her pace slowed as the morning sun played on the ripples of the lake, and she thought about her father and mother. A sad smile lingered on her lips.

It's only been a few weeks since they left, but how I long to see them!

She tossed a wild curl away from her face and resumed her gait, until the image of Matthias intruded into her thoughts. She hadn't seen him since Deborah's death. A fish jumped between the flickering rays of light dancing on the shallow waves as she whispered a quick prayer for Matthias.

Rebekah's thoughts returned to seeing her parents in Jerusalem for Passover, giving birth to a lighter step and a joy in her heart. Soon, she would travel with Phoebe's family for the holy day. In fact, she needed to be there now, helping with preparations. With a last glance at the sea, she turned toward her destination.

"Rebekah." Phoebe greeted her friend in the doorway. Her face radiated life. "Shalom." She grabbed Rebekah's arm and pulled her inside. "We are drying some fruit ..."

"And I smell bread already baking," Rebekah said, as her mind wondered anew at her friend's healthy glow and the events that had made it happen.

"Yes. Unleavened for the holy day."

"Of course."

The two worked alongside Joanna and their two house servants preparing for the journey. Along the way, families would offer them housing. Between the towns and villages, tents under the night sky would serve as their lodging. On the road, they would need their own provisions, and in the homes where shelter was offered, they would need a gift for their host. The older women went to the smokehouse to check on the supply of fish they still needed to prepare.

"Tell me, Phoebe," Rebekah said, as she chopped the figs and laid them out to dry. "What was it like?"

"Dying?"

Rebekah paused in her task and turned to Phoebe. "That too. But what was it like to come back?"

Phoebe's busy hands stopped with her knife still poised over the figs. She turned her eyes toward the ceiling, as if something written there would explain what she had experienced. She moistened her lips.

"I will start with dying, because that came first. The journey is worse than the event. I knew my life, my spirit, was escaping me. I wanted to hold on to it." She paused. "But I had no power. When I realized this was death, and I had no strength to fight, I rested." She turned back to the figs and chopped a few more pieces.

Silence hung in the air like a gossamer veil. Rebekah waited. Following Phoebe's lead she chopped more figs, but her heart yearned to hear more. Without looking up, she asked, "You rested?"

Phoebe nodded and continued to work.

"I died. There was no more struggle. I can't tell you anything of that time, for there is no knowledge in death. There is only death. I can't tell you that it is the same for all of those who do not know life again. I can only tell you what I experienced."

"And then?"

Phoebe laid her knife down and wiped her hands on her apron. She placed her hand over Rebekah's, stopping her work. Rebekah turned to her.

"And then," said Phoebe, "the moment he touched me, life awoke in my spirit. The darkness fled at the sound of his voice, the voice of life, of light." The tone of her voice was unearthly, and her eyes sparkled. She seemed to look past Rebekah into another world.

Rebekah stood, as motionless and expectant as a lion ready to pounce on its prey, as her friend talked.

"When he spoke, what did he say to you?"

"'Maid, I tell you to arise.'" Her eyes grew wide. "Rebekah, in that instant life entered my whole body, and immediately I stood. I slept no more." A beam lit her face as she continued. "And I was *hungry*." She giggled. "Yeshua told them to feed me." She shook her head and returned to the figs, plopping one in her mouth.

Rebekah stared at her friend as she tried to grasp the fullness of Phoebe's words.

"I do wish the Lord could have been here when Deborah died."

"And I."

"Are you girls still chopping those figs?" Joanna bustled into the kitchen area to where they worked with the fruit. "There won't be much to take if you two don't get busy."

The two girls glanced at Joanna and returned to their chore, glancing at each other in unspoken communication.

By the end of the day, most of the preparations were done.

"Shalom," called Phoebe as Rebekah started her path home.

"Shalom." Rebekah glanced over her shoulder as she waved to Phoebe and her mother. She would not tell anyone else of the other's rebirth, but hold it in her heart as Phoebe had asked. It was what Yeshua had asked of her family. She would honor it as best she could.

Arriving at the marketplace, Rebekah stopped at Jacob's table.

"Rebekah!" greeted the jovial merchant. "I hope you have come to supply Gramma with much food while you are gone. You must take care of your Gramma."

Rebekah tilted her head.

"You, fine sir," she began with a smirk, "are overly concerned for my Gramma. Or could it be you are concerned about how much silver you make from my purchase?"

Jacob covered his heart with his hand, shook his head, and lowered his eyes. "You cause me great pain, Miss Rebekah. I only have your Gramma's best interest in my heart." Then he patted his chest and turned his sad eyes towards Rebekah.

Rebekah covered her mouth and tried to speak without laughing. "Of course you are concerned for Gramma. Please, I need a pound of lentils."

Jacob rapidly measured the lentils into a bag. "Gramma will be making stew to share with the poor while you are gone?"

Rebekah nodded, taking the bag and filling the merchant's hand with the required coins. "Gramma may not be able to make the journey this year, but always she has strength to care for the poor among us. I can only hope to have her compassionate heart."

"Shouldn't we all," returned Jacob as he placed the coins in his coin box. "God be with you, Rebekah."

"And with you, Jacob."

As she made her way through the marketplace, she spotted a familiar face standing by the fruit stand.

Where have I seen her?

The woman turned and lowered her gaze when she saw Rebekah watching her.

"Leah," whispered Rebekah to herself. She approached the woman. "Leah?"

"Yes," she answered and nodded. "How may I serve you?" she asked, never looking at Rebekah.

"First," said Rebekah as she lifted Leah's chin with her hand, "you can look at me. I am not your better. We are all God's children."

"Yes, Miss." A timid smile crossed Leah's lips.

"I have not seen Matthias for some time. Is he well? I only ask because the last time I saw him, he was filled with anger and grief."

"Yes. Deborah's death consumed him, as it did Eliezer and me."

"He told me of Deborah. I am sorry for the pain this has brought to his home and to you." Rebekah placed a hand on Leah's shoulder as she spoke. "The Lord is near to all of our suffering."

"It is not I that suffer. Deborah lives even as the Rabbi has said. Those who believe in him shall never die."

Rebekah sensed an uncommon confidence.

"Matthias?"

"Yes," answered Leah. "He suffers to find answers. He left Eliezer in charge of his affairs and has gone to find the Rabbi. He searches for truth, for life."

"The Lord is not far from those who desire the truth. He will find it."

"But will he receive it?"

Rebekah cocked her head. "Why wouldn't he, Leah?"

"I have spoken too much. Begging your leave, I must be on my way." Leah placed her basket of fruit over her arm and started toward her master's home. "I have a new maid to train in the household duties."

"But—"

"I must go. God be with you, Miss Rebekah."

"And with you," replied Rebekah, still trying to determine what Leah hadn't said. The urge to pray for Matthias reemerged.

She stopped along the shore of the Galilee. The water lapped at her feet. Her pondering replayed Phoebe's telling of her death and return to life. Then in a moment, Matthias and his search for answers strayed into her thoughts.

I'm not sure what he searches for. Truth? That is what Leah spoke of. Truth of the Messiah? Of life and death?

Rebekah wrinkled her forehead. She, too, searched for truth, especially of life and death. She believed Yeshua, the works he did, the testimonies of those around him. She believed him to be the Messiah.

"Oh!" She stepped back as two fish jumped from their cover, trying to catch the same bug. The larger found the prize. As both began their descent back into the water, a much larger one found the winner to be his own dinner.

"Run, little one," she shouted to the smallest. *Such are the Romans to us Jews. Always we try to find a hiding place, a savior.* She believed Yeshua to be that savior. She knelt at the water's edge and let it play over her fingertips. Her reflection showed her distorted image changing with each wave washing the shoreline.

"Lord God," she whispered, glancing from her image to the sky. "You have come to be our Savior, but from the Romans?" Rebekah glanced back at her reflection. "Or from ourselves? You desire to change our distorted image. But how? How will Yeshua save us from ourselves? Open our eyes, and Matthias's eyes, to see truth."

A shiver ran over Rebekah's spine. She stood and shook the water from her hand. Suddenly, she wasn't sure she wanted the answer. She picked up her bag of lentils and hurried up the rocky path homeward.

CHAPTER 23

Matthias trudged up the hill toward Nain. He rarely took his eyes off the trail as he followed the caravan of merchants with their parade of camels, donkeys, and oxen transporting their wares, leaving behind them a littered path smelling of the stench of a stable. The merchants cared only for profit, not conversation. This left Matthias to travel in the safety of their numbers while being left alone. By the looks of their cargo, the Passover had proved prosperous for them. He had hoped the same for himself.

"Not so," Matthias whispered to the evening breeze. In Jerusalem, the throngs of people converging around the Nazarene had made private contact impossible. All wanted something from him—all but the Pharisees.

The Pharisees wanted the Nazarene dead.

"You cast out demons by Beelzebub!" Their charge made no sense. The Nazarene's answer showed their foolishness. He didn't defend himself but answered their charge logically.

"A kingdom divided cannot stand. Neither can Satan be divided against himself."

Thunderclouds of anger had swept over the Pharisees' clench-jawed faces. If eyes could shoot lightning bolts, the Nazarene would have been struck many times as he continued with an ominous warning.

"Listen to me. All your sins will be forgiven except the blaspheming against the Holy Ghost. The one who speaks against the work of the Holy Ghost, attributing it to Satan, is in danger of eternal damnation."

Whispers rolled through the throng like a river current, streaming the Nazarene's words along. A stirring among the crowd parted the river as Yeshua's brothers tried to reach him. Matthias shook his head at the memory of James's words as he passed by.

"Our brother must be beside himself. He is courting not only their ire but his own death."

"Possibly ours, too," spoke one younger than James as they continued to push their way through the people.

Before his brothers could reach him, the Nazarene disappeared into the masses. Matthias searched the crowd but saw no sign of him or his followers. Once again his own opportunity had been lost.

"Ugh!" Matthias grumbled, lifting his foot from a smelly deposit left on the road. The caravan continued up the steep hill to seek shelter before nightfall while Matthias found a patch of grass to clean off his sandal and foot. He poured some of his water over the mess, its pungent odor causing his nose to burn. Now was when he missed Eliezer the most.

His body felt the years he had not yet lived. *Deborah.* Her death had left in his heart an empty hollow. He moved off the path, hoping to avoid any more unpleasant mishaps.

With clouds rolling in, he decided to stay in one of the several caves dotting the hillside. Most were tombs, but a few proved suitable for a night's rest. He fixed a small fire in the opening of one to discourage any animals from taking his home. Before he could settle in and eat some bread and dried fruit, a couple of travelers stopped to share his shelter. They shared informal greetings, then busied themselves preparing for rest.

Matthias lay on his mantle, trying to make himself as comfortable as possible. Jerusalem hadn't been a complete loss. He did meet one of Yeshua's disciples.

What was his name? ... Judas.

Judas Iscariot, that was it. He'd been on an errand for the Nazarene's entourage.

"Shalom." Matthias tried to greet him. "Haven't I seen you with Yeshua?"

Stone-colored eyes overshadowed by black bushy brows made the blood in Matthias's veins run cold.

"Yes. What is it to you?"

"You've witnessed marvelous things traveling with a great miracle worker, true? I hear most think he is the Messiah."

Judas's expression remained unchanged. "Yes. We have seen many mighty works that must be of God."

"You're not sure?" questioned Matthias.

"I am sure. What is your interest?"

"I too am seeking the Messiah." He leaned closer to Judas and whispered, "*Is* he the Messiah? Is he preparing to free us from Roman rule?"

Judas stepped quickly back and scowled at Matthias as he spit out his reply.

"You fool. No one talks openly of that. Ears are everywhere and tongues wag freely as easily as spilt blood flows."

Matthias stepped back and cocked his head. "But there is talk."

Judas had scanned his surroundings. He had moved closer to Matthias, continuing to focus on the movements of those around them.

"I know the one who can do it," he whispered, with a devilish smirk. "Just not the when."

Matthias rose from his bed and placed more wood on the fire. He lay back down and pulled a corner of his mantle over his feet. He went to sleep remembering Judas's words, thinking the man with the bushy eyebrows might be one to stay close to.

But not too close.

The morning chill and dawning light roused Matthias from his bed. He grabbed his water skins to replenish them from the village well. The wineskin had enough to make it to Nazareth, and then after Nazareth would be Capernaum and home. Home, walls of brick and mud. Empty.

He lowered his chin, tapped a forefinger to his mouth, and lifted his head high. A longing grew in his heart as he thought of Eliezer. "Yes, Eliezer," he whispered to the ashes, and stirred the remaining fire from the embers. The fire would die on its own.

He tossed the stick and started for Nain. The townspeople would be stirring by now. It was too early for anyone to have breakfast ready, but maybe a merchant would have his wares out. Fresh bread. He whiffed the air and his stomach grumbled.

"Shalom. I could smell your bread begging for a buyer before I entered the town," called Matthias.

The merchant smiled a toothless grin.

"You are an answer to my prayers. The fishermen who fish the earliest have the biggest catch." The old man guffawed at his own wisdom, allowing a line of drool to escape between the missing teeth. He wiped it out of his beard with a swish of his hand.

Matthias eyed the merchant suspiciously as he reconsidered his decision, thinking if there was another choice of merchants, he would have taken it. "You are a businessman after my own heart. I'll take four of your freshest loaves, a few fish, and some dried figs." Matthias opened his bag for the man to fill.

The merchant's hands and mouth moved at the same speed as he filled Matthias's order. "You are mighty hungry, or else you still have a journey ahead of you. You won't be sorry for your purchase. My wife is the best cook in Nain ..."

Matthias intersected his chatter. "I'm sure she is. You know the townspeople well?"

The merchant cocked his head to one side with a quizzical look. "No one knows them better. I have lived here all my life."

Before the old man could finish his ramblings and baptize Matthias's purchase with spittle, he cut off the merchant's talk.

"Then you know of the widow whose son was supposedly raised from the dead?" Matthias handed the merchant his pay, with a couple of extra coins.

The old man's eyes grew bright as he jingled the money in his hand. "Yes, yes. But there is no supposing. It was along this very road, not far from here it happened. The young man was dead. Those bearing his bier passed right by here." The merchant's volume and spit spray increased with the retelling. Coming out from behind his table, he pointed out the path taken that day. "The poor widow," he shook his head. "Her husband had died but a few weeks earlier and now her son. She was destined for poverty."

"Yes," snapped Matthias. "What happened?"

Matthias arched his back as the merchant leaned forward to relate the amazing story.

"Yeshua." He spoke the name with a hushed reverence. "He came walking up the hill. A great crowd followed him. As they entered the city, the procession carrying the young man to his resting place was leaving."

The shopkeeper hesitated. He drew his hand over his thick graying beard as a tear rolled down his face. "Yeshua, the prophet, stopped the procession to speak to the widow. He touched her cheek."

The merchant reached his hand toward Matthias, who took a step back, leaving the man's hand hanging in the air. "He said the strangest thing. He told the widow not to cry." The seller let his arm drop to his side. "Even I thought this was heartless. But I did not understand."

"Understand what?"

"What this prophet from Nazareth would do next."

"And what was that?" asked Matthias, knowing what he was about to hear but not fully believing it.

"He went to the funeral bier and touched it. All waited in silent expectation, not knowing what they expected."

"What did the Nazarene do?" demanded Matthias.

"He spoke to the dead man. He told the young man to get up." The merchant stopped.

Matthias stiffened his back, as the old man searched his face for a reaction. The vendor wouldn't find one.

"Don't you want to know what happened next?"

"I already know, but tell me anyway."

"The moment the Master told the young man to rise, he sat straight up right there on the bier. The mourners stopped wailing and stared. I feared those bearing the bier would drop the lad, especially when the young man started speaking to the Master."

"He spoke? What did he say?"

"I couldn't hear, but some say he called him the Messiah and pledged to follow him."

"Is he with the Nazarene?"

The merchant shook his head. "No. The Master helped him off the bier and returned him to his mother. In truth, the Master gave life back to both the young man and his mother."

Matthias searched the merchant's face. A voice called out from behind them.

"Jonas, shalom."

A broad smile accentuated the merchant's missing teeth. "Shalom, Isaac."

Matthias glanced behind him. Then he addressed the merchant. "One last question before I take my leave. Does the young man live today?"

The merchant nodded behind them, in the direction from which the voice had greeted them. "That was him."

"Him?"

"Yes. Isaac."

Matthias spun around in search of the young man. He had vanished. Matthias grabbed his bag and headed back the way he came. It didn't matter, not really. The stories were all the same. The Nazarene was either the Prophet or he was not.

Matthias traveled on to Nazareth alone after the caravans and pilgrims went by way of Capernaum. Matthias wanted to talk with James, the Nazarene's brother. If anyone knew the truth about this self-proclaimed prophet, his family would know. If he couldn't talk to the Nazarene, maybe James could settle his doubts.

CHAPTER 24

Nazareth, the village no one visited, lay hidden in a basin between tall hills at the end of a mountain chain. Its seclusion left it without notoriety or desire. Matthias topped the last hill before his destination, where trees created hiding places for small insignificant homes. It held a simple and quiet beauty of its own. Matthias shook his head.

What is beauty without profit?

"Not a place I would want to live." He scanned the area as he sought a house to take shelter in for the night. Suddenly, across the valley, angry shouts of a mob erupted into a volcanic cacophony of voices. Matthias ran down the hill toward the commotion. The crowd vomited out murderous threats, as they pushed farther up the opposite hill.

"Who do you think you are?"

"You are only the son of Joseph and Mary! A charlatan full of trickery!"

"The Pharisees knew from the start. You do no work of God, only Beelzebub!"

Matthias forced his way into the edge of the crowd, trying to see for certain who received the hatred of this small village. A familiar voice rang across the crowd, halting his steps.

"No prophet is welcome in his home town."

Matthias caught a glimpse of the Nazarene. His followers worked to surround him. Simon made an imposing figure with his arms stretched out as if to protect the Nazarene. As quickly as he put his arms up, the Nazarene pushed them down. The crowd kept advancing on him, inching him closer to the precipice ahead. Matthias spotted Rebekah and Sarah holding onto one another, trying not to get trampled underfoot.

"Throw him off the cliff," shouted one irate man. "That is what we do to false prophets!"

At the admonition, the crowd in one motion moved on the Nazarene. No one could stop the wave of hate. Confusion ensued. The body of people turned every way searching for their prey.

"Where is he?"

"Where did he go?"

Matthias searched the crowd. The Nazarene had vanished. Surely his disciples had whisked him away from the madness. He caught sight of the women moving, trying to free themselves of the crowd, but nowhere did he see the Nazarene or the men with him. Matthias tried to reach the women, but to no avail. Before he could reach them, they hurried down the hillside and out of sight.

Their quarry gone, the angry mob grew disenchanted with the hunt, and one by one they returned to the relative peace of the village. Matthias watched, turning from side to side as different ones passed by. Then he found the one he sought, standing on the edge of the dispersing crowd. He wanted to run to him but feared being conspicuous. Making his way carefully across and down through the mass of people, he grabbed the man's sleeve.

Angry eyes turned on him.

"Remove your hand or lose it," James growled between clenched teeth, his hand raised in readiness to defend himself.

"No, James, no," pleaded Matthias, releasing the other's arm. "I mean you no harm. I am Matthias. We talked on the journey to Jerusalem. I came to—"

"To find answers." James, his voice tightly controlled, finished Matthias's sentence for him. "Everyone wants answers. Did you find them here today, Matthias? Or do you need more?" James turned and stomped down the hill.

Matthias lengthened his stride to keep pace with him. "What happened here?"

James looked from side to side, never slowing his speed as he answered.

"Come with me. I'll fill your head with answers—answers that will only raise more questions."

The two continued down the hill with Matthias taking two steps for James's one. His large, muscular frame hid Matthias from those ahead of them, and probably provided protection from any behind them. He noticed James continually watching those around them as they entered the village, as if someone might be lurking about waiting for the opportunity to attack.

"This way." James jerked his head to the right. "At the end of this path there is a small house where we can sit and not be bothered."

Matthias wondered how small the house would be. He didn't remember seeing any large ones in the village. "May I lodge there for the night?"

"Stay if you like," retorted James.

"Will you be staying?"

"Yes," he answered. "I'll stay tonight. Mother will be safe with my brothers, if she is not already with Yeshua." James pointed to a house planted on the hillside. "There, up ahead."

The house was surrounded by trees, with vines growing up its walls. No lamps invited visitors to enter, or even to knock on the door.

"It's empty?"

"Yes," answered James flatly. "It was a leper's house. No one—"

Matthias latched onto James's sleeve. James returned a threatening glare. "That is the second time you have seized hold of me."

Matthias released his grip. He believed James could and would hurt him if necessary.

"Forgive me, but we *cannot* stay in the house of a leper."

"Then you find another," answered James. He turned toward the house.

"We will be unclean and have to present ourselves to the priests. I can't stay here," pleaded Matthias.

"Then don't. But I am. The house has been pronounced clean."

"Then why doesn't the leper live here? Has he died? And if he died, how can this place be clean?" Matthias's eyes were wide with fear. Fear of leprosy. Fear of being unclean. Fear of being an outcast. *Fear.*

James pushed open the door. His large frame filled the opening. He turned to Matthias with a smirk on his face.

"The leper lives," replied James. He cocked his head to one side. "He lives. He is healed. He follows Yeshua, who healed him." James lit a lamp and held it next to his face, creating eerie shadows around him. "That's why he doesn't live here. Now will you come in or not?" He left Matthias with no option but to follow.

Matthias searched the doorpost for a mezuzah. There was none. His heart sank. He rehearsed it quickly in his mind as he entered the leper's house, careful to touch as little as possible.

"Have you any food in that pouch, Matthias?" asked James. "And how about sharing one of those wineskins?"

Matthias threw his mantle on the floor and sat on it. He opened his pouch and shared his travel supply with James.

He thanked the God of the universe for his provision of food, friend and even lodging, all the while praying silently not to get leprosy, nor be seen in this place.

James sat cross-legged across from Matthias, eating in silence. Occasionally, he shut his eyes and turned his neck from side to side and back and forth. Matthias could see the muscles in his face and neck begin to relax.

"Why are you here in this place?" asked James. "Same reason anybody comes to Nazareth these days? In search of the Messiah?"

Matthias noted the dark circles and bags under the other's eyes. "Yes and no."

James's puzzled look encouraged him to continue.

"I came looking for you. I knew your own uncertainty concerning your brother the last time we talked. I wanted to learn what truth you now hold about the man people are calling the prophet from Nazareth."

"Umph," snorted James. "The prophet from Nazareth? You saw with your own eyes and heard with your own ears what Nazareth thinks of him."

"Has this always been the people's opinion?"

James rubbed his eyes as if rubbing away weariness. He massaged his temples and gazed past Matthias into a distant place.

"No," he answered. "The people favored Yeshua wherever he went. He astonished them with his wisdom. Sometimes it was hard being his little brother." James smiled a half-grin that was quickly replaced by a scowl. "Then it all changed. John the Baptizer, our cousin, announced Yeshua to be the Lamb of God. His popularity grew. Many believed him to be the promised Messiah who would free Israel from Rome and be crowned our king."

"What changed the people into what we saw today?"

"Yeshua. He is not the Messiah the people want."

Matthias frowned. "Then who is he?"

James sat silent a long time before he answered.

"He is Jesus of Nazareth, the son of a carpenter now dead, the son of Mary. He is my brother. I love him, but he puts us all in danger, especially himself. His death would break my mother's heart, piercing it through as with a sword." James lay down on the sod floor, his arms underneath his head serving as his pillow. "I'm tired. I want to sleep." He closed his eyes, leaving Matthias with only questions, fears, and a flickering lamp.

James's words remained as solid in Matthias's head as words chiseled into a stone tablet. He turned the wick on the lamp down, extinguishing its flame like the hope extinguished from his heart. As he rested his head on his pouch and turned onto his side, quiet reigned everywhere but in his soul. A year gave rise to hope, and a year had snatched it away.

Will I ever know the truth about this prophet of Nazareth—and his promise of eternal life? Or maybe he did know the truth, and to follow it any further would be futile, expending his coffers and his life. His eyelids grew heavy and the weariness of his body, mind, and spirit pushed him into sleep.

PART THREE

"Jesus beholding him loved him ..."
—Mark 10:21 (KJV)

CHAPTER 25

"Gramma, I am going." Rebekah shoved bread, fruit, and a few dried fish in the leather bag.

"Child," Gramma pleaded, as she filled a wineskin for her headstrong granddaughter, "it's a day's journey. One you should not make alone. I would go with you, but I can't make the long walk." She handed the wineskin to Rebekah. "You don't even know what you will find."

Rebekah slung the bag and wineskin over her shoulder with one hand as she grabbed her embroidered blue mantle with the other. When she turned, Gramma's grim face displayed her disapproval. A smile played across Rebekah's lips.

"Gramma, you are right. I don't know what I will find, but I must seek." She touched the mantle to her face. "You will be as near to me as this mantle I wear. Remember, I am not a child, and I will not be alone. The marketplace is filled with people who have heard Yeshua has returned to the region. I'll follow the multitude."

"You try to ease an old woman's concern." Gramma laid a wrinkled hand on Rebekah's cheek. "Even as her heart desires to make the trip with you."

"I will tell you everything when I return." Rebekah covered the old woman's hand with her own. "And wouldn't it be wonderful if Immah and Papa returned with me?"

she added, as she wrapped her arms around her Gramma's bony shoulders.

Gramma smiled. "That would be a great surprise I don't expect to see. They will follow Yeshua as they should."

Rebekah pushed the door open and turned one last time. "May the Lord God watch over us while we are apart."

"God be with you, Rebekah. I will pray your journey ends with finding the Master."

Rebekah hurried down the rocky path as she called back over her shoulder. "I only need follow the crowd of hurting people. He will be there."

She edged through the crowded winding streets of Capernaum and waved a hand at Jacob behind his vending table. He looked quite pleased. A good day for sales, no doubt.

"Phoebe!" Rebekah stretched her neck, trying to see past Delilah's imposing figure.

"Rebekah?"

Phoebe's joy glowed against Delilah's dark scowl. The two girls pushed through the people into each other's arms.

"Where have you been?" A cloud of concern stole the glow in Phoebe's face. "Or should I say, where are you going?"

Rebekah grabbed Phoebe's arm and pulled her to the edge of the road. Delilah followed on their heels. "I followed Yeshua for a time with my parents, but they wanted me to return home to see about Gramma."

"You found her well?"

"Quite. I've missed you. I hoped to see you before I left again."

"To follow Yeshua?"

"Yes, if I can find him. He's somewhere to the north, I think."

"Papa's leaving today as well," answered Phoebe, tugging at the other's sleeve. "Come, you can travel with him." The girls scampered up the road, wedging themselves between other seekers. A disgruntled Delilah struggled to keep pace with them.

"Are you going too?" asked Rebekah.

"No. I want to, but Papa has forbidden it."

"But you are completely well and strong. Why—"

"He is my papa," answered Phoebe. "I will do as he says."

Rebekah admired her friend's unquestioned obedience. *If only I could be more like that.*

Impossible. No, my lessons are learned by the doing and the chastening.

The girls found Jairus where the road leading out of Capernaum met the path to his house.

"The Lord God carry you and all those on the way safely," called Phoebe as Rebekah and Jairus headed northward, joined by an ever-growing population of afflicted ones seeking the touch of the Master.

"Lord Jairus," Rebekah said. "Isn't that Eliezer up ahead? Matthias's servant?" She pointed him out.

Jairus raised his chin in the air trying to look over the heads of those in front of them.

"There," said Rebekah, indicating a man walking in the middle of the crowd.

"Yes, I believe it is."

Rebekah scanned the group. "But I don't see Matthias."

"Nor do I."

"In fact, I haven't seen Matthias since my return from Nazareth." Rebekah noticed Jairus's sideward glance. "It's not that I see him often," she explained. "On occasion I would see him walking along the shore or through the marketplace in the early morning hours." She leaned her head sideways, a frown shading her eyes. "I haven't seen him on Sabbath, either." she added. "Do you know? Is he well?"

Jairus looked straight ahead. His jaw was set. Rebekah was uncertain whether or not he would answer.

"I can't tell you what I don't know—"

Rebekah abruptly jammed against his side, pushed by someone behind her. They both turned. A girl with beads of sweat on her forehead clutched a cloth sling hanging around her shoulders.

"Forgive me," she whispered. Her eyes began to roll in her head. She swayed. Color drained from her face, and she tottered.

Jairus and Rebekah grabbed for her. A muffled cry escaped from within the sling, and Rebekah peeked inside. A small red-faced infant slept fitfully. Rebekah felt the infant's forehead.

"Lord Jairus, this baby is burning up with fever. If you can hold the girl, I'll take the baby." Carefully she lifted the little bundle before the girl fainted in Jairus's arms.

He lifted her effortlessly. Her head swayed in a circle, as she tried to focus on her benefactors before finally resting on his shoulder.

"My baby," she whispered, as she tried to reach for the infant nestled against Rebekah's breast.

Rebekah cradled the restless infant in her arms as she turned toward the mother, wondering how one so young could be this child's mother. The worry in Rebekah's eyes betrayed the smile on her lips. "I'll carry him for you. What's your name?" she asked.

"Eunice."

Jairus and Rebekah exchanged questioning glances. Rebekah knew by the size of the infant that Eunice would still be in her time of impurity, but Jairus didn't hesitate to help her.

"And I'll carry you. What's his name?" he asked.

"Timothy. He is not well. I must find the Healer. My husband is away."

Rebekah wondered if there was a husband. The girl looked younger than Rebekah in age, but not life. At this moment none of that mattered. She and the baby needed help. Before any more questions could be asked or answered, Eunice fell asleep in Jairus's arms.

"I don't think she's much older than Phoebe," Jairus said, his voice cracking as he surveyed the small frame he cradled.

Tears filled his eyes, as they did Rebekah's own. The baby's fever stained the sling with sweat. But Rebekah knew he would be better held by the fabric than in her arms, where her body heat would be against his skin.

"We need to find some way of shading this little one."

"And his mother," Jairus said.

Jairus seemed to carry Eunice without effort, but his face grew red in the heat. Rebekah searched the area as they walked.

"Can we not make a bed to carry them? Surely there are some broken limbs or something we can use." She lifted the corner of her mantle Gramma had embroidered for her. "And I can tie my mantle around it for her to lie on."

The grove that appeared ahead was a gift from God.

"Up ahead, Jairus. There's a small grove of trees. We can stop and share our food with Eunice. While she eats, we'll make a bed to pull her on."

Jairus nodded. "Yes, that's good. How is the infant?"

Rebekah's chin quivered. "I—I don't really know. I fear for him."

"And I for his mother," said Jairus. "But I believe all she really needs is rest."

Under the trees many travelers rested, those who were not strong enough to press on, seeking a drink or bite of food from those around them. Rebekah offered encouragement and help to those she could, while Jairus constructed a portable bed. All sought the same thing—the prophet whose touch could heal. Rebekah returned to Eunice's side.

"Here," she offered. "Wash down the bread with a little wine." Eunice closed her eyes as she swallowed the sweet liquid. Color returned to her face.

"He won't nurse," said Eunice. Desperation showed in her tired eyes.

"Let's try to relieve his fever with a wet cloth," suggested Rebekah as she took off her shawl and poured more wine over it. She laid it on the infant's hot forehead. She trickled a few drops of wine on Timothy's lips, and the baby responded with a faint sucking sound.

"Once this fever is gone, he will eat," Rebekah said. "We'll try to keep him as cool as possible by putting a little wine or water on the end of a finger. Like so." Rebekah poured a drop of wine on her forefinger and put it in the infant's mouth. "Look, Eunice, he likes wine."

"You gave him wine?"

Both women jumped at the sound of Jairus's voice.

"Only a bit, to help him keep some moisture in his body," explained Rebekah. "It's sweet and weak."

Jairus shook his bare head. "You look better, Eunice. Are you ready to travel?"

Eunice turned from Jairus to Rebekah and back.

"I don't mean walk, Eunice. See?" Jairus pointed behind him to the crudely constructed travel bed made from tying Rebekah's mantle to both poles and using his unwound turban as a canopy for shade. "It may be bumpy, but I will try to miss the rocks. Rebekah, help her and little Timothy onto the litter."

Once Eunice and her baby were settled, Jairus began pulling the cradle along while Rebekah walked beside them. Each bump evoked a whimper from Eunice.

"Wait, Jairus," called Rebekah, going to the back of the litter. "I believe I can help carry Eunice and make this easier." She leaned down to pick up the two poles.

"Miss Rebekah." Startled by the deep voice behind her, Rebekah dropped the poles, causing Eunice to cry out. "I can be of help if you wish."

At the sound of another male voice, Jairus turned to see who offered the much needed aid.

"Eliezer." Jairus's broad grin welcomed the assistance. "We thank our Lord God for you."

"May I suggest, Lord Jairus, we place the poles on our shoulders. We will bear the weight easier and for a longer period. And the ride will be smoother." Eliezer smiled at Eunice. She returned a nod of gratitude.

"I believe you are right," answered Jairus. "On the count of three."

The two men lifted Eunice easily to their shoulders. She glanced from Rebekah to Eliezer and back again, but as the journey continued, she relaxed. It didn't take long for her to fall asleep. Occasionally, Rebekah would give Timothy a bit of wine and pray for his strength to last until they reached the Master.

Rebekah slid her hand into the bag of food hanging from her shoulder. Nothing remained. She pursed her lips and stared up at the side of the mountain dotted with plateaus and plains. A multitude of people, thousands, she thought, traveled in a long line ahead of them. Some walked alone. Some, like Eunice, were carried. Others leaned on one another as they struggled to make the climb. She shook her head and bit her bottom lip. Never had she seen so many hurting people in one place. She glanced into the leather bag to be sure of what she'd felt. Nothing. She patted the wineskin hanging from her shoulder. The liquid jostled at her touch. Relief swept through her mind.

At least we have this.

"Lord Jairus." It took her took a couple of long strides to walk by his side. "Have you any food left?"

Jairus shook his head. "I gave my last morsel away down by the trees."

Rebekah glanced back at Eliezer. He carried nothing but a determined look on his face. He looked well. Her curiosity rose. Why was he so desperate to reach the Master?

CHAPTER 26

"Le-ah! Abi, Abi-gail! Eli, Eliez, Eliezer," Matthias's words swirled in his mouth as he searched the room for any movement. His head felt like it might fall off his neck. He shut his eyes and opened them again. The room no longer spun, but his eyes still refused to focus. He straightened his back, raised his hand high over his head and brought it down on the table with a thunderous blow. "Where …" he shouted, trying to form his words.

"Master?" Abigail stood beside him with a pitcher in her hands. She held it up for him to see. "This is what you are wanting?"

He didn't like the disdain he heard, but his head hurt and the spinning returned. She had what he wanted. That was all that mattered. He raised his mug in her direction, looking somewhere and nowhere.

"Will that be all, Master?"

Matthias shook his tottering head and waved a command for her to leave him alone. He didn't notice if she left, nor did he hear her footsteps quickly retreating. He put the cold mug against his head for a moment before lowering it to his lips.

He spewed the putrid stuff across the table and slammed the mug against the wood. "Abigail!" He shouted without a slur, his eyes wide. "Bring my wine and bring it now."

Abigail entered without a pitcher. She stood with her back straight and her chin held high. Matthias glared at her as he held his mug in front of her face. "What is this? Where is my wine?" The temptation to have her beaten entered his thoughts.

"This," Abigail replied, taking the mug, and speaking with a measured tone, "is buttermilk."

Matthias withdrew his hand, fearing she would notice the evidence of his plague. "I said I wanted wine. Where is it?"

Abigail lowered her gaze. "Master, there is no more wine. Would you like for me to go for some?"

Matthias continued to focus on the lovely young maiden Eliezer had hired after Deborah's death. Her black hair shone like it had stars hidden within it. Her face was petite but certainly not weak. He had to admit, she had a courage Leah lacked. So much like Deborah. His focus began to give way to the effects of too much wine.

"What do you mean there's no more wine? I own a vineyard. There has to be wine," he said. He turned from her and put his head on the wooden table. Before she could answer, he continued. "No. Don't get more. Leave me. Just leave me."

"Master ...."

"I said, leave," he muttered into his crossed arms. He heard soft footsteps moving away ... always away.

His shoulders began to tremble. Tears spilled onto the boards under his chin. Eliezer had left him, left him to face his plight, his living death alone. As he drowned in his self-pity, the weariness of body, mind, and soul, coupled with too much fruit of the vine gave way not to rest, but only to sleep.

No matter. In sleep there was no consciousness, no pain.

The mixture of joyous shouts and pleas for mercy urged Rebekah to run ahead of the two men carrying the litter. She reached the top of the knoll. Her knees buckled.

A sea of people filled the basin between the hills and the side of the mountain. Some stood, some lay on pallets, others sat on the grass. All looked in one direction. Rebekah followed their line of sight to Yeshua on the opposite hillside standing high above the masses, his frame outlined by the majestic mountain behind him. It had to be him. Who else could it be? A contingent of men stood in a semicircle around him trying to make some order of those seeking his touch.

Rebekah blinked back tears at the sight of desperate people stepping over those lying on the ground and wedging themselves between others, seeking to reach the Healer. Then she caught sight of her father. She could never mistake the square-shouldered figure of a man standing a head above the others.

"Give thanks to the Lord, for his mercy endures forever ... forever ... forever." The praises of the healed mixed with the moans of the waiting.

"Have mercy on me!"

"Praise the Lord for his goodness, and for his wonderful works."

As one praise floated away on the wind, another filled the basin and rose to the heavens.

Rebekah wanted to run to her father, but her body wouldn't obey. Her flesh crawled with a multitude of sensations. She lifted her hands toward the vast ocean of blue sky. The magnitude of compassion and grace filled her with praise, but the words stuck in her heart. Her arms fell to the ground as she bowed before the great Shepherd of Israel.

Not knowing how long she lay prostrate before the Lord, Rebekah lifted her head at the faint cry.

"No." Rebekah grabbed her skirt and raced down the hill, as she suddenly remembered those she'd left behind. Their questions flew in her face as she approached the three travelers.

"What is it, Rebekah? What did you see?" asked Jairus as he and Eliezer rested the litter on the ground.

Eunice clutched little Timothy to her breast "Is he there, Rebekah? Is the Master there?" The hope in her heart rose to her eyes.

Eliezer stood in silence and waited for the answer. Rebekah's heart pounded from the exertion.

"Yes. He is there, across the basin."

Eunice didn't wait for further explanation but raised her slight body from its resting place and started up the hill. Rebekah grabbed her arm. "Wait, Eunice."

Her desperation pleaded for Rebekah to let her go. She glanced at Timothy, then back to Rebekah. "You must let me go. I'm stronger now. I can make the rest of the trip. My baby grows weaker with each moment."

"I understand," said Rebekah. "But over that hill a multitude of sick and diseased people stand in your way. I believe I can get to the Master. My papa is one of his disciples. Let me take Timothy to my papa. He will take him to Yeshua."

Eunice hesitated, kissed her little one's burning forehead, and relinquished him to Rebekah.

"Eliezer and I will stay," said Jairus, as he turned to where the servant had been standing moments before.

"Eliezer?" Rebekah frowned. "Where is he, Jairus?"

Jairus shook his head. "I don't see him. He must have gone on. Now you must go." Jairus put his arm around Eunice's slender shoulders to give her some extra support.

"How will I find you?" asked Eunice.

Rebekah smiled. "The Lord God brought us this far. He will bring us back together." She turned and hurried up the hill once again. The scene on the other side hadn't changed, but she couldn't stand in awe this time. Little Timothy's life depended on the Master's touch.

Rebekah stayed to the edge of the multitude, keeping her eyes on her father. Many times Yeshua was hidden from sight as the needy continued to flow in his direction. But her father remained in view. Once across the basin she started up the opposite hill hoping, and yes, their eyes met.

"Papa," she pleaded, lifting the little one high enough for him to see.

Simon's size parted those before him like Moses's rod parting the Red Sea. Rebekah placed the infant in her father's large hands.

"Take him, Papa. Take him to Yeshua. His fever burns away his strength."

Simon nestled the infant against his side cradled like a bundle of wet clothing, using his free arm to part the way back to the Master. Rebekah followed close behind. They reached the semicircle where the infirm lay at Yeshua's feet.

Simon held the baby above his head. "Lord!"

Yeshua turned and nodded.

Simon returned the gesture and lowered the baby back to his chest.

Rebekah opened her mouth to protest. Wasn't Yeshua going to do anything?

Will you not heal this littlest of the lambs of Israel?

Simon handed Timothy back to Rebekah. The infant lay quiet in her arms. A healthy pink replaced the red feverish face of moments ago. Rebekah's mouth gaped with wonder as she searched her father's face.

Simon nodded.

"His mercy endures forever. 'Oh, that men would praise the Lord for his goodness, and for his wonderful works to the children of men!" Simon kissed Rebekah's cheek. "Now, child, go. Take the infant back to his immah. Tell her to give the little lamb some nourishment. I will find you later, and I'll let your immah know you are here."

Rebekah grappled with what had just happened as she returned across the basin, halting for a moment when she caught a glimpse of Eliezer approaching the Master. She watched long enough to see him kneel before the Lord, making a mental note to speak with him on the journey home. She scanned the crowd for Jairus and Eunice, trusting she would find them, as she returned the way she had come.

Elbows propped on the table, Matthias held his head in his hands. The room would not stop spinning. He pushed away from the table and lifted himself from his seat. His throat tightened as he forced himself to stand straight. With one hand he braced himself, with the other he reached for his mantle and slung it over his shoulders. He didn't remember it being so heavy. He inhaled deeply, slowly, and exhaled the same way, trying to get his bearings. With measured steps he walked toward the door. Fresh air might clear his muddled brain. He would have to be careful not to let anyone see him or come near. He opened the door to a setting sun. Its brightness blinded him for a moment. He shaded his eyes, blinking quickly to adjust to the light, then stepped into the world from which he had been forced to retreat.

The city would be closing for the evening. Most of the townspeople would either be at home enjoying their families after evening prayers, or off following the Nazarene. "Hmph," he muttered to himself. "That's probably where Eliezer is now."

Matthias hadn't seen him for two days, or was it three? He couldn't really remember. Didn't matter. Eliezer had left him alone to face his certain future. Soon, he would have to present himself to the priests. His unsteady steps took him to the one place of solitude where he thought he might find peace—his favorite seat on the large boulder planted by the sea. Ripples of water the color of sunset lapped at the shoreline.

Matthias searched the far shores. He was alone. He slipped off the rock and edged toward the water. He removed his sandals and tossed his mantle to the side.

"Woo!" He jerked his foot from the cool water. "I'll try this again," he said aloud as he put one foot in, then the other. He slowly waded deeper, cupped some water in his hands, and splashed his face. The evening sea breeze and fresh water slapped his skin.

If this doesn't clear my head, nothing will. He shook the water from his arms and head, but stopped as quickly as he had started, and listened. Did someone call his name?

I must have been mistaken. No one is here.

He waded to his waist and dunked his head under the surface. As he emerged, Matthias raised his hands to push his hair away from his face. He'd never felt so alive. His hands. He raised them in front of his face, examining them as if they belonged to another.

"My hands!" The sound ricocheted off the sea. His cry rang out once more. "My hands!" He held them up to the sinking sun. Did the dimming light hide the truth? He pushed the sleeves of his tunic up. The spots were gone, his skin as smooth and pink as a newborn baby's. He grabbed armfuls of water, splashing the fresh clean water over his body. "They are gone!" He shouted. "Gone!" His laughter filled the air as he pushed his way back through the water. Grabbing his mantle, he threw it around his shivering shoulders, picked up his sandals, and ran towards home.

At the doorpost of his house, Matthias reached for the Shema. Its words filled his heart, "Hear, O Israel: The

Lord our God is the Lord," as he completed the familiar scriptures.

I am back from the living dead. He smiled. "And the Nazarene isn't anywhere around."

"Leah, Abigail, I'm hungry." A broad grin filled his face. His servants exchanged bewildered glances. He stretched his arms out.

"I'm home." The women stood motionless. "Go," Matthias waved them toward the cooking area. "Go, fix me some food. I'm hungry." The women exited, speechless with wonder.

Matthias tossed his sandals and damp mantle across the table. His step was light as he entered his sleeping quarters and changed into a dry tunic. The evening breeze had dried his hair, and now he made his way to the hearth. He tossed a couple of logs in the fireplace, raised a lamp, and lit some dry grass, placing it under the smaller kindling. In a moment, a fire would warm his body. It was good to be home, to be alive.

CHAPTER 27

People rummaged through their leather bags, searching for a morsel to quiet their growling bellies. Philip stood near the Master with a small portion of food. Simon and the other disciples whispered among themselves, stopping as the Master spoke to Philip, who appeared puzzled. Philip shrugged his shoulders and extended his offering to Yeshua.

Yeshua's voice floated across the basin. "You have followed me for these three days."

"Rebekah." Eunice interrupted Rebekah's rapt attention to the Master's words. "I know you wish to talk more with your immah and papa, but we are out of food. Everyone is without food and have been for two days."

"Yes, but let's hear what the Master has to say," suggested Rebekah.

"Everyone sit," commanded Yeshua, "and my followers will bring you food."

Rebekah smiled at Eunice and patted the bundle squirming in its sling around her shoulders. "We are all hungry, but he said to sit. So, sit we will." Rebekah found a patch of thick green grass trampled down by the multitude.

Jairus nodded in agreement as he sat crossed-legged beside her. Eunice glanced around, then followed their example. The basin, filled moments ago with praises to the Lord God, grew still. Little Timothy lay quiet, and the children around them sat wide-eyed watching Yeshua.

He stood high above the crowd, his hands filled with a few loaves and fishes raised to the heavens. "Father, you are the giver of all good gifts, and we thank you for what you provide from your abundant storehouse."

Whispers breezed through the crowd. Rebekah watched as the Master put a portion of the bread and fish in baskets, and gave one basket to each of his disciples. He kept another container by his side, spoke to his followers, then nodded for them to begin passing out food among the groups. Jairus, Rebekah, and Eunice took their portion, while the men continued to share until all stomachs were satisfied.

Seven large baskets filled with fish and bread sat near the Master. Yeshua addressed the multitude.

"It's late. Many of you have a day's journey to reach home, but you go whole and filled. Go with the Father, remembering to labor for the food that does not perish."

The crowd rose to their feet. Some went to the baskets to fill their pouches. Fathers and mothers gathered their children. Friends that had been carried in walked out, and rejoicing filled the air from those who once were unable to speak.

Jairus offered Eunice help up. Rebekah watched the crowd disperse.

"We'll wait until the way clears. Eunice, if you're strong enough, we'll try to make it back to Capernaum by nightfall," said Jairus.

"And Gramma would welcome you and Timothy to stay with us as long as you need," added Rebekah.

Eunice sniffled, her tears threatening to fall. "I'm grateful for your kindness."

"Where is your home?" asked Rebekah, shaking out her skirt.

"I'm from Magdala, about a Sabbath day's journey from Capernaum."

Rebekah, knowing Magdala's reputation, guarded her expression and changed the subject.

"And Jairus, did you see Eliezer after he met with the Master?"

"No. I suppose he needed to return to Matthias."

She played with an auburn curl. "Has Matthias been ill? Is that why Eliezer sought the Master?"

"Rebekah!" A familiar voice intercepted Jairus's answer.

At the sight of her mother, Rebekah's curiosity fled as quickly as her feet could carry her to Sarah's embrace.

After a few moments of sharing pieces of their lives, Rebekah asked the question she wasn't sure she wanted answered. "When will I see you and Papa again?"

"I don't know," answered Sarah, reaching down for the bundle of food and the wineskin on the ground. "We never know where the Master's footsteps will take us. We just follow. Here." She held the food out. "This will take you home, enough for ... I thought there was a girl with you?" She nodded towards Jairus cradling the infant in his arms.

Rebekah shaded her eyes from the sun and scanned the area.

"Yes, there was." She and Sarah hurried toward Jairus. "Where is Eunice? Why do you have little Timothy?"

"I—I don't know," he answered, turning from side to side. "She asked me to hold him and said she would return shortly. I thought she was going to thank Yeshua, but ..."

"What will we do with this baby?" Rebekah pleaded with her mother for an answer.

Sarah rubbed her hand across her head, then nodded. "I know. When you return to Capernaum, take him to Jacob and his wife."

"Jacob the merchant?"

"His wife was with child. Her newborn didn't survive. Timothy will need a mother, at least for a time, and she needs a son to return her joy."

"And if she doesn't want ...?"

"She will. Now be on your way."

Rebekah and Jairus, cradling Timothy, started up the side of the basin. As they reached the top, she cast a longing glance back at Sarah, waved and scanned the area hoping for a glimpse of Eunice. A heavy foreboding weighed down her heart. She glanced at Timothy, snuggled safe and innocent against Jairus's chest, oblivious to the loss of his mother. Rebekah couldn't imagine what secret would cause a mother to abandon her baby. The trio slipped over the hill and out of sight of those left behind, not knowing what the future held for any of them—especially Timothy.

CHAPTER 28

Matthias studied the figures on the papyrus. The lines on his forehead drew together into a deep V. His time in seclusion had cost him profits. He pushed away from the table, leaving the numbers that revealed his losses. He tilted his head to the side and grimaced. "I should have known it was nothing," he muttered.

He reached for his mantle and threw it over his shoulders.

"Leah." Her name had barely escaped his lips when he heard the light patter of her feet.

"Yes, Master, how may I serve you?"

It bothered him that she would never look at him. Servants weren't allowed to, but that had never stopped Eliezer or Deborah, or even the new servant, Abigail.

"I'm going out," he said. "I've not examined my vines or figs since ... far too long. I'll return before the sun sets."

"Will that be all, Master?" croaked Leah. She stood with hands folded in front of her.

Not at all like Abigail.

"No. When I return, have my meal ready. Have Abigail go to the marketplace and purchase some smoked fish, leeks, and eggs. And bake some fresh bread." As he reached the door, he turned. "That will be all," he barked, and shook his head as the mousy figure fled.

Matthias pulled the door open, his mind so focused on what he might find in the vineyard and grove of figs that he did not notice the man standing to the side.

"Master."

Matthias jerked toward the voice. He didn't know whether to shout for joy or reprimand his prodigal servant. The latter choice erupted before he gave the decision thought.

"Eliezer." The name as it came from his lips judged Eliezer without question. "You have returned. Tell me why I should not have you punished."

"Yes, Master," answered Eliezer, his head bowed low. "I have no answer."

"I see you do remember I am your master."

Eliezer gave a slight nod. Matthias regretted his harsh words when Eliezer lifted eyes of compassion to meet his glare. His gaze engulfed Matthias with love.

"I have never forgotten you are my master, my friend, my only son. As your servant, I deserve whatever punishment you deem appropriate."

Matthias bit his lower lip. Emotion ruled over position as he grabbed Eliezer and pulled him to his chest. After embracing him, Matthias pulled back. He placed his hands on Eliezer's shoulders and showered both his cheeks with a salty-teared kiss.

"I have missed you, my friend. I thought you left me. I—I—" Matthias stuttered.

"Master," Eliezer spoke with tenderness. "I would never leave you. I love you as my own."

Matthias swallowed the shame in his throat.

Eliezer stepped back. "You look well, Master."

"I am, Eliezer. I'm whole again." Matthias raised his arms above his head, allowing his mantle to slide past his elbows. "Clean, Eliezer, clean," he whispered. Joy danced on each word. "I can't explain it, but one moment the scales dotted my arms, and the next they were gone."

"I can, with your permission, Master." Eliezer beamed with a secret he couldn't contain.

"Can what?"

"I can explain what happened."

Matthias's half-grin dared Eliezer to continue. "How can you explain it, Eliezer? You weren't here. The best I remember, you went following after the Nazarene." Before allowing Eliezer an opportunity to answer, he continued. "Besides, I'm convinced I was wrong. No one is healed in an instant of that dreadful plight."

"Do you want to hear the truth?" asked Eliezer.

Matthias stood motionless as he studied his wide-eyed servant ready to pour out the story. He pulled the door shut and turned to walk down the rocky path. "Walk with me. Tell me what you believe happened."

The two began their walk down the path to its fork. They turned to the left and started across the field to the grove of figs. Eliezer relayed his story.

"The Rabbi ...."

"The Nazarene?"

"Yes. I heard he taught near here, only a day's journey away. By the size of the crowd filling the road north, I was certain of it. I followed."

"Umph," grunted Matthias. "You did leave me to follow the Nazarene."

"Yes, Master, but not as you think," defended Eliezer. "I went for you."

Matthias stopped on top of the hill and surveyed the stand of fig trees. "I want to examine the fruit. Let's walk through the trees. It'll be cooler there and I can take a closer look." The two started through the grove. A slight breeze played with the leaves, causing them to whisper as the men walked by. "You went for me? Why?"

Eliezer walked a step behind Matthias. He cleared his throat and explained. "Your"—he hesitated—"your illness left you unable to help yourself."

Matthias stopped, crossed his arms, and leaned against the rough bark of an ancient tree. "Those days are not totally lost to me, Eliezer. I told you I would not go searching for a false prophet to heal me. But you chose to defy me and go anyway."

Eliezer lowered his head.

"Yes, Master." The rustling leaves grew silent as the gentle breeze hushed its whispering. Eliezer raised his head and faced Matthias. "Do with me as you please, Master, but know this. For you, I would do it again and yet again after that, even if doing so meant facing a whip."

Eliezer's love and loyalty chipped away at Matthias's stony heart. He twisted his mouth from side to side as he swallowed a piece of pride.

"In all fairness, I didn't say you couldn't go." He turned and continued through the grove, with Eliezer following close behind. "Finish your story."

"On the journey, I met with Jairus and Rebekah ..."

Matthias spun in a rage to face his servant. "You told them of my—my condition?"

"Certainly not. Although I am not sure Lord Jairus did not know."

"How could he know, if you didn't tell him?"

"By your own words, Master. Jairus came by when you did not attend synagogue and left your duties undone. He was concerned you might lose your position."

"I don't remember this."

"It was a particularly bad day for you, as were many of those days."

Matthias turned around and followed the path through the grove.

"Never mind that." He shut his eyes and gave his head a shake, trying to rid his mind of too many dark days. "What do Jairus and Rebekah have to do with this?"

"They are the reason my journey took longer. I helped them carry a young mother and her infant to the Rabbi. When we arrived, Rebekah found her father. I took my leave of them to approach the Rabbi, but the multitude was so great I could not get through immediately. People with every kind of illness and malady lay at his feet. The Rabbi healed each one. When I came, I fell to the ground and sought him to make you whole, to return your life to you."

"And what did he say, Eliezer? Did he chide me for not coming myself? For my unbelief?" asked Matthias without missing a step.

"No, Master, he did not. The Rabbi lifted me to my feet. Then he said something strange."

Matthias halted in front of his servant, causing him to bump into him.

"My pardon, Master. I beg your forgiveness."

Matthias turned and waved his hand in dismissal of the incident. "What strange thing did the Nazarene say?" A scowl clouded his face, daring his servant to amaze him.

"The Rabbi told me to return to you, and I would find you well."

"Is that not what he tells everyone who comes to him? I don't find that strange."

"There was more, Master," continued Eliezer. "The Rabbi said if you want to be whole, have new life, eternal life, you must believe, as he said, 'I Am'."

Matthias understood fully the meaning behind the Nazarene's words. He studied his servant's face.

"When? At what time did this conversation take place?" He was not yet ready to acknowledge the words of new life and wholeness, nor the deity expressed in the Nazarene's taking of the Lord God's most holy name.

"After the ninth hour on the third day after I left you. I know because before I could leave and return, the Rabbi had us sit on the ground. After giving of himself for others throughout the days, he would not let us leave until he fed us."

"How many people did you say were there?" asked Matthias, trying to ignore the possibility that his skin became clear at the time Eliezer said. The stupor he had wrapped around himself clouded his memory of the exact time.

"A great multitude, Master," Eliezer's voice grew in excitement. "I heard one of the Rabbi's disciples say there were four thousand."

"That's preposterous. Where could he obtain food for so many?"

"From a few fish and loaves of bread, and there were several basketfuls left over when we all had our fill." The awe of it all drowned Eliezer's countenance in light.

The two men stood face to face. Eliezer looked like a child filled with wonderment. Matthias tried to capture the whirlwind of thought coursing through his head. After what seemed to Matthias like time melted into eternity, he spoke.

"Eliezer, my servant, my friend," he said, placing both hands on his servant's shoulders. "I am grateful for one who would go to such lengths for me. However it came to pass, I praise God for my returned health, and for you who loves me so."

Matthias moved one hand to his servant's back as he turned to the path. "Come, let's return home. You must be weary from your journey. Leah and Abigail will have food waiting for us. You'll eat with me tonight, and we will rejoice."

As Matthias and Eliezer made their way home, the evening sun cast firebrands of orange and red across the sky. Undefinable shapes pooled in swirling colors on the sea's surface. The fusion of color reflected the spinning words of the Nazarene.

If you want to be whole and to have new life, eternal life, you must believe, as he said, 'I Am.'

Matthias stared at the sea as if its depth could answer all his doubts—but it didn't.

"Master, did you need something?" asked Eliezer.

"No, nothing, Eliezer, nothing." Matthias didn't speak the truth. What if the Nazarene's brother was wrong and Deborah had been right? What if the Nazarene did hold the secret of life?

To say he is the Messiah or the promised Prophet is one thing. But to say he is 'I Am'?

Matthias shook his head as the varied scenes of the Nazarene's works passed through his mind. The works were undeniable.

What cost held his heart in its grip of unbelief?

CHAPTER 29

Rebekah set the bag of grapes, figs, and olives on the table.

"I'm sorry to be so long, but I stopped to check on Timothy, and the city is full of excited people." She stepped toward the fireplace and placed her hands over the flat cooking stone. "The stone is hot, Gramma. How much bread do we still need to bake?"

Gramma joined her granddaughter and tossed a square of dough on the stone. "The two ready to bake will be the last of them," she replied. "The Feast of Booths has begun in the heart of all Israel. And how is the baby?"

"He is growing as plump as grapes bursting on the vines," answered Rebekah, "and with the excitement of the feast, I doubt my eyes will close even once tonight."

The bread began to brown on the bottom. "All this bread and fruit should last until we reach Jerusalem." Rebekah brushed a pesky curl from her face.

"I've packed smoked fish, too."

"Of course, you did, Gramma. And we can pick up palm and cedar boughs for our booths as we draw near to Jerusalem."

Gramma turned the bread over. "I'm sure Simon will have a booth built and waiting for us."

Rebekah frowned. "But I heard tales Yeshua would not be going to the feast. Won't Papa stay with him?"

Gramma smiled as she slid the bread onto the flat board. "Yeshua will be there, child. Of that you can be sure."

With the last loaves finished, Rebekah stirred the embers so they would burn out. "Good night, Gramma." She wrapped the old woman in her arms and kissed her cheek.

"Good night, my child," she answered. "My weary bones need rest. Morning will come fast, and we must meet Jairus's company early."

Gramma shuffled across the dirt floor to the nearby room, and Rebekah smiled.

"I do look forward to the journey with Phoebe," she responded.

But Matthias's group would be traveling with them.

He came to mind often, more than she liked. Each time she would turn her thoughts to prayer, hoping Matthias would finally release whatever tormented him. Phoebe had mentioned some of his unusual behavior.

She shrugged. Last time she ran into him he seemed fine, or as fine as he could be. She determined to think on other things and headed to her room on the roof.

The evening breeze cooled her face and played with her curls.

"Lord God, Master of the universe, is this the year?" she prayed, as the night sky winked at her. "Will Yeshua make clear he is the Messiah and draw all Israel to himself?" She hoped. Soon her hope would turn to sight, for tomorrow their journey to the holy city would begin.

Phoebe and Rebekah bundled broken willow branches from the roadside and tossed them into the cart. "Tomorrow we make Jerusalem," chattered Phoebe. "Rebekah?"

"Phoebe?"

Phoebe tilted her head to the side and quizzed her friend, "Where did we leave you?"

"What?"

"I've done most of the talking today. And I don't believe you could tell me a word that was said ... by me or you."

"You're right," answered Rebekah. She glanced around her. Gramma sat by the fire. Children who had joined the pilgrimage with their parents played around the trees, hiding from one another. But her glance stopped when she saw Matthias and Jairus talking by the edge of the spring.

"He troubles you, doesn't he?" asked Phoebe.

"Who?" Rebekah shifted her attention to her friend.

"Matthias. He troubles you."

"Troubles me? He pays me no mind, nor I him."

Phoebe cocked a slender eyebrow. "Who do you try to convince, Rebekah? Will you not admit he interests you?"

Rebekah reached for some more boughs to bundle. "His wellbeing is all that interests me."

"If you don't want to share with me, that's fine. But be sure you're truthful with yourself." Phoebe grabbed a few more willows and a couple of smaller cedar branches. "I'm going to use these for a bed tonight and bundle them in the morning."

"Phoebe," Rebekah grabbed Phoebe's arm. "I can't tell you what I don't know. I am torn and don't understand why."

"Torn?"

"Yes," answered Rebekah, fixing her stare on the ground. "I've secretly hoped, for as long as I've been of marrying age, that James would seek my papa's blessing concerning a union between us."

Phoebe dropped her branches and stared at Rebekah.

"That's why I've kept it to myself."

"I thought all along you were interested in Matthias."

"That's what troubles me." Rebekah picked up her friend's dropped branches. "I'll carry these for you. Where to?"

"No," interrupted Phoebe, grabbing the branches from Rebekah. "No, I will take them and fix my bed. May Adonai bless you with rest." Phoebe rushed away from Rebekah.

Rebekah knew she shouldn't have shared her thoughts with the one who did seek Matthias's attention. With hands on her hips, she stared after her friend.

Tomorrow I need to straighten things out between us.

"And may he bless you as well," she mumbled.

"Is that blessing for me or another?"

Rebekah twisted toward the man's voice. "Matthias, I thought—I mean, you were—"

"What is it you mean, Rebekah?"

She crossed her arms. "I mean you shouldn't sneak up on someone in the dark."

Matthias ran his hand over his beard.

"That's a bad attempt to cover your enjoyment of my discomfort," she huffed.

"Why do I bring you discomfort, Rebekah?"

"You don't. I was surprised. That's all."

"Let's begin again. Agree?" He offered his hand to seal the covenant.

"Agreed." Rebekah received his offer. Matthias covered both her hands with his free one. The warmth caused a chill to race through her. She wanted to retrieve her own but yet she didn't. Heat rose in her face, and she pulled away from him.

"And where shall we begin, Matthias?"

"Here. Where we are now."

"And that would be where?"

"I can only speak for myself, and I will," he began. "You will need to answer as to your whereabouts."

Rebekah nodded.

"I am a ruler of the synagogue and have a great amount of wealth. I have a house with my own servants and workers under me. You are beautiful with a strong will, and I believe an even stronger faith in Adonai. I need someone like that in my life."

Rebekah blinked, trying to cover the frown creeping onto her face.

Where is he taking this conversation?

Matthias continued listing their qualities. Was he asking her to marry him? She stood expressionless, her hands clenched in fists at her sides, her mouth closed.

"I want to seek Simon's blessing in a union between us, but not until I know you are agreeable. I don't want to force you into any arrangement you don't want."

Rebekah clamped her bottom lip between her teeth as she gathered her thoughts.

"I am not interested in this or any arrangement with you. As for asking Papa," she added, "don't bother. I will marry for love, not status, money, or ease. More importantly, my first love is Adonai, and my future husband's first love needs to be the same." She turned to walk away, but Matthias grabbed her arm and made her face him.

"I don't understand. I am a ruler of the synagogue. Does that not tell you where I stand with Adonai? I keep his commandments, following all the law and traditions of the elders. I am offering you everything."

"Release my arm," she whispered as compassion slowly drove away her anger. "You don't understand, do you?" She continued without giving him an opportunity to answer. "Matthias, I care for you. You know the law and the traditions, but you do not know the Lord God of the law. You go about seeking to prove your righteousness."

"I understand now," he answered. "This is about Yeshua, the Nazarene, his claims to be the Messiah, God the Son. I tell you I do believe he is a man sent from God. I believe it because of the works he does. No one else could do those works."

"If you believe, why do I see doubt in your eyes?"

"That's why I need you," he pleaded. "Adonai took my papa from me, then Deborah. She believed Yeshua has the words of life, life eternal. You have that same faith."

"I do, Matthias, but it is my faith. You must find your own." Rebekah turned away from him, then stopped. "I will pray for you, Matthias. Your search for truth will lead you to Adonai. I will pray you receive it."

Rebekah left him alone. She found herself a place between Gramma and Phoebe. As she settled for the night, she hoped Phoebe wouldn't be worried by the attention Matthias paid her. She wanted nothing to hurt their friendship. As she turned on her side to sleep, Rebekah noticed Matthias's shadow at the edge of the fire's light. He had not moved from his place.

Rebekah understood her feelings for him now.

He is a lost lamb of Israel. But I cannot save him.

Her meandering notions jumped ship and turned to James.

Would there be room in his life for a family—a family with me? Following Yeshua didn't come without cost.

The caravan of travelers began the steep climb toward Jerusalem before the sun managed to touch them. Soon it would be up and warming their backs. Rebekah helped Gramma get comfortable on the donkey, settling her between the bundles of palm fronds and willow branches tied to its sides.

"It makes quite a comfortable saddle," said Gramma with a grin.

Rebekah couldn't recall a time when she heard her Gramma complain. She always had something good to say. She smiled, remembering the time she tested Gramma by challenging her to say something good about Satan, the serpent of old. Gramma tilted her head to one side and continued stitching on her cloth. She stopped, blinked her eyes, and answered, "He's good at what he does." Without hesitation she returned to her embroidery.

"Soon," said Rebekah, returning to the present, "we will be in Jerusalem and will meet Immah and Papa. I hope Papa has our booth made."

"I hope there is room for us to be beside you," said Phoebe, joining in the conversation.

Rebekah clasped the other girl's hand and gave it a squeeze. They had talked earlier, easing Phoebe's mind about any earthly interest Rebekah had for Matthias, beyond concern for his soul.

"I am grateful the Lord has brought us together."

"As am I," replied Phoebe. "Did you sleep well?"

A smile spread across Rebekah's face. "Yes, I did. And," she added, "this is a new day the Lord has given us. I for one intend to rejoice in it. After all, it is time to celebrate the gathering of his children." With her arms raised over her head, she twirled in dance until her feet tangled in her skirt. If it had not been for the donkey nearby, she would have found herself on the ground.

Phoebe steadied her friend as their laughter broke the early morning stillness.

"You two better save some of that energy for the climb, or my little donkey will have to carry the both of you and leave me to walk," warned Gramma good-naturedly.

As they made their way towards Bethany and up the Mount of Olives, the two girls passed the time trading stories about past celebrations, and what it would be like if the Messiah did proclaim himself at this feast. It would surely be a celebration as never before. Occasionally, Rebekah watched Matthias as he walked and talked with Jairus. She wondered if he shared their conversation from the night before. It didn't matter. She would do what she knew to do and pray for him.

By the fourth watch, the caravan topped the Mount of Olives. From there they could see inside the walled city. At the highest point stood the temple of God bathed in the gold of the sun. Rebekah shaded her eyes against the shimmering jewel of the sky.

"It is magnificent, isn't it?"

"Made more glorious by his presence," commented Gramma from behind them.

"Who, Gramma?" asked Rebekah. "The Messiah?"

"Adonai, Yeshua?" asked Phoebe.

"Yes," answered Gramma, still gazing at its beauty.

The girls exchanged glances and shrugged.

"Look at the lower city, Rebekah." Phoebe pointed to the south. "The rooftops are full of booths. And there to the east."

"And all around the city," Rebekah said. "Come on, little donkey," she encouraged, tugging on its lead. "We are off to Jerusalem, the city of our God."

As the pilgrims entered the gates, each went in a different direction searching for family, a place to build their booth, and the best produce to share with those who would stop by as the week progressed. As Rebekah and Gramma entered the lower city, Jairus, Matthias, and their company continued around to the upper city where most of the Pharisees and other temple officials lived.

Rebekah led the donkey through the winding streets, looking for her family.

"It was kind of Jairus to leave his donkey with us," she said, scanning the rooftops.

"There, child, over there. I see your papa." Gramma pointed out the tall figure.

"Immah, Papa," called Rebekah, waving wildly with one hand and tugged on the donkey's rope with the other. When they ran toward her, she dropped the lead and ran into their full embrace, leaving Gramma sitting alone on the donkey.

"Gramma," cried Sarah, seeing her mother perched like a forgotten queen in the middle of the narrow street. The three hurried to her rescue. Simon lifted her easily from the beast's back.

"I see you brought branches for your own booth, Gramma," teased Simon.

"I brought the *best* branches for mine," she retorted as they exchanged hugs and kisses.

"Come," said Sarah, placing an arm around Gramma's shoulder. "You must be tired. Be our guest tonight. Tomorrow we will build your shelter."

Gramma laughed. "I believe I will. I may be the guest that does not know when to leave."

Rebekah glanced over the other booths, wondering who might be near.

"Rebekah, Gramma." James and John greeted the pair in unison as they exited Simon's booth. They grabbed each in turn by the shoulders and kissed each cheek. Rebekah scrunched up her nose as James's beard tickled her chin. She wondered if he still saw her as Simon's little girl. Her eyes met his and for a moment hope sprang up within her, not sure what she saw, but liking it.

The booth stood tall enough for the men to stand and wide enough for all to sit and enjoy one another's company.

"Judas has taken the money bag and is buying some provisions. The men will stay in the booth over there at night. You ladies will sleep here along with Mary, Mary of Magdala, Susannah, and Salome. Others will join us throughout the celebration," explained Simon.

"And Yeshua, when will he arrive?" asked Gramma.

"We don't know …"

"And will he proclaim openly that he is the Messiah?" interrupted Rebekah.

"We don't know that, either. Only he knows the time. He does as the Lord God directs him and only as he directs."

"But Yeshua is coming, yes?"

James reached across the makeshift table to place his hand on hers. Rebekah felt her blood rising to the surface as he spoke without moving it.

"He will come. His brothers are here already. Sabbath begins shortly. He won't travel then, but wait. In the meantime, we need to be cautious what we speak and to whom." He removed his hand from hers. Rebekah slid her own to her lap and glanced sideways at her father. She couldn't determine his look. Approval? Concern? Nothing? After all, James was only reassuring her, or perhaps reprimanding her like a child not knowing when and where to speak.

She lifted her chin and popped another grape in her mouth.

CHAPTER 30

"Do you not agree," asked Nicodemus, "this is the best view of the temple mount?"

Jairus grabbed his host's shoulders and kissed both his cheeks. "It is a grand site. Don't you think so, Matthias?"

"It will be a wonder to see when the seven-branched candelabras are lit."

"Nicodemus and I are going to the temple and witness it up close," said Jairus, "would you like to join us?"

"I will remain here, and enjoy the view and the music."

"Master, may Abigail, Leah, and I join in the celebration at the temple?" asked Eliezer.

After all had left, Matthias sat cross-legged on the soft willow branches to watch the festivities in peace. The women's courtyard came alive as each of the candelabras received fire. Each new glow brought the light of life into the mesmerizing *hallel* sung by the thousands of chanting voices.

"Praise the Lord, Praise O servants of the Lord, praise the name of the Lord. Blessed be the name of the Lord from this time forth and forevermore ..."

With each phrase the praise rose like yeast in rising bread.

A semblance of peace washed through Matthias as the light carried the music into the night. He closed his eyes and listened. With the last line of the hallel, a vision of Rebekah's face and the memory of her stinging words chased the light away, giving way to anger's seed of darkness.

"Best offer she will ever get," he muttered. A movement on the cobblestone street below caught his attention. He followed the man's course. The pilgrim investigated his surroundings, then blended into a shadowless alley where a disreputable inn entertained zealots and Samaritans along with prostitutes and thieves.

He dismissed the scene, and strained to grasp the final words of the hallel in hope of recapturing the peace he had lost.

"I will praise you for you have heard me and are become my salvation. The stone which the builders refused is become the head stone of the corner ..."

He ran the palm of his hand across his chin. He didn't understand this stone. He recalled the prophet Daniel speaking of a stone that crushed all other kingdoms—*that* stone he grasped. The Messiah would come. He would crush to pieces this Roman empire wielding its strong arm against God's people. The Messiah would end their tyranny once and for all as he set up his everlasting kingdom.

The Messiah? An everlasting kingdom?

He nodded. "I do believe in eternal life," he whispered to the emptiness around him.

But if life reigns in me, why do I feel like an empty tomb?

And the Messiah? Where is he? Wouldn't Yeshua of Nazareth be here to set up his kingdom if indeed he was the Messiah?

The street below filled with songs and praise from the pilgrims returning from the lighting ceremony, disrupting Matthias's pondering. He had enjoyed the brilliance of the candelabras and music from a distance. Torches lit the streets and buildings in front of the rejoicing crowd.

The man he'd seen earlier came out of the alley and hurried toward the lower city. In the torchlight, Matthias glimpsed his face.

"Judas? Judas Iscariot?" He angled his head for a better view. "Does that mean Yeshua of Nazareth is here?" he spoke aloud, searching the scene for any sign of the Nazarene.

"Master? Did you require something?"

Matthias did an about-face. Eliezer, Leah, and Abigail approached him.

"You startled me," he responded. "But, no, I require nothing." He returned to his view of the temple. "The lights are beautiful, are they not?"

"They are," replied the three as one. Abigail and Leah suppressed rising giggles as Eliezer took the lead. "More beautiful here than in the courtyard."

"I do believe I had the best view," said Matthias, taking another look at the light and shadows the menorahs cast on the city. "Did I miss anything by not being there?"

"Nothing, Master," offered Eliezer, still gazing at the beauty of the dancing firelight against the gold of the temple. "And," he continued turning his attention to Matthias, "if you need nothing, may we enter our hut and rest for the night?"

"Certainly. I'm waiting for Jairus and our host to return before I lie down. We may take a goblet of wine before retiring."

"Would you have me wait and serve you, Master?"

"Always the servant, Eliezer, but not tonight. Tonight, and throughout the week, we celebrate freedom, our release from bondage, even as we look forward to our future release. So tonight you sleep."

Eliezer bowed his head. The trio entered their three-sided booth. It was divided into two sections and covered with enough palm fronds and willow branches to provide cover, yet not hide the merriment of heaven's lights.

Matthias waited in vain for Nicodemus and Jairus. Their servants returned, but none of Jairus's family. He poured himself a cup of wine and drank alone. Cup emptied, he shifted on his pallet and slept.

Shouts rumbling in the streets roused Matthias from his bed of willows and pine needles. He blinked, adjusting his eyes to the morning sun.

"He's going to the temple!"

"Yeshua, Yeshua of Nazareth, he is here!"

Matthias jumped to his feet and wrapped his belt around his tunic. He tied the leather money pouch securely within the belt. He didn't want a repeat of the Passover theft. He threw on his cloak and followed the crowd.

Yeshua stood in the court of women as the crowd amassed around him. His disciples encircled him, protecting him. No wonder. Anyone with eyes could see members of the Sanhedrin circling like vultures waiting to feast, their beaks never shut, biting their own lips, waiting for the right moment to pounce.

Hypocrites. It is the one thing where I agree with Yeshua.

A sudden tidal wave of rulers at the edge of the crowd divided the sea of people as they roiled through them, waving their hands as if they held the rod of Moses.

"Rabbi, Rabbi." Their cries crashed through the air.

Matthias glanced toward Yeshua. A storm brewed here, but Matthias was unsure of where the wind came from. Clouds of disgust shadowed the Nazarene's face. Thunder rolled from the rulers' mouths, but the fire of the lightning flashed from the Rabbi's eyes.

With a sudden motion from the rulers, a woman appearing to be more child than adult fell at the Rabbi's feet. She lay in a heap, sobbing, her hair stringing over her face. Her accusers continued pointing fingers and filling the air with charges. One jerked her to her feet.

"What should we do with her, Rabbi?" he challenged. And from another, "We caught her. Caught her in the very act of adultery."

A lawyer from the crowd craned his neck and joined the storm. "Moses says stone her."

The quiet belied the brewing tempest, as the crowd waited for the Rabbi's answer. He stepped forward past the young woman. Kneeling, he scribbled in the dust. Matthias stretched to his full height.

"Well, Rabbi?" Impatient anger shattered the silence. "What do you say?"

"Yes, what is your answer?"

"The law of Moses states she is worthy of death. What do you say?"

The rulers' faces glowed with certain confidence, shining as the sun before an oncoming tempest, as the Rabbi stood. The storm clouds gathered with the Rabbi's words. Matthias didn't want to miss any part of this.

"If any one of you standing there is not guilty of sin," replied the Rabbi, standing tall, his voice clear and calm, "you throw the first stone at her." Without hesitation, he knelt and began writing again.

A stone dropped. One accuser exited. Another stone dropped. Another accuser exited. Again and again the action repeated itself, until only the Rabbi and the woman were left in the middle of a widened circle none dared enter.

"Is that—? ... it *is*."

The loud utterance behind him caught Matthias's attention.

Rebekah?

Matthias frowned as he followed her stare of recognition. She knew the woman. How could she know her? He glanced back at the woman standing in her shame. A second look confirmed he'd never seen her before.

The Rabbi stood, facing the prostitute who still covered her face with her hands, shivering from fear. "Woman." She looked up at him, dirt and tears streaking down her cheeks. "Look around you."

She obeyed as the Rabbi continued. "Where are those who accused you? Has no one condemned you?"

"No ... man ... Lord." The words tremored with unbelief.

"Neither do I condemn you." His words flowed sweeter than the waters of Marah. "Go, and don't sin anymore."

The young woman wrapped her torn tunic tight around her. Fear, relief, and wonder washed over her face. With hesitant steps, she walked back the way she had come, repeatedly glancing over her shoulder at the one who freed her soul to live.

The storm changed course. The Rabbi continued teaching. Ears were eager to hear, but eyes were curious to follow the woman. Rebekah, Matthias noticed, had run to the woman's side, wrapped her arms around her shoulders, and walked with her as if sheltering her from the accusing hearts that had been stopped by the Rabbi's words. Another older woman joined them before they disappeared.

The Rabbi continued. "I am the light of the world: If you follow me, you shall not walk in darkness, but shall have the light of life."

The huddled Pharisees stepped out again from the shadows like lions seeking a feast, teeth bared, ready to tear apart their prey. "Who are you to speak such words? You testify of yourself."

"Yes, your testimony is false."

Yeshua answered. "I am my own witness, and the Father, who sent me, is another witness."

He never shrank from their threats, but continued to speak with an authority impossible to refute.

"I am from above. You," he said, pointing them out, "are from beneath. You are of this world: I am not."

One Pharisee sauntered closer to the Rabbi. Hatred spewed as he spoke.

"Who are you? Tell us plainly."

The Rabbi's stare was void of anger but mixed with a warning plea.

"I told you from the beginning who I am, but you can't understand. When you have lifted up me, the Son of man, then you will know that I am who I say I am, and that I don't do anything of myself ... but always what pleases my Father."

The clouds of displeasure darkened over the Pharisees as the Rabbi continued to challenge their self-righteousness. Matthias unobtrusively searched for the best place to escape should the full force of the Pharisees' hatred be unleashed.

"You are of your father, the devil." The Nazarene's words thundered, igniting the lightning in their dark hearts. The clouds finally burst when he declared, "As surely as I stand here now, I'm telling you, before Abraham was, I am."

Suddenly stones meant to condemn the adulterous woman were hurtling toward the Rabbi. His disciples formed a shield around him as they skirted in and out of the marble columns seeking escape. The likelihood of a riotous mob sent Matthias running in the opposite direction, pushing his way through the throng. He expected to hear at any moment the boots of legionnaires stamping across the courtyard, bringing a bloodbath with them. He exited the temple and headed for his shelter atop Nicodemus's house. Along the way pilgrims shared excited whispers of fear and hope as they sought to put distance between them and the brewing storm.

"Do you think he is the Messiah?"

"Will he set up his kingdom?"

"Quiet, you fools, unless you want to be thrown out of the temple for good."

Matthias kept his mouth shut while his brain roiled. He would wait this out. Tomorrow would be another day. He wondered if the rulers believed Yeshua to be the Messiah and feared him. Why else would they tolerate his teaching? If they knew he wasn't, why wasn't he arrested, or at least thrown out of the temple?

He made to exit the crowd for the lane to Nicodemus's house when a cloaked figure ducked into the alleyway leading to the disreputable inn. Matthias stopped.

Judas.

With the cloak covering his head, Matthias wasn't sure. He trudged through the pilgrims who still filled the street. He couldn't imagine what business Judas would have for Yeshua in such a place.

Maybe following Judas is not such a good idea.

Loud drunken voices mixed with the high-pitched twitters of the city prostitutes swept through the window. He crept to the opening, stepped on a wooden crate, and peered into the dimly lit room.

There he is.

Judas sat at a table with several men Matthias didn't know. Judas spoke to them in harsh tones. He scanned the crowd as if looking for those who might betray him.

"I tell you, be ready. It's coming, and coming soon. Our dreams will be realized. We will have a king."

A burly man, once muscle-bound but now mostly blubber, slammed his mug on the table.

"You've been telling this same tale for months. We're growing tired of waiting. We will be in the crowd tomorrow." He lifted something from inside his cloak. "With daggers ready. We will have a king or die trying."

"You fool. Put that thing away. Keep your voice down. The Sanhedrin has spies everywhere. We must wait for his word, but it will be soon. Look for it by Passover." Judas reached inside his cloak. "Here." He shoved something into the burly man's hand. "Take this. Recruit more to the cause. Make sure every man has a sword."

Judas stood. Matthias carefully left his perch but could hear his final words. "And then *wait*."

As Matthias hurried down the lane, he heard the inn door slam.

"You! You there!" Judas cried out.

Matthias stopped and answered with a fake calmness.

"Me? Were you hailing me, sir?"

"Yes, you," answered Judas, taking long strides to join Matthias. "I've seen you before, but where? What is one like you doing here?"

"I could ask you the same question, Judas. Isn't that your name?" questioned Matthias with more bravado then he possessed. "You are one of Yeshua's disciples, yes?"

The suspicion in Judas's eyes was palpable as he answered. "What is that to you? What if I am?"

Matthias walked on as he talked. "You're close to him. You see him in public and in private. What do you make of him?"

"How do I know you're not a spy of the Sanhedrin seeking to end the mission of Yeshua?"

"I am a ruler in the Capernaum synagogue. I desire only to know the truth. Is Yeshua the long-awaited Messiah?"

"Examine his works and his words and you'll have the answer," answered Judas curtly.

"The tide of favor is turning against him. When will he set up his kingdom and free us from Roman rule?"

Judas grabbed Matthias by the shoulders. "Be careful what you say and to whom. Just be ready." Judas dropped his hold on Matthias, pulled his hood over his head, and disappeared into the crowded street.

Matthias worked his way to Nicodemus's rooftop. His mind wrestled with the possibilities, the probabilities, and the plans in the minds of others who sought peace at any price.

CHAPTER 31

Eunice raised her eyes to meet Rebekah's.

"Is there somewhere I can go? I'm afraid I won't be welcome among so many. And look at my clothes. It's obvious what I am." She swept her hands over her torn clothing, trying to cover where ripped cloth revealed naked skin. The older woman with them worked at pulling the torn cloth together.

"It's what you *did*, Eunice, isn't that right, Lois?" answered Rebekah. Lois, Eunice's mother, nodded as tears clouded her vision.

"Did you not hear Yeshua's words of forgiveness?" Rebekah said. "You are a lamb of Israel, found by the loving Shepherd."

"Is it truly that easy?" Eunice pleaded for affirmation.

Rebekah smiled. "It is that easy to begin. It's the journey that sometimes grows hard." She reached out to the young woman and lifted her to her feet. "But you won't have to take the journey alone. You have God, your immah, and me. Come."

She led Eunice and Lois to the extra bedchamber. "I have another change of garments. We'll wash your face, and you can change into them. That's where we will begin."

"I can't stay in such a fine home. I'll sleep in the stable if they'll allow me."

"Nonsense. They would give you their own sleeping rooms, but I have my booth along the courtyard wall. I want you to be my honored guest, and Lazarus and his sisters will welcome you at their table anytime."

"A little big, but they'll do the job. Here's a tunic."

A question burned in Rebekah's heart, and as usual, what was in her heart came out her mouth. "You haven't spoken a word about Timothy."

A cry caught in Eunice's throat as she slipped the tunic over her head.

"Eunice?"

"I—I—" She dropped to Rebekah's feet, grasping her ankles, tears flowing. "Is he doing well? I was too afraid to ask. I know the Master healed him but—but—"

Rebekah lifted her to her feet. "He's well. Plump as a melon."

"Do you understand why I left him with you and ran away?"

"I believe so," answered Rebekah.

"Tell me who has him. When I didn't see you with him, I worried ..."

"A shopkeeper and his wife love him as their own," explained Rebekah. "He has all daughters, and he received Timothy as a precious gift from the Lord."

Eunice grew quiet.

"What is it? I thought the news would bring you joy."

"Nothing. I'm grateful for all you have done for him." Her pensive smile betrayed her heart, but Rebekah let it go for the moment.

The two women sat in Rebekah's booth facing the city of Jerusalem. The giant candelabras were a pale imitation of the glory of the Lord against the deepening blue sky of night. Tomorrow all would hear the trumpets and answer the call for the last day of the feast.

At dawn, the priests lifted trumpets to their lips, chasing away the night shadows with their calls. Three times as they proceeded up the steps toward the Court of Women, the blasts echoed throughout the city and beyond its walls.

Matthias threw his cloak over his tunic and secured the leather pouch inside his belt. Today he would make his biggest offering yet. As he descended the steps, smoke from the sacrifices swirled its way to the throne of the Lord God Most High. He wondered how this last great day would unfold. The priests would carry the water from Siloam's Pool to pour on the altar, a symbol of the outpouring of the Lord. Tonight there would be no light.

Would there be a king?

He hastened to the temple, making his way to Solomon's Porch, the most likely place the Rabbi would teach if he dared to return after yesterday's attempted stoning. The people gathered by the thousands as the trumpets finished their call. He was right. A band of pilgrims made their way toward the great king's porch, Yeshua among them with his disciples close by. A burning knotted Matthias's stomach when he glimpsed Rebekah walking near James.

So that is my rival.

He moved his attention from James to the women walking with Rebekah. He was certain one of them was the harlot who had faced her own stoning. Dressed differently, he thought, but the garments changed nothing. If she takes that kind in, better he put Rebekah completely out of his mind. He didn't recognize the elderly woman walking arm in arm with the adulteress.

A sudden halt of the group as they came to Nicanor Gate caused Matthias to return his attention to the Rabbi. One of the many beggars piqued the disciples' curiosity with a question. Matthias stretched his neck to see above the others as he made his way forward. He tried to edge his way through when one of the men turned and eyed him suspiciously.

"You," the man hissed. "What do you want?"

"Judas, I mean no harm to the Rabbi," Matthias said.

Matthias felt the disdain in Judas's perusal. Matthias's eyes turned to slits as he tried to understand this one so unlike the others following the Nazarene.

It was James who spoke. "Master, whose sin caused this man's blindness, his parents' or his own?" The others nodded, waiting for the Rabbi's answer.

"Neither," answered Yeshua.

The disciples glanced at each other. Matthias was puzzled.

How could the Rabbi be so mistaken? He would know this curse came from sin if he was the Messiah.

"This man's blindness isn't because of his sin or his parents'. But it's so God could show his power working in the man."

The multitude watched and waited.

Yeshua surveyed the crowd, then spoke. "My Father sent me to do his work while it's day—there's coming a night when no man can work. As long as I'm in the world, I *am* the light of the world and must work his works."

The Rabbi spat in the dust around his feet and proceeded to make clay from the spit. He took a small portion in each hand, gently rubbed it over the beggar's blinded eyes, and said, "Go wash in the pool of Siloam."

Without hesitation the blind beggar, arms outstretched, started making his way to the pool. Yeshua began teaching again as if nothing had happened.

"... as Moses lifted up the bronze serpent on a pole in the wilderness, so the Son of man must be lifted up on a cross: Any who believe in him won't die, but will live forever."

Tears pooled in the Rabbi's eyes as he raised his face toward heaven. The next moment pulled a moan from somewhere deep within him. Time paused as he beheld the multitude. He opened his arms to the people, as if inviting them into himself and spoke. "God loved you all with so great a love, he planned and gave his one and only Son," Yeshua paused, with his hands folded as if in prayer, then continued, "so that anyone who believes in the Son should not die, but have everlasting life." He shook his head and continued. "God didn't send his Son into the world to condemn you but to save you. The one believing on him is not condemned."

His teaching stopped, but his eyes—Matthias felt the intensity of the Nazarene's gaze peering into his soul. The multitude disappeared into the recesses of his mind, as he stood alone before the Rabbi.

Am I one of the dying?

Matthias felt the stares of each person fastened on him, as the Nazarene resumed teaching.

"But know this, the person who *does not* believe in the one and only Son of God is condemned already because of his unbelief in the Son—the light that's here with you—and that one has loved the darkness, the evil deeds of the heart, rather than the light."

The Rabbi addressed a group of whispering Pharisees. "Every one that does evil hates the light, neither comes to the light, because he's afraid the light will expose what's in his heart. He that works truth comes to the light, and the light shows his works are brought about in God."

The words rambled through Matthias's head.

I tithe, I give to the poor, I offer the required sacrifices. Is this not enough? I always thought so, but why now does it not seem true?

As the Rabbi continued to teach, Matthias tried to evade his piercing words and watch for the blind beggar to return. Many in the crowd began to disperse. Matthias started to leave, thinking the beggar must still be blind or ungrateful.

"I was blind, but now I see! All praise to the Lord God Almighty!"

The shouts of the once-blind man halted all other activity as he ran across the Court of the Gentiles. "The eyes of the blind shall be opened, and the ears of the deaf shall be unstopped ... the lame man leaps as a deer ... the ransomed of the Lord shall return, and come to Zion with songs and everlasting joy upon their heads: they shall obtain joy and gladness, and sorrow and sighing shall flee away." His words filled the temple court as they bounced back and forth in happy song declaring the glory of God.

"You," cried a Pharisee with his contingency in tow. "You," the Pharisee said again, pointing at the Nazarene with a bony finger. "Are you claiming *this* man healed you? That he is of God?"

The accusatory question could not squelch the joy on the man's face or the glory in his voice.

"I know that now I see where before I could not, and Yeshua of Nazareth worked a work never before done."

The Pharisee grabbed his ears. "Blasphemous words! By the authority of the council, leave the holy temple, and do not return until you can denounce this name and give the Lord God glory!"

The sighted rejoicing beggar left the temple through the Golden Gate, praising God for his newfound sight. Yeshua exited by the Eastern Gate. Matthias followed as he made his way with Yeshua's disciples. Outside the temple, the Rabbi found the healed man with a few Pharisees still ushering him on his way, their mouths yapping like hungry dogs. At Yeshua's approach the snarls died away.

The Rabbi addressed the beggar as if he stood alone. "Do you believe in the Son of God?"

"Lord, who is he that I might believe on him?"

"You have now seen him, and it is he that talks with you."

The man dropped to his knees. "Lord, I believe."

As the man worshipped, the Rabbi spoke to those around him. "I have come into this world for judgment. That those which don't see might see; and those which see might be made blind."

"We have a question for you, Rabbi," called out one of the Pharisees.

"Yes," cried another, issuing his own challenge. "Are we blind, too?"

"If you were blind, you wouldn't have sin," replied Yeshua. "But because you say you see, then your sin remains."

The turban-crowned Pharisees in their robes hemmed with tinkling bells announcing their righteousness, stalked away mumbling how a man who did not follow the Sabbath could not possibly do any work except by Beelzebub.

Matthias stood alone with his thoughts as Yeshua, his followers, and the newly sighted man took their leave. The words of Isaiah, the prophet spoke to his heart.

And I will bring the blind by a way that they knew not; I will lead them in paths that they have not known: I will make darkness light before them, and crooked things straight. These things will I do unto them, and not forsake them ... hear, you deaf and look, you blind that you may see ... who is blind as he that is perfect ....

CHAPTER 32

Travelers bound for home trudged up the banks of the Jordan River. Their steps became slower and their numbers fewer with each village they passed. The setting sun brought a chill to the autumn air.

"Papa!" Rebekah called out to Simon as she ran to catch him. "Will we go by way of Samaria? It's easier and shorter." Rebekah had hoped this would be their route, but not with expectation. The Jews' and Samaritans' common hatred for one another meant most would avoid it.

"We need to take the Jordan way, as the Lord wants to go into Perea." Simon returned to walk beside his wife and the disciples as Rebekah rejoined Phoebe and Eunice.

"You look tired, Phoebe."

"My behind is numb. This donkey's backbone has no cushion. "She hoped off the beast. "I'm going to walk a bit."

"I lost feeling in my feet an hour ago," said Eunice. "Do you think we will go much farther this evening?" She wrapped her arms around herself as if trying to ward off the chill.

"I'll trot back to Papa and ask."

As Rebekah approached her father, an involuntary shiver coursed through her body, and it wasn't from the air. Without turning her head, she scanned the group around her. She and Matthias locked eyes. She offered him a nod, then continued to her father. She couldn't shake the feeling Matthias was watching her.

"Papa?"

Simon turned. "Rebekah." His smile melted her chill. "Back so soon. What is it?"

"In all truth, Papa, I'm tired. Can't we stop here for the night? The shore is wide and there is wood for the taking along the shoreline, and ..."

"Sshh," answered Simon as he put a finger to her lips. "We *are* stopping." He nodded towards Yeshua sitting on a small boulder next to his mother.

Rebekah silently thanked the Lord God for weary mothers.

The children scurried up and down the river gathering dried driftwood and brush. Soon smoke spirals filled the air and nostrils as several campfires dotted the river's edge. Families with small children gathered around some, the women around others, and the men around them all. Bread, dried figs, and smoked fish appeared from cloth bags and baskets as everyone settled down for the evening.

"My son, has anyone seen my son?" A woman's frantic cry shattered the peace and alerted those nearest Rebekah. "He's only a small child. I turned and he was gone. Have you seen him?"

The tired pilgrims began searching the crowd. Rebekah stood with Sarah and Gramma.

"Tell us what he looks like. There are many small children," said Sarah as she put her arm around the mother's shoulders. "We'll help you find him."

"The river ... I am afraid ... I don't see him anywhere."

Sarah coaxed the mother to walk along with her, heading her toward Yeshua and his disciples. Rebekah followed as Sarah continued to comfort the woman. As they approached Yeshua's fireside, laughter welcomed them. Rebekah craned her neck to see what caused the lightheartedness among the tired entourage.

"Here, Aaron, maybe you'll find this to your liking," said Yeshua to a yet unseen person. Sarah and the woman made a path through the group.

"Aaron," called the youngster's mother. Her outstretched arms invited him to take refuge. Kisses filled his little cheeks as he protested.

"Immah, stop it, stop it," he whined, trying to wriggle from her arms. "Yeshua gave me some bread and honey. See?" A syrupy grin spread across his face.

The homecoming ended abruptly as she turned to Yeshua, her head bowed. "Master, forgive my Aaron. I turned ..."

Yeshua smiled and took Aaron in his arms. "This little one has brought laughter to our hearts. He told us you brought nothing but leeks and stale bread."

The mother's mouth closed tightly in silent dismay as Yeshua continued. "Then Aaron told us he knew I would have good food."

"And I was right, Immah," chimed in the youngster as he ripped another piece of sweet bread and popped it into his mouth.

Chuckles rippled through the group as Yeshua handed the boy back to his mother. "Next time," he added with a smile, "ask Immah to bring you to me, so we don't worry her."

Aaron nodded as his mother clutched his hand. "Master, thank you."

As she walked away with Rebekah and Sarah, Yeshua addressed the crowd.

"Unless you become like little children, you will not enter the Kingdom of Heaven."

Rebekah caught Matthias's reaction to Yeshua's words as they passed by him, relieved he was not staring at her. "Lord God, help him hear," she whispered.

Rebekah and Sarah joined their group as Aaron and his mother continued to the next. Yeshua's words resounded among the pilgrims. Rebekah devoured his words more quickly than Aaron had eaten his sweet bread.

"When you welcome a child like this one in my name, you welcome me." Love colored his face with a light as bright as the noonday sun. As he surveyed the crowd, a threatening cloud shadowed the light. He spoke again.

"But if you hurt one of these little ones who trust me, you would be better off having a millstone hung around your neck and being drowned in the sea. Hurts happen, but be warned—grief will come to the one who does the hurting ..." The firelight cast moody shadows over the listeners. Silence hung as a heavy curtain.

With the women out of his sight, Matthias turned his full attention to the Rabbi's words.

"Don't treat even one little one with hate, for their angels are continually before my Father in heaven."

There was that phrase again, "My Father." Matthias did not understand. No one dared call God their Father, no one except this carpenter.

"The Son of man is come to save the lost."

Matthias felt as if a boulder sat on his chest, crushing him from within. He moved away from the firelight as the Rabbi continued.

"What do you think?"

Matthias wanted to flee but his feet refused to obey, the weight of the imagined boulder making it impossible to move.

"If a man has a hundred sheep and one wanders away, won't the man leave the ninety-nine, go into the mountains, and seek the lost one? The shepherd would give his life for his lost sheep."

Matthias turned from the Rabbi's face, fearing what he would see in the mirror of his soul. It was there. Death, suffering, pleading. Sorrow seeped from the Rabbi's heart and rained on the band of pilgrims.

Then like a bolt of lightning, the Rabbi's voice burst through the gloom with a joyous refrain, as he leaped on top of the large, flat-topped rock. "When the shepherd finds the lost one, rejoicing springs from his soul, even more than over the ninety-nine safe in the fold."

The Rabbi hesitated. Matthias shrank deeper into the shadows.

"It's not the will of your heavenly Father that a one of these little ones perish. I am the good shepherd."

My Father. The good shepherd.

Not even the darkness could hide Matthias from the one whose eyes searched his heart.

"There is nothing hidden that will not be revealed. It's late, but there is one last story to tell."

Matthias remained in the darkness.

"The land of a certain rich man produced an abundance of crops."

No. How could he know?

"In fact, he needed to build new larger barns to hold them all. He decided that was exactly what he would do. So he did. Then the rich man said to himself, 'Soul, you have more than enough goods to last for many years. It's time to take life easy, eat, drink, and enjoy.'"

Those closest to the fire nodded in agreement. They liked the story, but Matthias was not taken in. Something was coming.

"But," continued the Rabbi, jumping from the boulder, "God said to him, 'You fool! Tonight your soul is required of you. You will die. Now who will own what you've worked so hard for?'"

The Rabbi let his words find a resting place in the hearts that would hear before finishing his tale. "The man who lays up treasure here and is not rich toward God, is this man."

Matthias felt as if he stood naked before the Rabbi. Why him? There were other rich landowners on this march.

"Listen, my little flock," continued the Rabbi. "Your Father in heaven knows all your needs. Seek his kingdom, and the things you need will be given to you. Don't fear, your Father has chosen gladly to give you the kingdom."

The kingdom? Matthias caressed his beard. What kingdom? Was Yeshua going to set up his kingdom?

"Sell your possessions and give to charity; don't waste your time gathering things that wear out. Seek the lasting treasures of heaven—where your treasure is, that's what owns your heart."

Matthias moved back by the fire. He heard the words, but became deaf after he heard "Sell your possessions." He would have to hear more than this if he were to sell all he owned for the hope of a kingdom—with a carpenter for a king.

"Eliezer," whispered Matthias.

"Yes, Master."

"Tomorrow we'll reach the crossing into Perea. You go on to Capernaum with Abigail and Leah. I'll follow the Rabbi." Eliezer's look of concern caused Matthias to hesitate. "You question my wisdom?" he challenged.

"No, Master," answered Eliezer with his head slightly bowed.

"What is it, then?"

"With your permission, Master."

Matthias nodded and with a flip of his hand invited Eliezer to continue.

"Have you forgotten what is at stake, Master?"

Matthias shook his head. "How could I when you remind me daily? Work is done in the vineyard and the grove. You're capable of caring for my matters while I"— he hesitated— "while I find whatever I'm searching for. I'll not lose what I have for nothing more than a dream." Instinctively his hand lay against the leather money pouch hidden within his belt. "I'll return before work begins in the spring with all the answers I need."

"As you say, Master. I will take care of your affairs."

"I know you will. I trust you with more than my possessions. I trust you with my life."

Both men rested on their pine needle beds and let the fire's warmth lull them to sleep.

"Eunice, are you crying?" asked Rebekah as she turned on her bed of willow limbs. The sniffling stopped. Maybe she was sleeping? A moan told her otherwise. She raised herself on one elbow. "Eunice, what's wrong?"

Eunice faced Rebekah with trails of tears etched down her cheeks. "That woman with Aaron ... I want my son, Rebekah." Her words came between whimpers. "I want to be Immah to Timothy. I want him to know I love him, that God loves him."

Rebekah wrapped her arms around Eunice as the girl sobbed into her cloak. "Something will work out," Rebekah said.

Eunice pulled back. "Will anyone believe I've changed? Will they let me have him?"

"Your immah believes you've changed," answered Rebekah as she nodded in Lois's direction. "And she will help you teach little Timothy, even as she teaches you."

Eunice glanced at her mother sleeping across from her. "She prayed for me often. Her prayers and the Lord's grace have made me a new person. We will make it, won't we?"

"Yes. God has some wonderful things in store for your family. Just watch and see. What he starts, he completes."

Eunice squeezed Rebekah's hand. "He has already done so much for me. Thank you, Rebekah."

"Sleep now. Tomorrow is another day."

CHAPTER 33

Rebekah paused at the river's edge. Her band of pilgrims traveled north to Capernaum following the dirt road toward Tiberius. Her heart traveled east across the Jordan with those following Yeshua. All she loved traveled that way—her parents, Yeshua, and yes, she admitted to herself, James.

"Rebekah, child, come along."

Not all she loved. Gramma's high-pitched cajoling made her reluctant feet follow the path home. "Coming, Gramma. I just needed one more moment."

"This old woman may be wrinkled, but she still has eyes that see more than her ears may hear." Her Gramma wrapped an arm around Rebekah's waist. "The winter months will pass quickly. Then you will be able to join them all again back in Jerusalem for Passover."

Rebekah's heart betrayed her smile. She knew the seasons would change and life with them, but now was now.

"First thing we must do, Gramma, is find Eunice and Lois a home."

Gramma waved a leathery weathered hand in the air. "Nonsense, child. Did ever one of God's children not offer strangers a roof? Surely Moses would come off his mountain graveyard if we did not give shelter to these children of Israel."

Rebekah kissed the top of Gramma's head. "I hoped you would say that."

"Hoped? You doubted?"

"Not for a minute. Do you care if I catch up with Eunice and Phoebe? I'll ask Lois to come walk with you."

"Go, child, go. Lois and I can plan how we'll spoil little Timothy."

Rebekah's mind swam with ideas as she extended the invitation to Eunice. Once the dust had been washed from their feet and little Timothy reunited with his mother and grandmother, Rebekah planned on a trip to Perea.

Eunice grabbed Rebekah's hand as they walked and talked.

"How the Lord has blessed me today with such good friends. I'm certain Immah will agree. And this means each step takes us one step closer to Timothy."

Rebekah's smile faded when she noticed Phoebe chewing on her lower lip. She questioned Phoebe with her eyes.

"What about Jacob and Naomi?" mouthed Phoebe.

Rebekah shrugged. She had no answer for the hurt the couple would know in returning the little one, but she would not steal Eunice's hope.

Entering Capernaum, Rebekah hugged Phoebe farewell as her family headed through the city and Rebekah, Gramma, Eunice, and Lois climbed the rocky path home.

"When will you take us to Timothy?" asked Eunice.

"I'll need to go to the market in the morning," Rebekah said, "and speak with Jacob. I'll ask him and Naomi to come meet you and take the evening meal with us."

"You will explain why he is coming, and that he is to bring Timothy?"

At the top of the hill, Lois and Gramma went inside the house as Rebekah talked.

"Eunice, I know you are anxious to see your baby again. But try to think how much Jacob and Naomi have come to love him in your absence. It won't be easy for them."

Eunice lowered her gaze. "I know. I know how hard it was for me to leave him." She held her head up and continued. "I am forever grateful for their care of my baby. I will try to be patient."

Rebekah sandwiched Eunice's hands between her own. "Soon, you'll have your son."

"When will they get here, Rebekah?" asked Eunice for the hundredth time as she peered out the door.

Rebekah shoved the door shut and pulled her friend back into the house. "As I told you."

"I know," she said with a nod. "They will be here as soon as Jacob closes his shop. Forgive me. I just can't imagine how much Timothy has grown. And—" Eunice hesitated as she fidgeted with her long brown braid.

"And what?"

"He won't know me. He may cry for the woman who has been immah to him for these four months."

"As you care for Timothy, he will learn you are immah. He's not old enough to hold a memory of Jacob and Naomi."

Eunice grabbed Rebekah's arm. "No. I *want* him to know them. They have loved and cared for him when I couldn't. He must always remember them."

Rebekah put her arm around the young woman's shoulder. "I'm sure they will rejoice to hear that."

A muffled cry from outside caught their attention. Eunice flung open the door. Standing before her stood Jacob and Naomi, but Eunice saw nothing except the bundle wrapped in a blanket, cradled in Naomi's arms.

A tear trailed down Eunice's cheek as Rebekah edged her way around her to the door.

"Shalom, dear friends. We won't make you stand out in the cool evening air. Come join our table."

"Forgive me. Yes, won't you come in?" chimed in an embarrassed Eunice, as Lois and Gramma joined them.

"These children," scolded Gramma, "keeping our guests in the cold. Scoot out of the doorway and let them in."

At Gramma's orders all moved toward the table in the center of the room nestled near the small hearth.

"Ah, Gramma," greeted Jacob with arms wide and a kiss for the old woman's cheek. "Am I to enjoy some of my produce cooked superbly by your hands?" The sadness clouding his face did not match the jovial greeting. Gramma gave him a friendly push away.

"As always, full of nonsense. But before we eat, we must peek at this babe." Gramma lifted a corner of the blanket covering the sleeping little one and planted a kiss on his forehead "As soft as the silky hair of a baby goat. He is beautiful, Naomi, and looks to have as much of an appetite as Jacob."

Nervous laughter coursed through the group. Naomi stepped towards Eunice. "Would you like to hold your son?" she asked, offering the cocooned baby to his mother.

Eunice's eyes overflowed. She sucked in her bottom lip and nodded, as she reached for her son. Lois moved closer to her daughter and to the grandson she had never seen. Naomi laid the baby in his mother's arms. Eunice nuzzled his soft velvety cheek.

"He is more beautiful than I remembered. Look, Immah. How is it possible?" she asked as she looked back at Naomi. "How can I ever repay your kindness and love?"

Naomi smiled. "By raising him in the knowledge and faith of our Lord." The older woman hid quivering lips behind her hand but couldn't conceal the glistening tears threatening to fall.

"And," interrupted Jacob, striving to keep his cheerful countenance, "make us his honorary family. Maybe your immah would allow us to be his adopted grandparents."

Lois reached out to Naomi. The hug squeezed sniffles from both women.

Lois's voice filled with emotion. "The more people in his life who love him, the more blessed he will be."

Jacob and Naomi shared stories with Eunice about Timothy's habits, likes, and dislikes as they enjoyed the meal with their extended family. He had recently learned to blow spit bubbles. Too quickly the evening came to an end. As the couple walked to the door, Eunice followed, clutching little Timothy to her chest.

Reluctantly, she offered her son to Naomi. "I know I must give him back for a time ..."

"Why is that?" asked Naomi. "He's your son. We've given you the knowledge you need to start you on this journey of being his immah. It won't take him long to know he is loved by you."

Eunice leaned into Naomi, holding Timothy between them. "May the Lord's peace and blessing be upon you. I vow before you and the God of heaven to raise him knowing the Lord."

The reunited family watched as Jacob and Naomi made their way down the path. Naomi pulled her shawl closer around her shoulders, stopped, and turned. "Shalom," she cried with a wave. "And know this, Eunice—as his gramma I will make a pest of myself."

Eunice smiled. "Come anytime."

Timothy filled the house of Simon Peter with joy as he grew through the rainy cold winter months. Eunice proved herself a good mother, and Lois faithfully and patiently guided her daughter into motherhood while enjoying her grandson. Rebekah had never seen her own Gramma so full of life.

Rebekah's spirit grew more restless. She knew where she wanted to be. And soon the cold would give way to warmer weather. The time had come to speak to Gramma.

The old woman sat in silence, weaving a wool blanket as Rebekah related her plans.

"Gramma, did you hear what I said?"

The loom slowed and then sat silent. Gramma faced her granddaughter.

"I heard." She straightened one of Rebekah's sleeves. "You're no longer a child, yet always a child in your Gramma's heart." She patted the girl's cheek.

Rebekah covered her Gramma's hand with her own. "I love you, Gramma."

"And I love you. You are a comfort to this old woman while Sarah and Simon are away." Gramma looked off as if into a distant land. "The Lord is good. He has blessed me with many years and filled my life with joy." She turned back to Rebekah. "I know you must go. You must find your way, make the journey the Lord has for you. I'm certain you'll find it following Yeshua. But child," she continued, lightly touching Rebekah's face, seeing something Rebekah did not understand, "remember his words. The journey will grow hard, but you will never be alone."

Rebekah tried to understand but couldn't see what older and wiser woman saw. She only knew she must go.

"I don't plan on returning until after Passover, Gramma, unless Yeshua comes this way. Knowing your prayers go with me gives me comfort, and knowing Eunice and Lois are with you helps me leave in peace."

Rebekah stood outside the door of her home with a shoulder bag full of bread, dried fruits, and even some smoked fish. Gramma, Lois, and Eunice each shared hugs and kisses with her. Little Timothy bounced on his mother's hip, his chubby arms waving at the air. Rebekah kissed his cherub cheeks and pressed a finger on his nose.

Next time I see him, he will probably be walking and talking.

"You're the man of the house now."

"Finally, one we can handle," retorted Gramma, and their chuckles eased the pain of good-bye.

"Shalom," said Rebekah, and she turned and walked away from the only life she had ever known.

"Shalom," echoed the voices of those she left behind.

She didn't look back, but set her steps for the road she must travel. Soon she would meet with Jairus, Joanna, and Phoebe, and, of course, Delilah. At the thought she shook her head and smiled. She repositioned the sling bag and wineskin on her shoulder as she tugged at the goatskin water bottle hanging from her belt. She hoped Jairus's donkey could handle a little more.

CHAPTER 34

"You better listen to what I say." Judas's spew of foul breath punctuated his threat. "The Master must make a move and soon. Look around you. What do you see?"

Matthias heard but kept looking toward the Rabbi. He tilted his head towards Judas as he surveyed his surroundings. "The masses, and the thunderclouds."

"Are you speaking about the storm clouds above or around us?" Judas nodded right, then left.

"They are always on the fringes. What more can they do?"

Judas shook his head and rolled his eyes. "You call yourself a ruler and ask that question? They've already tried to silence the people by banning them from the temple if they speak Yeshua's name. At every turn, they test the Master, trying to make him look the fool. You can see their self-righteous angry faces as well as I when he speaks."

"This kingdom you speak of ..." cried one predatory Pharisee.

Judas and Matthias turned to the challenging voice.

"When will this kingdom of God come?" The Pharisee's companions nodded their heads at his words, their lips pushed out, anticipating a victory.

"Listen," Judas snarled through gritted teeth. "I tell you the time is near. Now is not the time to leave."

Matthias heard, but said nothing as he turned to hear the Rabbi. His heart and mind wrestled with truth, not sure he would recognize it if he heard it. Thunder rolled in the distance.

Yeshua stood on the sandy dirt of the Jordan River's washed-out banks. "You can't see the kingdom of God here or there," he called to his challengers as he pointed first to the south, then to the north.

Another Pharisee swung his arm in a wide circle. "You are saying we are blind?" His voice dripped with sarcasm, sour as bad wine. "I believe we see clearly."

"Because you say you see, your sin remains in you. The kingdom of heaven is come for the unrighteous, and is even now among you, but you don't see it."

The flock of robed and turbaned vultures grew darker than the ominous clouds overhead.

"There is a day coming ..." The Rabbi continued speaking in lower tones, turning from his challengers to those who would hear, but his stare stopped with Matthias. "You will long to see the days of the Son of man, but you won't see it. There will be people here and there saying they're him. Don't go after them or follow them ..."

A streak of lightning parted the sky and thunder shook the earth. Stifled screams emanated from the crowd. The Pharisees haggled among themselves as they wandered away like a pack of whipped dogs.

The Rabbi stood unmoved. Looking at the crowd, he pointed behind him. "As the lightning lights the sky in one place and shines to another, that's what it will be like when the Son of man comes in his day."

The roar of his voice halted the panic as stillness settled on the people, heavy as the morning fog over the Galilee. "But first, he must suffer many things and be rejected by this generation."

Matthias whispered to Judas, "That doesn't sound like a king ready to set up his kingdom."

Judas stood grim-faced. "He may need a little help to see it's time."

Matthias glanced at the surly disciple beside him. A terror seized his heart.

"Eating and drinking, marrying, buying, and selling, planting ..." continued the Rabbi. "All these things will still be going on. But just like Sodom and Gomorrah received the rain of fire and brimstone from heaven in one day and were destroyed, that's how it will be in the day when the Son of man is revealed. Be ready. Don't turn back." The plea vibrated from deep within the Rabbi as it was planted in those who receive it.

Matthias knew the Scriptures, the prophets, but this one's words cut through to the bones. He wondered how ready he would be for that day.

"I tell you the truth, whoever seeks to save his own life, his own way, will lose it, and whoever loses his life for my sake shall preserve it. The first will be last and the last first. Many will go into everlasting torment, but those who believe in the Son of man will go into eternal life."

Yeshua started walking toward the village. "If you would be my disciple, follow me."

The crowd followed like hungering children seeking a morsel of bread. Matthias followed, fleeing the approaching storm. He hoped to find shelter in Bethabara along with the Rabbi and his followers.

The late winter rain beat against the stable. Matthias curled inside his mantle on a soft bed of hay, tucking himself into the far dark corner. He covered his nose with a corner of the mantle to stifle the overpowering stench of animals, and rested his head on his bag of belongings. His last thought was of the leather purse strapped to his belt which would not leave his person. The constant rhythm and drip of water leaking through the roof lulled Matthias to sleep.

Orange, yellow, and blue intertwining split tongues swirled around his head. A scream filled his mouth but no sound came out, racking his body with a choking sensation. A hand with fingers of fire burst through the sheet of colors as it grabbed for his throat. Crawling like a crab, Matthias scrambled to find a place beyond the reach of the threatening flames. He was falling, tumbling into a deep abyss. He grabbed his ears and tried to block the agonized cries in the darkness beyond the relentless pursuing flames. A voice called his name.

"Matthias! Matthias!"

Someone, something grabbed his shoulders and shook him violently.

"Get up! Get out!" the voice screeched.

His body jerked him out of the nightmare, only to face another. Judas stood over him, smoke swirling around his feet. The man grabbed his arm and began dragging him across the dirt floor.

"We have to get out! The stable is on fire! Get up or we'll both die here! No, you will die. Alone. I'm getting out!" Judas left Matthias and vanished in the flames and smoke.

Reality eradicated the lingering images from Matthias's sleep. He leaped to his feet.

"I'm up," he shouted, dodging burning timbers and running for the door. Behind them a blazing beam fell, consuming the place where Matthias had slept.

Once out the door, both men gulped the crisp night air into their burning lungs. The rain fell in a slow steady stream, washing the two men and their companions of the ash and smoke. But it could not provide enough water to stay the lightning's wrath on their shelter. They stood dripping, watching as the hissing fire turned its victim to ash.

The village had awakened. Men came to examine lives and damage. Women gathered at doors and windows. One of the men approached Yeshua.

"Barnabas has offered us his home and a warm fire," announced Yeshua to his followers.

"I'm thankful for his offer," said Matthias to Judas. "But I must admit I'm a little leery of the warm fire."

Judas smirked. "It'll feel good and dry us off."

Barnabas's home proved to be sufficient to hold his new guests, along with the several women and children already there. His servants and the women provided the men with some wine as they stood around the open fireplace. The flames provoked memories of Matthias's nightmare. A foreboding wrapped around him like a heavy cloak.

"Matthias?" A familiar voice freed him for the moment.

"Rebekah. I didn't know you were here."

"We arrived just before the storm exploded. But here," she said, holding out a pitcher. "Have some more wine. It will warm you."

Matthias held his cup for her to fill. "You said we. Who did you travel with, if I may ask?"

"Jairus and Phoebe." She motioned across the room to the two coming their way.

Matthias smiled at the welcome sight of his mentor. Then his attention moved to Phoebe.

"It's good to see them," he commented. His focus remained on Phoebe. *She is no longer Jairus's sickly little girl. She's grown into a beautiful young woman—inside and out.*

Jairus grabbed Matthias's shoulders and pulled him close, kissing each cheek. "Shalom, my friend."

Matthias returned the greeting as Jairus continued to talk.

"I hear Judas saved you from certain death tonight."

The fear that had gripped him in the barn tied a knot in his chest. He nodded as he tried to regain his voice.

"Yes, Judas pulled me from the fire. I will be forever grateful to him. I owe him my life." Speaking of the fire fueled the terror in his heart. His body began to shake.

"I brought an extra cloak. It's dry. Would you want it?" asked Jairus.

"Uh, thank you. I lost what little I brought, as did the others," he answered. "I do have some coinage." He instinctively reached for its hiding place in his belt. "It's gone." He patted around his belt, glanced behind him toward the rubble, then back to Jairus. "My leather pouch is gone. Maybe when Judas dragged me across the floor ..."

Jairus laid a comforting hand on the younger man's shoulder. "We'll look for it in the morning light. Maybe it survived. But my friend, I thank our Lord *you* survived."

"Of course, Jairus. I'm thankful to be alive." He clenched his fingers around the naked leather belt.

One by one the guests in Barnabas's home retired for the night. Matthias found himself a place near the door. Each time the promise of sleep slipped over his heavy eyelids, the fiery hand of his nightmare hurled them open. When movement ceased in the house and silence was replaced with snores, Matthias rose. He inched his way around Jairus and stepped out into the chilly night. The rain had stopped, leaving a few embers glowing and a whirl of rising smoke where the barn once stood. He grabbed a pole and carefully shuffled the ash, not wanting to encourage a new flame.

He stepped over the cooling residue as he made his way to the corner that had been his resting place. *Nothing.*

"Matthias."

He turned with a start. "Rabbi? I hope I didn't wake you. I ... I couldn't sleep, and I had lost ... wanted to see if anything survived the fire."

Yeshua stepped through the dust. He held something in his hand. As he neared Matthias, he let it dangle.

"Would this be yours?" he asked, holding up a leather pouch heavy with coins.

"I—yes, I believe it is, Master."

Yeshua took his hand and laid the bag in it.

"I thought it was lost forever. Please take my offering of gratitude and a few of the coins for your travels." He pulled three coins from the bag.

"You are gracious." The Master took the coins. "But if you could only believe, I would give you treasure without measure."

Matthias wanted to know more, but words wouldn't come. The two stood in silence among the ashes. Finally, Yeshua turned to go.

"It's late," he said, as he walked out of the rubble. "When morning comes, we'll work to help our brother rebuild his stable." As he reached the road, he turned to Matthias. "Morning comes quickly."

Only for those who can sleep.

Matthias stared after the Rabbi as he secured the leather pouch inside his belt. Shortly he followed in hopes of finding rest, but rest was consumed among the flames and cries, the darkness and falling that kept jolting him awake. The night lingered like an unwanted guest.

Matthias rubbed his hand over his face, trying to wipe away the sleepless night. He worked like a slave with the others on the burned-out stable, hoping a weary body would drive away the horrors of the recurring dream. He leaned over a bucket of water and splashed a handful of cold water on his face. The work was done, and today the Rabbi would continue teaching. Matthias shook his head. When didn't the Rabbi teach? He recalled the story the Rabbi told about the rich man who built bigger and better barns to hold all his goods. Matthias's image in the water bucket mocked him as he remembered the end of the story. That night the rich man's soul was required of him. His riches had done him no good.

A crowd gathered near the village well. Children played around the Master's feet. He hoisted one of the boisterous lads over his head like an eagle and laughed at his hawk-like shrieks for, "More!" When the play ended, each child received a blessing from Yeshua, as he gathered them one by one into his arms.

"To enter the kingdom of God, you must receive it like a little child," said the Rabbi before offering a final blessing on their hosts. "Bless these, Father, who fed us and gave us shelter."

Then began their trek south towards Jerusalem.

Matthias's parched soul longed for relief. He understood the thirst of the psalmist's spirit like the deer panting for water. He yearned to be blessed, to be held, to laugh again— to have peace in knowing he would be a part of the kingdom of God. He watched the Master walking farther and farther away from him. He held up the hems of his cloak and ran after the only one who could answer the hungering of his heart.

"Rabbi! Rabbi!" As Matthias reached the edge of the group of followers, they stopped to see what caused the sudden commotion. Matthias pushed through them and fell at the Nazarene's feet. The pent-up words tumbled from his mouth like a land side.

"Good Master, what do I need to do to know eternal life is mine?" He didn't care that those around him knew him as a ruler of the synagogue, one who should already know the answer.

Yeshua took Matthias's folded hands and raised him to speak with him face to face. "Why do you call me good, Matthias? You know only God is good."

Matthias didn't know how to answer.

Yeshua continued. "You know the commandments."

Matthias nodded, his heart growing hopeful.

"Don't commit adultery, don't kill, don't steal or bear false witness. Don't cheat anyone, and honor your father and mother."

When the Master paused, Matthias's answer burst out. "Master, I have done all these things since I was a small boy." He waited, wringing his fists under his chin, for the words he ached to hear.

Yeshua laid his palm against Matthias's bearded face. "There is one thing you lack, Matthias."

Matthias's soul screamed *no, there couldn't be*. Whatever it was he would do it.

"Go home." Yeshua paused before continuing. "Sell all you have and give it to the poor—then you will have treasure in heaven. After doing this, come, take up the cross, and follow me."

Matthias's chest deflated like a bellows squeezed of its air. He searched the Nazarene's eyes. Those deep brown eyes seared through flesh and bone into his heart with a tenderness of a father holding his newborn son. How could that be? Had he heard correctly? He instinctively fingered the leather bag tied inside his belt. How would he survive? How could the Rabbi ask such a thing? Why?

A needling voice whispered in Matthias's ear.

"He doesn't care about you," it hissed. "Only your silver."

A passing moment froze itself in eternity. What did he believe? He lowered his gaze. Tears of doubt and despair threatened to overflow. He would remember forever the cries of love brimming in the Rabbi's eyes as he walked away from hope, from life.

The Rabbi's next words followed him, growing weaker with each step.

"It's hard for those trusting in riches to enter the kingdom of God ... With men it is impossible, but not with God, for with God all things are possible."

Not with him, thought Matthias. The Nazarene's price was too high. As any good child of Israel, he would attend Passover. He would return home. And one day he would die, and because he was a child of Abraham, he would be raised in the last day.

Wouldn't he?

CHAPTER 35

Sweat beaded on his forehead. He lay staring at the roof above him, clamped his mouth shut, and fought to control the rapid rise and fall of his chest. Matthias closed his eyes and braced himself on his bed as he got up. He took a minute to get his bearings, then stepped to the washstand. He splashed cold water on his face and wiped away the water and the sweat. Leaving the Rabbi had not rid him of the nightmares. He rubbed his temples as if trying to erase the images taunting the darkness inside his head.

"Eliezer!" Matthias stood in the doorway, searching the courtyard for his servant. "Come," he said, motioning his servant to his side. "Get my cloak and walk with me to the grove. I've come to a decision and want you to have knowledge of it."

Matthias ignored Eliezer's frown, knowing he had unasked questions when he simply replied, "Yes, Master and would you have me instruct Leah and Abigail to have your breakfast ready on our return?"

Matthias put his folded hands to his mouth, bowed his head and nodded. "Yes, but only a small serving of dried fruit, some bread and a little wine." He could no longer bring himself to eat the sweet cakes and dibs Deborah use to make for him.

Silence hung heavy between the men as they walked.

"Eliezer." Matthias broke the silence. The gnarled arthritic trees dotted with the white flowers of spring produced hope of a fruitful harvest in early summer. Soon the budding flowers would fall like snow on Mount Hermon, creating a white carpet on the rocky hills of green grass.

"Yes, Master."

Matthias gestured toward the grove, his chin held high and his eyes questioning the vision in front of him. "Surely, this promise of a bountiful crop attests to my righteousness. I leave the fallen figs for the poor to gather. I tithe my profits and produce, do I not?"

"You follow the laws, Master, giving out of your abundance."

Matthias stopped and faced his servant. "Do my workers complain that I am unfair in their hire? And you, Eliezer, did I not offer you freedom after my father died? Do you or any of my servants have complaints concerning my treatment of them?"

"Master Matthias, you are a fair man. You do not cheat your buyers and you deal honestly with all your workers. I have heard no complaints from any of your servants."

"And you, Eliezer, have you changed your mind? Do you want to be released from your vow?"

"If you released me, I would never leave you. I have no wish to be released." He paused. "How can one be released from a bond of love?"

The old man wiped the moisture escaping down his cheeks. Matthias's stoic demeanor threatened to collapse. He turned his attention back to the grove.

"The Rabbi told me I must sell everything and give it to the poor if I wanted eternal life."

Eliezer made no response as the two proceeded through the stand of trees.

"I walked away from him, but I've been considering his words. Do you believe in the resurrection of the dead, Eliezer?"

"Yes, Master, I do."

"I do as well, but I am not certain I will be raised to life. I follow the commandments. Even you testify to that. But if this Rabbi wants me to sell my grove and give him the money, then surely he would be satisfied if I sold half of it and gave it to the promise of his kingdom. Once the kingdom is established, I will gladly sell it all if he would give me a place in the kingdom—and ensure my eternal life."

"Master, may I have permission to speak freely?"

"Surely. Let's return home. I know which trees I will sell," answered Matthias. "And I would have you speak nothing but honest words."

Eliezer walked a step behind Matthias as they proceeded across the hillside. "I do not believe that is what the Rabbi meant, Master."

"What do you think he meant?" Matthias fiddled with the dangling sidelock.

What else could he mean?

The Rabbi needed money to finance his kingdom. He certainly was among the poorest of the people. He had no home or income of any kind. His band of men had no way to prepare for the battle that would take place if he tried to defy the Romans, not to mention the Pharisees.

"I believe the Rabbi tested you, Master."

Matthias's sudden turn caused Eliezer to stumble.

"Tested? And I failed the test. Is that what you're saying?"

Eliezer intertwined his fingers, his head bowed. "You did not answer the test, Master."

"Explain," demanded Matthias as he resumed his steps.

"The Rabbi asked you about commandments you have kept from your youth up. The one he asked you about was the first one. You shall have no other gods before the one true God."

"I have never worshipped idols, Eliezer. Never."

"Master, idols are not necessarily statues made of wood or silver or gold. I believe the Rabbi wanted you to know where the Lord God stands in your heart. That you trust and love the Lord God more than you trust in your many possessions."

"I may have failed the first test, but selling half my grove should show my heart, my devotion," defended Matthias, knowing selling a portion of his inheritance would give him first rights to redeem it if the new owner desired to sell.

"Yes, Master, I am sure it will."

Matthias felt the sting of resignation in his servant's reply. No matter. He dismissed the squeezing in his chest. He would secure his way to eternal life.

Matthias busied himself the next few days drawing up the deed for the farthest part of the grove. Once signed, witnessed, and handed over to the new owner, he only had to give the money into the hands of the Rabbi. No doubt it would go into the common money bag which Judas held. A twinge of uncertainty grasped his spirit.

Judas saved my life, but ...

Matthias shook his head.

He could have left me to die.

No, he would trust Judas. And soon he would prove his devotion. Then eternal life would be his.

Hopefully, the transaction would free him of the nightmares, the dreams of the haunting hand of flames plunging him into the dark abyss. He closed his eyes against the vision but opened them in an instant, as the darkness served only to heighten the glow of the flames swirling around his head.

An uncertain hope, but hope nonetheless, rested in Matthias's heart after he returned from delivering the deed to the new owner.

"Eliezer, it's time to prepare for Passover."

"You are anxious to be on your way, Master?"

"Yes, I feel like an eagle soaring above the winds of change. And I believe I'm ready to secure my place in the change." He shook the leather pouch full of gold coins. "I would like you to travel with me to Jerusalem for the Passover. You have waited more years than me for this Messiah King. Accompany me and see it take place before your eyes."

"Master, what makes you so certain this is about to take place?"

"One of the Rabbi's men is certain of the timing, and now I am certain to be a part of it." He bounced the leather pouch one last time before securing it inside his belt. "Do Leah and Abigail have our preparations made? Tomorrow the caravan arrives, and I intend to travel with them. There's safety in numbers."

"Yes, Master, the women have everything ready. And of course, I am honored to travel with you."

"We should arrive in Jerusalem a week prior to the celebration."

Matthias, with Eliezer close behind, pushed a path past camels, donkeys, and carts as they entered the village of Bethphage.

"Up ahead, Eliezer. Over there. See them?" Matthias lifted the bottom of his tunic and quickened his pace. "Isn't that the Rabbi? I'm sure it is. There is Simon, standing a head taller than the others," he called back to his servant. "What's going on? Can you tell?"

If Eliezer answered, Matthias couldn't hear amidst all the pilgrims heading for the same place—Jerusalem. Eliezer finally caught up with him, and they both craned their necks to get a better view. The gathering crowd moved as a river flowing down the mountainside. Swept along with the flow, they continued to push their way forward. As the head of the movement reached the other side of the valley pushing towards the Beautiful City, Matthias began running ahead, leaving his servant to keep up if he could.

"Eliezer, it's the Rabbi! He's riding on a donkey. The people are hailing him as king. Do you not hear them? We must hurry."

"Yes, Master, I see their excitement and hear their song."

As the pair drew near the throng, Matthias and Eliezer joined the volume of voices in their praise.

"Blessed is he that comes in the name of the Lord! Hosanna to the Son of David. Hosanna in the highest!" As the river of praise rushed along the road to the City of God, Matthias joined the others in grabbing branches from the nearby willows and waving them in praise to the Messiah. The King would take his throne. They would finally be free from Roman rule.

By the time the masses entered the Shushan Gate, Matthias had made his way to the edge of the faithful followers of the Rabbi, the King. He spotted Jairus, Joanna, and Phoebe. On the other side he saw Rebekah with her mother. Simon and the other disciples made a human barrier between the Rabbi and the masses, but to little avail. And there on the edge of the group stood a smug-looking Judas. He was right. Matthias smiled.

The Rabbi, the Son of David, will claim the throne.

"Jairus, shalom," called Matthias, edging his way through the throng.

As he approached the family, Phoebe suddenly grabbed his arm, and pumping it up and down exclaimed, "Oh, Matthias, it is happening. Finally, the people believe and rejoice. Is it not wonderful?"

Matthias smiled, distracted for the moment by the life in Phoebe's voice and the beauty that graced her. "Most wonderful," he answered.

"Shalom, friend," returned Jairus, breaking into their conversation. "You made it. You couldn't have arrived at a better time."

Phoebe dropped Matthias's arm as color shaded her cheeks.

"What do you make of it, Jairus?"

Matthias and Jairus, caught in the tide of pilgrims, pressed towards the grand stairway leading into the court of the temple. Merchants had their wares laid out on the ground on either side of the stairs, hawking their goods and haggling prices.

"I've given the Rabbi's words much thought," answered Jairus. "Everything points to him as the Messiah—his words, works, authority."

"But?" questioned Matthias, as the pilgrims began marching into the Royal Porch. They pressed their way into the outer court around the overflow of vendors of sacrifices and money changers.

"I'm not sure we're understanding his meaning," answered Jairus as he and Matthias followed the crowd.

The crack of a whip rang out. The cheering crowd anticipating their king began to scatter as pandemonium broke loose within the Royal Porch. In one motion, merchants grabbed their cages of doves and tried to protect their heads. Matthias's mouth opened but no words came out. He stood motionless, scanning the scene, remembering the same incident two years earlier.

Jairus grabbed his sleeve and pulled him behind one of the colonnades as the chaos continued. The high priests and their contingency ran for cover. Their visage expressed the wrath broiling inside. Tables were overturned. Bags of money clattered onto the floor. Men on all fours snatched what they could while brushing coins into their open bags and crawling away from the fiery sting of the whip.

"*It is written!*"

Matthias turned as Yeshua's voice rang through the colonnade and across the courtyard. Merchants and money changers loaded down with what they could salvage scrambled out of the outer gate. Two priests stood staring at the Rabbi, their jaws clenched, their shoulders rising and falling like the tide of the sea.

"My house is a house of prayer, but you have made it a den of thieves." The Prophet's eyes burned with fiery judgment. As he spoke, he emphatically pointed to each group of priests, Pharisees, and Sadducees. He turned, and with deliberate steps began to cross the courtyard to Nicanor Gate where the diseased, lame, and beggars sat waiting for mercy.

"Come, Jairus, I must hurry," said Matthias, clutching his leather purse. "I must give him this." He held it up for Jairus to see as they edged past two priests. Their angry words caught his attention.

"We must meet with the council. This self-proclaimed prophet must be destroyed."

Matthias tucked their words into the recesses of his mind.

They know as well as I, the Nazarene threatens their power. But would they go so far as to destroy him?

Maybe he should give this more thought.

No. This money will go to the King of the Jews.

"They're dangerous, Matthias," Jairus whispered into his ear as they made their way onto the courtyard.

Matthias nodded.

Many brought their sick to the Rabbi. He healed each one as the numbers continued to grow. Matthias could not get near him.

"I must give this to him, Jairus," said Matthias, leaning his head toward his friend but not taking his eyes off the Rabbi.

"Soon Yeshua will return to Bethany. Come with us. You can give him your gift there."

CHAPTER 36

The scowl on Matthias's face didn't compare with the raging anger in his heart. He squeezed the leather bag repeatedly, grinding its contents between his fingers—a continuous reminder of the Nazarene's rejection of his gift, after he had struggled so hard to get to Yeshua to offer it.

"Matthias?"

At the sound of Rebekah's voice, he spun around, tucking the bag into his girdle.

"Rebekah, Phoebe, shalom." A forced smile accompanied his stilted greeting.

"Shalom. We're following Yeshua back to Jerusalem. Will you be going?" she asked.

"Of course. I need to prepare for Passover."

Phoebe rested her hand on Matthias's arm. "Papa asked me to extend an invitation to you and Eliezer to be our guests for Passover tonight. You will come, yes?"

Her invitation pushed his inner turmoil under the surface.

"Yes, we would be glad to join your family. Have you already secured a place?"

"We'll join Nicodemus."

"I know of his place. When the three stars appear in the night sky I will be there," Matthias said with a nod. "And Rebekah? Your family? Where will you be sharing Paschal?"

"Yeshua told his twelve chosen ones he desires to spend this Passover with them. He sent Papa and John ahead to secure a room."

At the mention of Yeshua, Matthias instinctively reached for his leather bag as the simmering in his soul returned. The women shared a confused look, making him aware of his reaction. He released the pouch and motioned to the group of disciples starting their walk back to Jerusalem.

"It appears they're leaving." He nodded toward the departing men, hoping to separate himself from the awkward moment.

Both women turned. Rebekah hurried to follow. "Shalom," she called, looking back over her shoulder. "May you find peace, Matthias."

As she joined the band of disciples, he noticed she stayed close to James.

"I, too, must leave," Phoebe said. "Papa and Immah are going with Yeshua to hear him teach and make final preparations." She inclined her head ever so slightly toward Matthias. "Shalom."

He smiled at the child turned woman. Her gentleness warmed his soul. "Shalom, Phoebe. I'll join Jairus and we can prepare together. Eliezer will be a great help."

Matthias watched her join her parents, then rubbed his hand over his forehead, down his face, and across his beard. He began the walk down the road leading to Jerusalem. Pilgrims joined them along the route. Lost in his personal war, he didn't realize he had caught up with the Rabbi's group until Judas came alongside him.

"Matthias, you're walking alone, and not at all in a festive mood."

Matthias threw Judas a look that dared him to reveal something to be festive about.

"I overheard your conversation with the Lord. Is that what has you looking like a thundercloud, or could it be watching Simon's daughter with James?"

"Rebekah is of no concern to me. She can walk with whomever she wishes."

"So it is your conversation with the Lord."

Matthias kept walking. Surely Judas would have to quit talking and watch his step while they crossed the Kidron Valley. If he didn't, he'd end up slipping on the scattered stones and picking himself up out of the brook. That didn't sound too bad either.

"You should have known you could not buy his favor," accused Judas.

So much for not talking.

"I wasn't trying to buy anyone's favor."

"But didn't you?" asked Judas, offering him a hand from the other side of the brook. His smile made Matthias's skin crawl.

"No, I did not," he said. "I did what the Rabbi told me to do. Then he tells me he doesn't want my gift. Tell me, Judas—if you know—what does he want?"

"The Lord will need swords, weapons, men to set up his kingdom." Judas darted his eyes from side to side checking out those who walked nearest them. "Give me your gift. It will help when the Lord claims his throne. I'll tell him it's from you. You'll secure your place in his kingdom."

"Judas!" James called from near the front of the group. "The Master needs you to go on ahead and purchase what is required for the Passover meal. Simon and John will show you where to take the supplies."

Judas nodded his head and waved to James in assent. "Think about what I said, Matthias. But don't think too long," he warned. Pebbles slipped under his steps as he hurried away.

"Master?"

"Eliezer. I had lost sight of you," answered Matthias.

"I have been close by. May I speak freely?"

Matthias motioned for Eliezer to come closer. "Don't you always?"

Eliezer lowered his glance as he spoke. "Be careful whom you trust."

Matthias shifted his eyes to the side.

"Do I need to explain, Master? For I am not sure I can."

"No, Eliezer. No not at all, but we should put our distrust aside and join Jairus. The crowd continues to grow. We don't want to lose him until we know what preparations we need to make for this evening."

Eliezer fell in behind Matthias as they crossed the stream of pilgrims to reach Jairus.

The evening star sang a bright solo in the sky. Pilgrims entering the homes of strangers became family for a night as they joined in the celebration of Israel's liberation from Egypt. Matthias yearned to share in the laughter and celebration, but Judas's words, mixed with the Rabbi's words and refusal of his gift, were enough to drain any gaiety from his heart.

Remembering the Rabbi's approval earlier of a poor widow's meager temple offering served only to twist the gall in his stomach at his rejected generous gift. Then as others praised the beauty of the temple, a distant look had filled the Rabbi's eyes as he spoke.

"There is a day coming when there will not be one stone left upon another. They will all be thrown down ... when you see Jerusalem surrounded with armies ... This generation shall not pass away, until all is fulfilled ..."

Perhaps Judas was right. The Rabbi needed men, weapons, and those ready to fight if indeed this kingdom was to appear. Matthias longed to be a part of that kingdom, one free of Roman rule.

"Master?" Eliezer disrupted Matthias's pondering. "Is this not the home of Nicodemus?"

"Yes," answered Matthias with a half-smile. "The door is open, and the festivities are beginning." As the two men entered, Matthias decided to meet with Judas as soon as possible.

Matthias felt an air of expectancy among the host and guests from the first blessing of wine, the sharing in the bitter herbs, and the retelling of the fateful night when God's people were saved from the death angel through the shedding of the lamb's blood. John the Baptizer's words from three years ago passed through his mind.

The Lamb of God that takes away the sin of the world.

The hour grew late as the last blessing was given and the final hallel repeated.

Each man reclined on his pillow surrounding the table. Propped on his left arm and holding his cup in his right hand, each raised the cup and repeated, "God is the Lord, which has showed us light. Bind the sacrifice with cords to the horns of the altar. You are my God, and I will praise you. You are my God. I will exalt you. O give thanks to the Lord for he is good, for his mercy endures forever."

Matthias frowned. Nicodemus had risen and moved to his open door in the middle of the exaltation. Jairus had continued it without missing a word. Matthias mouthed the words but watched Nicodemus. Who would dare interrupt at such a time?

"My honored guests." Nicodemus returned to the table. "Please stay, enjoy your fellowship until you tire and need rest. I must excuse myself. It seems"—he hesitated—"there is some urgent business with the council, and I must take my leave." His eyes darted around the room as he whispered to Jairus before leaving.

Matthias started for the door to see if he could surmise who had come for their host. There couldn't possibly be council business this late. The midnight hour was approaching, when the gates would be open and early sacrifices would begin. Before he reached the entrance, Phoebe intercepted him.

"Matthias?"

He faced her. Dressed in her festive garments, with a blonde curl hanging over one shoulder, she glowed in the candlelight. Ordinarily it would give him pleasure to stay and talk with her, but not now. He glanced from her to his escape route and back.

"You were like a stranger tonight, wandering in a distant land, here but yet not truly here," she continued. "Are you feeling well?"

Matthias took one of her slim hands in his. "I'm fine," he lied. "Just tired. I will take my leave for tonight. Tomorrow maybe we can speak more."

Instead of going to the sleeping quarters prepared by Nicodemus's servants, Matthias exited the house. An urgency drove him toward the temple.

As he approached the steps, a contingency of soldiers, temple guards, and what he thought were the high priest's servants exited the area. He craned his neck, hesitating to get too close, but then he saw Judas surrounded by the group.

Surrounded? Or leading?

He couldn't tell. Matthias quickened his pace, trying to catch up to the fringe of the group and hear whispers blowing through the entourage. Could it be these men would take the Rabbi and force him to ascend the throne? He shook his head.

Not with Roman soldiers in the mix.

"This Judas is one of Yeshua of Nazareth's own men."

Matthias caught pieces of conversation as the group pressed on through the streets of Jerusalem to a destination unknown to him.

"I heard the high priest gave him thirty pieces of silver for the information," offered one of the temple guards. "He told them this teacher is celebrating the Passover with the rest of his disciples."

The guard's rumored information made no sense to Matthias. Yet he followed, as a lamb follows its shepherd, until the mob stopped. Judas pointed to a room on the rooftop of someone's house. The soldiers' hobnailed sandals pounded the steps. They threw open the door. Shrill screams came from inside but stopped the instant the soldiers exited.

"You!" shouted a legionnaire as he bounded down the steps and grabbed Judas by his cloak. "He is not here."

Matthias moved as close as he dared, hiding behind others.

"If you want to live with a tongue and your two feet, you better start talking and walking," threatened the muscular Roman.

"If you remove your iron fist from my clothing, I will lead you to him. And when we get there, I will approach him and greet him with the kiss of a friend." The legionnaire loosed Judas's cloak. The disciple smoothed it out with both hands—a small smug smile on his face.

"Know this," the legionnaire growled. "My patience with you Jews is wearing thin. Lead on and pray to your God he is there."

The soldiers stayed close to Judas as the throng marched through the streets of Jerusalem and out of the eastern gate in the direction of Bethany. Matthias followed on the outer edge, hoping Judas knew as much as he'd said he knew.

When the mob entered the garden area of the Mount of Olives, Matthias pushed his way forward and waited for some sign from Judas to make sense of all this.

Without hesitation, Judas strode up to the Nazarene and kissed each cheek. The Nazarene said something that made Judas jerk his head back. Then Yeshua spoke to the crowd.

"Who are you searching for?"

The muscular centurion at the head of the group answered, his spear planted firmly beside him. "We seek Yeshua, the Nazarene." His voice crackled like lightning in the cool night air.

"I am he."

The Nazarene's declaration shot out like a catapult's ammunition, knocking the mob and the soldiers backwards on their heels. Matthias stumbled under the weight of those in front of him. He didn't understand what had happened, but he did understand the Nazarene's answer proclaimed him to be *I Am*— the most holy name of God Almighty, the self-sustaining, covenant-keeping God of Israel.

As the soldiers assumed their previous positions, Yeshua locked eyes with Matthias. He wanted to run, to hide, but there was no place to go. The Nazarene responded again to the centurion. "As I said, I am he. Let these others go free."

The guards rushed him. In one mighty motion, Simon drew his sword and with a swift swing cut off the ear of one of the high priest's servants. The servant's scream pierced the night. The soldiers drew their swords, and Matthias froze where he stood. Things looked as if a bloody confrontation was inevitable.

Yeshua raised a hand and cried out as he touched the servant.

"Put your swords away. Let these go free." Then he pulled his hand back, and Matthias's muscles grew taut. Whispers trailed through the mob.

"The Nazarene restored his ear."

"He is whole," whispered another. Then the centurion's order ended any further actions for the moment.

"*Seize him.*"

Not knowing what else to do, Yeshua's disciples fled, all except Judas. Matthias braced himself against the twisted trunk of an ancient olive tree as the soldiers led the bound Nazarene away from the garden. Judas trailed them. With cautious steps, Matthias followed and whispered to him.

"What happens now, Judas?"

Judas opened his cloak to reveal a small sword. His face clouded with confusion. "They didn't fight." His tone was dazed. "He was supposed to fight them, defeat them. I thought when Simon ... but then Yeshua—"

Judas's head jerked up, and his eyes, half-wild, bored into Matthias's.

"He let them take him. He didn't fight. He will die." Judas pulled a small leather pouch from his belt. He grabbed Matthias's shoulder as he shook the pouch in his face.

"*He will die at my hand for thirty pieces of silver.*"

CHAPTER 37

"Judas! Judas!"

His cry elicited no response from the fleeing figure of the wretched soul trying to escape his own betrayal. Matthias wrestled between following him and waiting to hear the end of the Nazarene's arrest. As he took a last glance toward the High Priest's palace, he caught sight of Simon warming himself by a fire in the reception room. Not willing to hesitate any longer, he ran after Judas. Maybe the council had revealed the end of this thing. Maybe the council wouldn't put the Nazarene to death. Maybe he would wake up from this living nightmare driving him to the end of—he didn't know what.

Finally, away from the commotion surrounding the arrest of the Nazarene, Matthias called out again.

"Judas! *Stop!*"

The man turned and faced his pursuer. His eyes were filled with doom and the flames that pursued Matthias in his dreams, causing him to halt his steps.

"Leave me, or follow me to my death."

The voice without a soul sent a foreboding of evil throughout Matthias's body, and yet pulled him after Judas. Judas outran him as he raced through the Valley of Hinnom and up the steep mountainside while Matthias slipped and stumbled on the rocky soil and clay. Up ahead, Judas stopped by a gnarled tree coming out of a jagged precipice. His shadowy figure moved methodically.

Matthias couldn't make out what he was doing until it didn't matter.

"No!"

Judas had tied his belt to the gnarled tree overhanging the edge of the outcropping.

"I have betrayed innocent blood."

The haunting cry followed the ghostly figure as he flung himself out from the rocks.

"No! No!" Matthias struggled up the rocky incline, his feet slipping on the pebbly clay. He reached out to the swinging body just as the limb gave way. Judas's body plunged down onto the jagged rocks. Matthias clung to the protruding tree roots as his own feet threatened to toss him off the mountain to join the betrayer's twisted and broken form. His intestines had spilled onto the rocks, testifying to the anguish of a condemned soul. Matthias's stomach lurched and mixed its contents with the darkness of death. A putrid stream spewed from his mouth.

He held tighter to the tree. Moving in slow motion, he wiped his mouth and carefully lifted himself to his feet. When he turned, he saw the pouch lying there in the path—Judas's leather money pouch. He picked it up.

Empty.

Judas had returned the silver as he said, but it had bought him no more peace than the life Matthias attempted to purchase with his gold coins.

As a man drunk, Matthias wandered back the way he came. The fiery fingers of death pursued his path. He wanted to find the Nazarene.

No. Life had proved worse than the nightmare invading his mind. It was too late to find the Nazarene.

Matthias entered the city called Beautiful at a dead run. The dark swirling clouds of night mingled with the purples and pinks of the sunrise straining to peek over the Mount of Olives. He rushed through the narrow streets of the lower city to the sounds of the donkey carts passing over the dusty roads to pick up overnight refuse. The refuse would be dumped in Hinnom valley and burned in a fire always smoldering. Matthias could taste the smell as he dodged buckets sitting outside the hovels the poor of the city called home. He forced himself to focus on Herod's palace complex in the upper city.

As Matthias drew closer to the outer courtyard of the justice hall, angry voices challenged the Roman governor, Pontius Pilate.

"Condemn him! He claims to be a king!"

Matthias entered the courtyard and struggled to push his way through the motley mob to the outer edge of the pack of religious wolves seeking their lamb. Pilate sat on the judgment seat on a raised platform. The priests, Sadducees, and Pharisees encircled the base of the raised area and yapped at him.

But where is the Nazarene?

"We have only one king—Caesar!" The throng joined the angry shouts with fists raised above their heads. The High Priest nodded at the infringing crowd. Bloodthirsty cries erupted through the stone edifice.

"Crucify him! Crucify him!"

Roman legionnaires, spears and shields at ready, stood between the judgment seat and the riotous pack of wild dogs. Pilate draped his purple cloak over one shoulder and across his arm as he rose from his seat and faced the mob. Shouts hushed. He gestured with a wave of his arm, and two soldiers half-dragged their prisoner across the stone floor. They stood the blood-soaked Nazarene to the side of Pilate.

Matthias strangled his short beard and sought to blink away the sight of the mangled body, crowned with thorns, beaten almost beyond recognition.

Pilate spoke. "I find no guilt in him."

He summoned a servant carrying a basin of water. He washed and slowly dried his hands.

"I wash my hands of this. Take him and crucify him." He exited the courtyard, never looking back.

Matthias grabbed his ears as the crowd's thirst for blood exploded into chanting. The soldiers reclaimed their prisoner and moved away. Matthias squinted, focusing his eyes on the Nazarene, and was suddenly overcome with sickness. He grabbed his mouth, shut his eyes, and struggled to curtail the rising bile threatening to hurl from his throat.

As the mob moved through the streets behind the Nazarene, Matthias unconsciously followed, as if a force beyond his control pushed him forward. The cries of the women echoed in his ears. One flooded his mind.

"My son!—the sword is piercing my heart!"

Matthias saw her—Mary, the Nazarene's mother—helped through the street, with John at her side. Tears streamed down her face. John held her close as they followed her son out of the city and up the dark, menacing hill called Golgotha, the Place of the Skull.

Matthias kept his distance. No other disciples, not even Simon, were anywhere to be seen. Mary of Magdala and a few other women known to travel with the Nazarene followed him to the place of his crucifixion.

The soldiers methodically did their job until three crosses, with a thief on each side and the Nazarene in the middle, stood starkly silhouetted against the morning sky. The soldiers gambled for the Nazarene's clothing, pitiful as it was.

"Father, forgive them," came a cry from the center cross. "They don't know what they're doing."

Beads of sweat gathered on Matthias's forehead as the sun moved across the sky. The Nazarene spoke to the thief hanging beside him.

"What did he say?" asked Matthias of a sneering bystander.

"Umph, something about being with him in paradise. Don't know I want that kind of paradise," answered the man. Then he spoke to the man on the center cross. "You saved others. Save yourself if you are the Son of God!"

"Come down from the cross!" shouted another. "Then we'll believe you!"

Matthias turned from side to side as he followed the shouts and insults filling the air. Shadows began to drape across the lowering sky until suddenly the sun went dark, as if it no longer had reason to shine. Matthias, shifting nervously on his feet, stopped at the echoing cry from the cross.

"My God, my God, why have you forsaken me?"

As Matthias gaped at the mutilated figure hanging upon the middle cross, the fingers of flame that haunted his nightmares grasped for the Nazarene. The darkness became the bottomless pit filled with ghostly figures wailing and thrashing as their cries shattered his ears. The earth began to swirl around him as the agony threatened to crush him under its weight. Like a madman he pushed his way down through the throng of onlookers who were oblivious to the battle taking place on this hill called the Skull.

Matthias didn't look back. There was nothing left to see, nothing he wanted to see. Life and hope were dying, both on the hill and in his soul. He wanted to go home. He wanted to hide from death. He wanted to live, but this day death surrounded him. He made his way to Nicodemus's house.

"Eliezer! Eliezer!" called Matthias, in hopes Eliezer might be near. The rapidly approaching footsteps changed his hope to reality.

"Master, I have …" Eliezer stopped midsentence. Concern etched his face. "You are shaken."

Matthias stared at his servant. "Shaken? Yes, Eliezer I am shaken to the core of my being. Have you not heard?"

"No, Master, I have not heard anything. I only know that Nicodemus left abruptly last night and has not returned, and you followed shortly after. There seemed to be some commotion in the early morning, but I have not left here. I have been waiting for your return."

"Eliezer," said Matthias, placing both hands on his servant's shoulders. "They have crucified the Nazarene. He is not the Messiah. There is none to save us from the Romans. There is none to save us from death, for the one we thought of as our Messiah hangs on a Roman cross, planted at the Place of the Skull."

Disbelief registered in the servant's eyes, but before he could speak, the earth began to rumble under their feet.

"Quickly, Eliezer. Gather our belongings. We must leave this place."

Within minutes the two men trudged through the crowded streets full of confused pilgrims and out the eastern gate, fleeing the city where hope had died on Golgotha.

"Master, what has happened?" asked Eliezer as the two men traveled along the empty road north and west. "Is Yeshua really dead?"

"Yes. Crucified on a Roman cross."

Eliezer's silence begged for further explanation, but Matthias would not, could not speak of it further. Death engulfed him, and his own seemed imminent. If he did not speak of it but fled from it, perhaps he could outrun it.

Death always finds its prey.

"Master?" Eliezer questioned hesitantly.

"If you seek to know more, I have no answers for you," snapped Matthias.

"I understand, Master. I only mention the setting of the sun so we can find a place to rest for the night. Sabbath is upon us, and we are nearing Samaria."

Matthias stopped on the well-traveled road and glanced westward.

What else can go wrong?

"I know where we are and the time of day," he muttered. It hadn't occurred to him that Sabbath was upon them. He hated traveling through Samaria as much as the Samaritans hated the true children of Abraham. He had taken Samaria's shorter route, forgetting Sabbath travel limited how far they could go before stopping. It would take most of the day to get across the dreadful land.

"Up ahead there is a grove of trees. We'll take our rest there." He wondered what purpose it served. No matter the number of laws one kept, there was always another broken. The law brought nothing but the knowledge of sin and with sin, death.

Matthias wrapped his cloak tight around him to shelter against the night air. Eliezer's fire had long gone out, but he would not wake his servant. Once home, he would explain the events of the memories he tried to flee. As his eyes grew heavy with sleep, he turned, trying not to give in. He desired a weary body over the visions of a fiery grave. His hip rested on a lump. He reached into his belt thinking to move his leather pouch. It was empty. He sat up. He slung the pouch to the side. It was Judas's. The image of the mangled disciple kidnapped his thoughts.

Matthias shook his head and pulled his knees under his chin, wrapping his arms around his legs.

The sun's bright oranges and yellows filled the sky. The colors began to dance and float together. Suddenly, they joined together into the flaming fingers that haunted Matthias's sleep. He scrambled backward spiderlike on his hands and feet, seeking an escape but finding none. Then a face, the beaten face of the Nazarene with his crown of thorns, appeared amid the flames.

"No!" He tried to cover his face from the vision. "Save me! Save me!"

"Master! Master, wake!"

Matthias opened his eyes to the face of Eliezer. Sobs of a lifetime shook his body, his faithful servant pulled him to his chest, and cradled him in his arms. Eliezer rocked him like a child until dawn gave way to the sun's bright light.

Matthias pulled away from his friend and rested his back against the tree. He rubbed his hand over his face and beard. Eliezer drew some dry fruit and a piece of bread from the shoulder bag and grabbed the wineskin, passing both to him. Matthias sat cross-legged, using his cloak as a table. He sat staring at the food before him.

Eliezer stood next to him, waiting. "Will you not speak God's blessing, Master?" he asked.

Matthias turned dead eyes toward his servant. He picked up the bread and lifted it to the heavens. "Lord ... God ... Creator of the universe ... we accept your provision ... with thanksgiving." He spoke the words and broke the bread, handing a piece to his servant. With each bite, the words of the Nazarene stuck in his throat.

"I am the living bread which came down from heaven: if any man eats of this bread, he shall live forever ..."

There was more, but what? He couldn't remember. No matter. The Nazarene was dead. He took a drink of wine and another bite of bread.

"... the bread that I will give is my flesh, which I will give for the life of the world."

Those were the words, but what did they mean? He died. A dead man gives nothing but food to the worms.

The slow travel on Sabbath took the men to the outskirts of Samaria. One more night under the sky and then they would be back in Capernaum, and home. Matthias didn't know what he thought he would find there, but surely it offered him more than this hopeless emptiness that was past feeling.

Death could not be worse than this.

CHAPTER 38

Matthias walked by the fig grove without stopping. The budding fruit promised a good crop. Unconcerned about the crop, he had one destination in mind, and it quietly rested in the hillside ahead. The white rock covering the entrance mocked the dead ones' bones inside. He squinted. Light. Life. Neither would be found here. Only death. Within the walls of the tomb lay the bodies of his father, Deborah, his mother, and the baby brother he had never known. He caressed the white rock, knowing it would make him unclean for the day. Traditions of men. None of it could bring life. Maybe the Sadducees were right. The bodies lying inside belied a resurrection.

"Father, if only I could speak with you, hear your voice telling me what to do. But the dead do not speak." Matthias turned and walked away as he spoke to the air. "Soon I will join you. Who will know, and who will care?"

Back home Abigail and Leah met him with a breakfast of cheese, fruit, and a mug of goat's milk.

"I'll take it in there." He nodded toward the desk and chair in the far corner as he slipped off his sandals and cloak. "Where is Eliezer?"

"He is taking care of the business you asked him to take care of, Master." Abigail set the plate of food on his desk.

Leah followed quietly, left his milk, and exited.

"Is there anything else we can do for you?" asked Abigail.

Matthias heard the concern in her voice. The servants had been stealing around him as if he had leprosy. He laughed to himself. Exactly like that. The memory of contracting the dreaded disease leaped into his mind.

"No," he answered. "You may leave." He remembered that dark period when he believed he would lose everything. "Then it was gone," he said to the plate of food. Eliezer believed the Nazarene had healed him. Probably not. He picked up a piece of cheese. If he was the Messiah, he would not be dead.

Matthias pushed the plate aside and placed a piece of papyrus in front of him. He began writing.

> To my dearest servant and friend, Eliezer:
>
> You will no longer be my servant but my heir. It is a strange thing for the son to leave his possessions to the father, but that is what you have been to me. Upon my death, all my properties and assets will be yours. All I ask of you is to free Leah and Abigail from service if they desire to go. Give them wages so they do not leave empty-handed. They have served me well.
>
> Signed,
>
> Matthias ben Zebulan
>
> This 24th day of Nisan in the 7th year of Governor Pontius Pilate

He quickly read it, then rolled it, and put his seal on it.

"Master!"

Matthias shoved the scroll to one side. "Eliezer, you look as if you have seen an apparition."

Abigail and Leah appeared, their hands covered in bread flour.

"What's wrong, Eliezer? What's going on?" asked Matthias.

"I have not seen him, but others have." Eliezer's face radiated hope. The women drew closer.

"What are you talking about, Eliezer? Who have others seen?"

In an uncommon gesture, Eliezer took Matthias's hands in his. "Yeshua, Master. Yeshua is alive."

"Alive? How can that be?" interrupted Abigail. Matthias shot her a disapproving look as she stepped back to her place. "Forgive me, Master."

He nodded, then answered, "It can't be, Abigail. I saw him crucified. No man could live through that. His sentence was death. Who told you these things, Eliezer? Servant's gossip? Have you gone mad?" Matthias moved toward the courtyard followed by his servants.

"Miss Phoebe and Miss Rebekah spoke in hushed tones of it in the marketplace, Master. Yeshua did die on that cross, but he rose from the dead. Simon and the others saw him and talked with him. He is alive."

"They revived him?"

"No, Master. Nicodemus and one named Joseph, a man of Arimathea, took his body and put it in Joseph's own tomb. It was sealed and a guard set. When the women went after Sabbath to anoint the body, he was gone."

"His body no doubt was stolen, or his disciples were just too overcome by grief and believed they saw him."

"Tell us more, Eliezer," begged Abigail, at the risk of being reprimanded.

"No," demanded Matthias. "You will not speak of this fable in my hearing again. Death is death. If there is a resurrection it will be at the end of the ages. And personally I am not even sure of that anymore." Matthias grabbed his cloak and left the house, not knowing where he would go. He thought of Jairus, but no doubt he too would believe this nonsense. He did not want to hear tales and fables. Those had taken him to his despair.

He walked as a man without a destination. The vineyard offered no peace, nor the grove of figs. The seashore with its gently lapping ripples belied peace. No matter where he found himself, Matthias was haunted by two images—the mangled body of Judas, and the tortured face of the Nazarene. As the sun began to sink behind the distant mountains, he headed home. He would try to find rest from the torment twisting his insides. If it didn't come ... he would make it come.

Sweat poured from his brow. The night terrors had left him drained. He rose from his bed and grabbed his belt and the leather pouch that lay next to it.

One last offering.

He bound the pouch in his belt and picked up his cloak. Before leaving the house, he laid the scroll atop the desk and scribbled Eliezer's name across it. He set his feet on his chosen path. The sea would become his tomb.

The mountain rested on the sea under the fullness of the moon, mocking Matthias's despondency. Gentle waves washed over his feet. He shut his eyes.

"No!" The flames engulfed his mind. His scream penetrated the quiet, dropping into the depths of the sea. No one listened. No one heard.

He raised defiant fists and shouted, "Who are you?"

The only answer came in the rhythmic sound of the undulating water. Its whisper dismissed his pain. The waves beckoned him to come, enter the depths, and know release. They promised he would have no more agony.

He knelt, letting the water run through his fingers. He looked to the sky.

"Are you there, Adonai? Will you meet me in the sea's depths?"

He hung his head.

There is no peace. No escape.

He clasped his dripping hands over his ears. His eyes closed against the relentless image pursuing him, haunting him.

He stood and turned his hopeless stare back to the sky. The flickering stars teased his tormented soul.

"Elohim, if you are there, show me the truth. Who is this Yeshua? Does he live? It is not possible. Almost I believed. Is it too late?" His words floated away like a leaf in the waters to nowhere. "If there is eternal life, show me. How may I possess it?"

Yeshua's words played in the playground of his tormented thoughts.

Sell all you have and follow me.

Matthias remembered the love reflected in the Nazarene's eyes, pleading with him to come, to receive his love. Even now, Matthias felt it, but the plea had produced death in him, not life. He had walked away clutching his leather bag of coins. What good were they now?

This day his search for truth would end. Truth would deliver him, or it would destroy him.

He cradled the leather pouch of gold coins as he stepped deeper into the water. He would carry them to his watery grave. The cold water numbed his senses as he waded into its depths.

"Matthias." The word was no more than a whisper on the wind.

That's not possible. No one knows I am here. No one cares.

He took another step.

"Matthias." There. Again, louder than before.

He turned. A shadowed figure stood on the shore. Panic and confusion wrestled with his mind, as he twisted the neck of his tunic. The voice called a third time.

"Matthias."

"Do I know you?" His words tumbled out in a hoarse whisper. "What do you want?"

"I want you, Matthias. Sell all you have, give it to the poor, and follow me."

The words pierced his heart just before it broke.

"Yeshua?"

"*I Am.*"

Matthias, clasping his leather bag, ran to the shore, even as the water tried to hold him back. His body shook as he fell at the Nazarene's feet. When he lifted his head, the Lord extended his hands, wounded by the nails of crucifixion—wounds that belonged to Matthias—and lifted him to his feet. Matthias swallowed the despair and grief lodged in his throat as the Lord wrapped him in his arms.

When he stopped shaking, the Lord released him. Matthias offered him the pouch.

"Take this, Lord. All I have is yours. There is no price too great to pay, for your love has bought me. Take my life. You alone will be my treasure. From this day forward I will follow you."

EPILOGUE

Matthias felt as if he sat on top of the world from his perch on Mount Arbel. He pondered over the events of the last several days. Simon Peter, James, John, and several of the disciples—all of the remaining eleven—had returned to Galilee, away from the din of confusion in Jerusalem, the constant threats and whispers. It was good to be home.

Not only had the Lord appeared to Matthias but to many others, several times. He remembered Peter's words.

"The women said we are to meet the Lord here, in Galilee."

So Matthias waited. He saw a group, barely visible in the dawn's light, starting up the mountain. He wondered if the Lord led them.

"Matthias."

He jumped from his seat. "Lord." He fell to his knees, no longer a master himself but a servant to the risen Lord.

The Lord touched his shoulder. "Join me." He extended his hand to the kneeling figure.

Matthias grasped it. "Yes, Lord."

He would always remember the tender love in the eyes of this One, the Lamb of God, God's own Son.

"You have followed me from afar for three years and now you have come near. Soon you will see me no more."

Matthias turned his head to one side. "No, Lord. You will leave me, too?"

The love and tenderness of Yeshua's voice put Matthias at ease, as he spoke.

"No, my son. I will never leave you nor forsake you. I will be out of sight but always near. I will send One to be your Comforter, to dwell in you and with you, and you in him. He will tell you more of me and the Father, my Father and yours."

"Yes, Lord. How will I know what to do, where to go?"

"When I have spoken to you all, I will leave for a time, but I will meet you in Bethany. You are to stay with the others. I will give you instructions now and again in Bethany before I leave to join my Father. All you need do is ask in my name, and I will give you whatever you need."

"Over there!" Simon Peter's cry rang in the crisp air. "Hurry, he is here, and Matthias is with him."

The rushing feet of the others and excited voices broke the peaceful quiet of the communion Matthias enjoyed with the Lord.

"The others are here," said Yeshua. "Remember always, follow me."

Matthias nodded, unable to speak the words of love lodged in his heart.

The group of men, along with their wives, and Jairus, Phoebe, and Rebekah gathered around the Messiah, along with a few others. Eliezer stood with Matthias as the Lord spoke.

"All power is given to me in heaven and in earth."

His words finished the picture the Father painted across the sky as the sun rose above the far horizon. Behind the Lord, it cast its image on the shimmering sheet of the Galilee far below, giving the lake the appearance of the eye of God. In the far distance the edge of the earth created an arc divided only by the sun.

"Go therefore and make disciples of all the nations, baptizing them in the name of the Father and the Son and the Holy Spirit. Teach them to observe all things that I have commanded you; and know this, I am with you always, even to the end of the age ..."

Matthias caught the Lord's attention toward him as he spoke, "I am with you always." As the sun reached its fullness and the blinding brightness surrounded the Lord, he vanished from their sight.

"What now, Peter? What shall we do? Are we to stay here?"

Peter shrugged his shoulders. "The Lord didn't say, John. I—I—"

"Peter?" Matthias approached him.

"Matthias, you were with the Lord when we arrived. Did he give you word as to what we are to do now?"

"He said to return to Jerusalem, and on the way meet him at Bethany."

"Then that is what we will do," Peter responded as he turned and led the group down the mountain.

Eliezer walked alongside Matthias. "Would you have me travel with you, Master?"

Matthias smiled a crooked smile.

"You have one Master now, Eliezer, and it is not I. You are free to serve him however and wherever he leads you. Would I want and enjoy having you journey with me? Of course."

As they made their way down the mountain, Matthias pondered.

What final instructions will the Lord leave with us before returning to his Father?

It didn't matter, really. They would carry out his instructions, no matter the cost. No price, no gold or silver, could ever repay the love, the hope, the life the Nazarene had given him. And no payment could ever equal what the Nazarene himself had paid in blood, the price Matthias himself had witnessed on Golgotha.

At that memory, Matthias bowed his head and said what was in his heart.

Thank you, Yeshua, Lamb of God. All mankind will bless your holy name, now and forevermore.

Thank you.

ABOUT THE AUTHOR

Donna Stearns finds her identity, as a child of the King, in Christ Jesus. He has blessed her with varied titles to encapsulate her life. Donna is the wife of a bi-vocational pastor, living in an empty nest in Southern Illinois. Their children have blessed her with the titles of, mom, mother-in-law, grandma, and great-grandma. Donna's love of God's word fills her life with directing a day camp for children, organizing summer mission trips for teens, and leading bible studies for adults. Donna is excited about this next chapter of her life as the Lord continues to lead her in a writing ministry. He promises to bless her with more fruit now than in her youth—Psalm 92:13,14. Donna is blessed with an abundant life—you are a portion of the abundance. If you would like to connect with Donna email her at dkstearns@hotmail.com or visit her website, "Meeting Jesus With Donna Stearns." at https://believe4147.wordpress.com.

If *The Nazarene's Price* has blessed you, would you consider leaving a review on Amazon and Goodreads, so others are encouraged to read the story of Jesus' love for Matthias and share in your blessing? Thank you.

QUESTIONS FOR PERSONAL OR SMALL GROUP DISCUSSION

This guide is for use over a three-week period as your group reads Matthias's story. The guide is easily adaptable to your group's needs. The contents can aid in personal study and reflection when no group is available. Either group study or personal will benefit from the inclusion of several Scripture references.

Part One: "Behold the Lamb of God which taketh away the sin of the world." John 1:29, KJV

1. John the Baptizer introduced Yeshua/Jesus as the Lamb of God. What does this title reveal about Jesus? (See John 1:29; 1 Peter 1:18-19. For further study see Isaiah 53:10-12.)

2. Why did this title bother Matthias?

3. What other reasons caused Matthias to be skeptical about the Nazarene?

4. What picture comes to mind when you hear Matthias call Jesus, the Nazarene? (See John 1:14-17; Philippians 2:5-8; Hebrews 2:14)

5. What reasons do people purpose today to justify believing Jesus was merely a man?

6. Matthias saw the Nazarene's miracles and heard his words. Why did it bother him to hear the Nazarene call God his Father? (See John 10:30-39; 15:8-11)

7. Do you believe the Nazarene to be who He claimed to be? Why/why not?

Part Two: "A prophet is not without honor but in his own country, and among his own kin, and in his own house." Mark 6:4

1. Yeshua's popularity grew with the people while his disapproval rating dropped among the religious elite. This disapproval causes Phoebe fear in proclaiming her belief in Yeshua. What fear inhabits Rebekah? What fear/s hinder you from speaking boldly concerning Jesus? What does God's say to our fear? (See Isaiah 41:10; Hebrews 13:5,6)

2. Rebekah thought, "How could one's tongue go from praising God one moment to berating another of his own?" What answer comes to mind? How is it overcome? (See Matthew 12:34-37; Ephesians 4:29; 1 John 3:18)

3. In chapter 14, Matthias heard the Nazarene proclaim himself one with God. He heard the demon declare Yeshua, the Holy One of God. He saw the Nazarene command the demon and it obey. Matthias remains unconvinced. If this scene played out before you—would you be skeptical, believe easily, or consider all you saw and heard? Why?

4. In chapter 16, Matthias "glanced over his shoulder at those seeking the Nazarene but not the man." What did he mean? (See John 6:26)

5. How are we alike or different from those same people?

6. What truth did the Nazarene want the people to believe? (John 14:8-11; John 6:29, 51)

7. Matthias sought to know truth. What did he look to for freedom from his doubts?

8. Where do people turn today to find truth? Where do you look?

9. Matthias witnessed Phoebe's resurrection and Deborah's healing. He almost believed. What held him back? What holds us back when we have a great witness before us?

10. Matthias didn't understand Deborah's sudden death. How do you handle what seems a senseless death? Any death?

11. Yeshua's brothers believe him to be mad. The Nazarene's hometown believes him to be a charlatan. The Pharisees believe him to be of the devil. Matthias remains confused. Yeshua's disciples believe him to be who he says, but without understanding what it means. Who do you believe the Nazarene to be? Why?

Part Three: "Jesus beholding him loved him ..." Mark 10:21

1. When Matthias contracts leprosy, he sinks into despair. When miraculously healed, Matthias is glad the Nazarene is nowhere near. Why, do you think that is? (Check out John 9:1,2 for insight.)

2. Matthias sought refuge by the sea. Do you have a special place to meet with the Lord when life is hard or when you want to be near Him? What makes it special? For Matthias it was memories of his father.

3. What does the name, "I Am" tell us about Yeshua? (See John 8:57-59 and Exodus 3:15)

4. How are the accusers and the accused alike in the account of the woman taken in adultery? How do they differ? (The biblical account is found in John 8:1-11)

5. How did Matthias plan to gain eternal life? In John 14:6, Jesus makes it clear he is the only way to the Father. Why do people stumble over this truth?

6. Matthias saw the fires of hell reaching for Yeshua, the Nazarene, as he hung on the cross. Imagine you are there, what do you see? (See John 15:12-13; Romans 11:30-33; 1 Corinthians 1:18)

7. The Nazarene is dead. Matthias loses all hope for he does not realize the Nazarene's love for him will not let him

go. Death couldn't kill his love but gave it strength. Matthias learns this as the Nazarene calls to him. When have you known the love of Jesus in your life? What difference did it make to you?

8. What hope is yours because Jesus lives? (1 Corinthians 15:51-58)

9. One last question: Jesus talked with Martha in John 11:25-26. He said to her, *"I am the resurrection, and the life: he that believeth in me, though he were dead, yet shall he live: And whosoever liveth and believeth in me shall never die, Believest thou this? (KJV)*

Write out your answer and explain it.

And many other signs truly did Jesus in the presence of his disciples, which are not written in this book: But these are written, that ye might believe that Jesus is the Christ, the Son of God; and that believing ye might have life through his name. John 20:30,31, KJV

REFERENCES

The New Manners & Customs of Bible Times, Full-Color Edition of the 175,000 Best Seller; Ralph Gower, author; Revised and updated edition © 2005; Published by Moody Publishers

The Life And Times of Jesus The Messiah, Complete and Unabridged in One Volume, by Alfred Edersheim, Hendrickson Publisher; New Updated Edition

Rose Guide to The Temple, Randall Price, ThM, PhD; Rose Publishing, Inc. Torrance, California

Jewish Literacy, Rabbi Joseph Telushkin; William Morrow, an imprint of Harper Collins Publishers

The International Inductive Study Bible, New American Standard; Published by Harvest House Publishers; Inductive study material compiled by Kay Arthur and the staff of Precept Ministries.